someone
else's
wife

JOLIE MOORE

Someone Else's Wife
Jolie Moore

This edition published by
Moore Digital Media Inc
1125 N Fairfax Ave
Unit #46071
West Hollywood, California 90046

ISBN 13: 978-1-64414-086-4
eISBN 13: 978-1-64414-085-7

Cover Designer: Damonza
Someone Else's Wife/Jolie Moore

for my son
This is the first book I've written since you
got here. You are my inspiration.

Acknowledgements

I'd like to thank my first readers, authors Casey Dawes, Andrea Wenger, and Monica Epstein. Your feedback was priceless. I'd also like to thank my dear friend Dr. Daniel Goodwin for his expertise on heart conditions I could inflict on Dr. Walter Cooper. Lastly, I would like to thank my fellow Keeper Shelf authors, the fabulous unicorns. Without you, it would have been an even tougher year. You are my New York.

1

"How's your butt?" Hannah Keesling's husband Michael palmed her ass, sliding his hand between her oversized sleep shirt and her bikini underwear. This was her least favorite way to wake up.

Hannah squeezed her eyes shut, the words of the one friend she'd confided her problems to, coming back to her. "Friendship is the foundation of a good marriage," she'd said piously. "When the going gets tough, remember why you chose him in the first place." She wondered what her friend would make of this.

"My butt's fine," she murmured, cracking one eye open. It was still dark. She hated how her body betrayed her, reacted to his clumsy seduction after all that had happened between them.

"You didn't ask how my cock feels." Michael prompted. Why did he have to be so coarse? Their marriage wasn't perfect, but she deserved a little respect, consideration. They'd started out as friends, added sex, then matrimony. Now it had morphed into a different thing altogether. And she was stuck in it, like a fossil in the tar pits.

Hannah fought her way from sleep, through drowsiness, to wakefulness like a diver pushing through heavy water desperate for air. She didn't have to ask how Michael's penis felt. His engorged flesh eagerly probed her back, her butt, and her legs.

"How does it feel?" she whispered, eyeing the bedside clock. It wasn't even five in the morning. The bright Southern California sun hadn't yet stolen the darkness from the room.

"Very lonely," he said. Hannah could hear a pout in his voice. The squeak of the metal springs and the rhythmic movement of the mattress told her that Michael's hand was keeping his organ company. "C'mon, turn over and take off your shirt."

Her weak flesh responded, while her stronger mind rebelled. Hannah knew she should have been more excited, more responsive, desired him like real wives wanted their husbands. Guilt flooded her veins. Her husband wanted her, and she didn't want him back. Hannah scooted away from her husband to the very edge of their bed. If this was all there was to marriage, she didn't want any part of it anymore. Michael didn't even try. Would it kill him to kiss her, light a few candles, tell her she was beautiful? The thought of thirty more years of frat boy groping killed any stirring he'd aroused.

Saying yes, pulling up her shirt, spreading her legs— that would be the easy thing. But Hannah was done. She was tired of being her husband's glorified whore. The finality of her decision made her next words come easy.

"So this is foreplay?" she asked, unable to keep the disgust from her voice.

Her remark hit the intended target. Cool air raised the gooseflesh on her naked legs and exposed back as Michael threw off the goose down duvet and stalked toward the bathroom.

"This is marriage?" he threw back at her. Michael's anger surprised her. He never fought back, just stalked off to finish the job himself. "You think I like having to beg my wife to touch me? To make me feel good?"

He was right, damn him. He couldn't know that she'd learned to steel herself against his touch. Guilt and obligation took the place of desire now. "You're right, Michael. This *isn't* a marriage. I don't think we can go on like this." There was no point in pointing fingers or placing blame. Reasoning with him hadn't worked no matter how many times she'd tried. Hannah knew what she had to do. She had made the decision to marry someone she wasn't in love with, and they'd both paid the price.

"God damn it, Hannah. Why do you make this so hard? I wanted a little quickie. You wouldn't have to do anything but lie there. This could have been a win-win morning. But you have to go make everything an all or nothing decision." He slammed the door. The angry squeak of the shower knobs and the unnecessary banging of razor against sink comforted her. He wouldn't be back in the bed today. She'd escaped for the moment.

Pulling suitcases from the walk-in closet, and angrily tossing in random clothes and underwear, Hannah couldn't help comparing herself to some past-her-peak actress on a bad Lifetime movie racing against time and bad music before the battering husband returned home. She stilled her movements, and sat on the bed pulling the cool, salt-tinged air into her lungs. Her life wasn't a burning bed situation. Between the move to the suburbs with all the consumer trappings, her change in career, and the relentless pressure she and Michael put on themselves to conceive a baby, Hannah's life felt wrong.

The unexplained infertility that had weighed upon them was a godsend now. She couldn't bring a baby into this hot mess of a marriage. She'd been that child. Been there, done that, had the psychiatric scars to prove it. An innocent baby deserved more.

With less urgency, she finished packing her bags. Hannah glanced outside. Still early, the sun hadn't yet burned the marine layer from the sky. She'd already done the research. Made all the calls. Ignored her friend's advice to try to work it out. If she left now, she could make it to Oregon in about twelve hours. Her friend's words echoed. "Once you decide, there won't be any turning back." Now that she knew what she had to do—leave Michael—she couldn't undo it. She couldn't go back to playing the dutiful and pliant wife, even if she wanted to.

Hannah's nine-month old Lab mix puppy Cody sniffed around her bags, his tail twitching nervously. Any disruption in the order of his life, threw Cody off. She'd never met a creature so hewn to routine.

She sifted through the fine hairs on the dog's smooth black head. "Don't worry, I'm not leaving you behind."

Cody's tongue left a wet trail on her palm. She took that as a sign of approval.

Bags loaded in the car, Hannah came back to the bedroom. Cody, unsure of what was going to happen next, jumped around her legs. Nudging him to his bed, she fished through her nightstand looking for the note she'd written out weeks before. Her fingers found the smooth surface of the cream envelope she'd addressed with one word: Michael.

Lifting the flap, Hannah shook the thick card, embossed with her name along the top, onto the bed, slowly turning it over.

Michael,

I'm going away for a few days. I need time and space to think about our future. Cody's with me.

Love,

Hannah

She hoped Michael didn't notice the odd way the 'v' in 'love' folded in on itself. Hannah had debated for days on whether to keep that word in the carefully thought out missive. The strong black script disappeared one line at a time when Hannah put the card back in the envelope, and propped the note against the pillows. She patted her thigh and Cody got up from the spot he'd taken up by the French doors. His tail wagged, ready for an adventure. Without a backward glance, Hannah closed the bedroom door.

"It's not you. It's me." Michael's voice burst the bubble of solitude that had cushioned Hannah for the last seven hours.

Hannah let out a long sigh. "What did Dr. Stern say?"

Rustling papers crackled through the car's speakers. In her mind's eye, she could see Michael sitting hunched over his desk reading from his carefully organized notes. "He called it immunological infertility," he said, stumbling over the alliteration.

"What does that mean?" Why couldn't Michael ever spell anything out without a nine-hundred-word recitation? If she came back, would they ever be able to have a baby?

"He said that my immune system is attacking my sperm. Treating them like a foreign invader, like it would treat a bacteria or virus."

"I guess I can stop taking Clomid," she said, relieved to drop that last pretense. Undecided about their future, she'd taken the drugs to mask her indecision. Michael was silent. The dog's panting and the whomp of the tires on the nearly deserted freeway filled the car with white noise. Hannah searched for the right thing to say. "Can this be fixed?"

More silence. Hannah glanced at the Bluetooth display on the dashboard to make sure the call had not been dropped. Nope, three solid blue bars.

Michael's answer came on a whoosh of breath. "There aren't really any standard treatments. The cause is unknown. So, the cures are experimental. The doctor mentioned one treatment that involved a high dose of steroids. But the side effects would be bad and the chances of pregnancy not much better."

"I'm really sorry, Michael." He had wanted a child as badly as she did. Hannah knew now that she would never have a baby with him. But, she hoped he could find someone else to have a family with one day.

"It's okay. Don't divorce me over this," he added only half-jokingly.

Hannah glanced at her left ring finger bare of its two-carat engagement ring and its companion wedding band. She had slipped the small gold circles from her fingers a few minutes into the trip before fate put this final nail in the coffin.

Hannah looked around, not having a clue in hell where she was. "Look, I'm still on the road, so I'll give you a call later tonight, and we can figure out what to do next. Okay?"

"Love you, Hannah," Michael said solemnly before disconnecting the call.

For a few impossibly long seconds, the road blurred in front of Hannah. Her marriage was really over. The end of something she'd put so much time, and hope into made her heartsick. But his news solidified the decision to leave Michael. She hadn't married him for his sperm, exactly. She had reached thirty-five and looked around, and decided to settle down. Hannah had truly loved him—in her own way.

Marrying one of her closest friends had seemed like such a reasonable idea. Hannah and Michael had met in New York in the heyday of their twenties, and after all the assholes had left her high and dry in her thirties, Michael was still around. And, most of her friends were married. Hannah had lived long enough to realize that she was never going to have the glamorous, worldly life that she expected, so she had made an adult decision.

She'd married Michael hoping to create the stability she'd never had as a child. If the world wasn't going to give her fireworks and sparks, at least she could have good enough. Looking around at her college girlfriends and their sports watching, weight gaining, workaholic husbands, good enough was more than most women got. Guilt flattened the bubble of giddy elation that started rising in her chest. Hannah mentally shoved Michael right out of her mind, vowing to think about the future she wanted, not the past she'd left behind in Newport Beach.

She fiddled with the car controls and put on her favorite Shay Morrison CD, *Scarlet Lady,* and sang until her throat was hoarse. Hannah had stopped singing when she'd married Michael. He'd called her passion impractical. But she'd missed expressing her feelings this way. She looked around. All that singing and she'd gotten lost. How long was an album, an hour, an hour and a half?

Where in the heck was she? She'd wanted to be near the ocean. Realizing she hadn't seen the green spade shaped sign designating the California One for some time, Hannah took her eyes off the relatively empty road to look more closely at the car's onboard navigation, to no avail. The point and click computer mouse like device that had seemed so futuristic at the dealership was of no help in figuring out where in the hell she was. But all these redwoods and not a lick of sand meant one thing. She'd lost the ocean again.

Hannah looked at the map one more time, but the colors, lines and squiggles meant nothing to her. Maybe she should pull over and figure it out. She wasn't a man. She would pull over and ask for directions at the first gas station or convenience store she saw. Skip the help, the sound of Cody's retching from the back of the car made pulling over right now a necessity. She should have known it was coming. The last few hours after passing the bustle of San Francisco and Marin County found the Sheprador looking a little green around the gills. The floppy-eared black and white dog, who'd always loved a car ride, wasn't looking so happy-go-lucky anymore. Wrenching the steering wheel to the right, Hannah sped down a random exit ramp off the 101 freeway, spraying gravel as she braked the SUV at the next turn out. She hoped she didn't ding the paint. With her luck, she would ruin the car that she and Michael had only leased.

Hitching the purple nylon leash to the dog's collar, Hannah helped Cody leap out of the car – in time. The dog upchucked the all-organic biscuits she'd bought at a pet boutique earlier in the day. Queasy herself, Hannah empathized with Cody. The combination of coffee shop muffin, the never-ending drive, and conversation with Michael, did not settle her stomach.

A few miles later, Cody forced Hannah to make another emergency stop on the shoulder of the freeway. He must have been at the end of his rope because thick yellow bile was all that came up before the dog shuddered with dry heaves. When Cody's face lost the vomit grimace, she plotted her next move. The dog was not having a good time. But there was no turning back now. If she found somewhere to stop for the night or two, maybe she could even out the dog's system. She hadn't made a reservation because the Oregon cabin owners said they were nowhere near being overbooked. Looking at her watch, Hannah realized she had been standing next to her car for ten minutes and she hadn't seen more than a handful of cars drive by. Northern California was not as traffic choked as San Francisco had been. She hoped there was some semblance of civilization, namely a vet, out here.

Hannah pulled her smartphone from the car's console and typed 'veterinarian,' into the search box. She waved the phone through the air, and got a signal. Only one vet came up in nearby Garberville. She'd never heard of the place, but assumed it was a town of at least two people – the vet, and a guy with a cow, who needed the vet.

Cody, now slightly foul smelling, jumped into the SUV on shaky legs. She navigated over to the address of the vet, glad the car's fancy computer at least worked this time. Pulling up in the parking lot, she was surprised how little the building differed from her vet in Newport Beach. The building was slightly more rustic, wood paneled instead of stuccoed, but it looked large, and well lit. Hannah took the first calming breath of the day. A vet who took pains with appearances would probably treat her dog well.

No receptionist stood behind the Formica and wood front desk. Not a lot of black granite here to impress pet lovers with open wallets. Hannah checked her watch against the hours posted on the door to make sure the clinic was still open. She hoped they didn't close early.

"Hello?" she called out tentatively.

"Back here," a deep male voice called back. "Just a second."

Cody slumped under her legs, lethargic. Hannah looked in the dog's miserable eyes. He couldn't die on her on this trip. That would be too much.

A tall, broad shouldered, dark-haired man robed in a white lab coat emerged from an unseen side door.

"Doctor Cooper." He extended his hand. Hannah thrust out her hand to shake his, her bangles jingling, but the doctor ignored her hand, instead leaning down to pet the dog. "How can I help you?" he asked *the dog*, raising his voice a few octaves. "What do we have here, buddy? You don't look so great. Let's get you into a room and get a closer look at you."

At Dr. Cooper's command, Cody, who could barely raise his head a minute before, roused himself and followed the doctor with a loyalty he usually reserved for those he knew well. Man and dog went through a door into a sterile looking examination room. With little choice but to follow, Hannah pulled her tired body from the wooden bench and brought up the rear.

When the vet finally looked at her, Hannah felt her butt hit the chair before she realized that she'd nearly lost her balance. Infinitely grateful the plastic bucket seat in the corner caught her, because she had landed hard enough for it to sting. Her stomach roiled, her hands shook, and her ears rang. Only one other time had an attraction so instant or intense shot through her like this. Twenty years ago she'd come undone when Lucas walked into freshman orientation.

Hannah hadn't thought it was humanly possible to feel this way again. She would be hard pressed to explain it to anyone, but something about Dr. Cooper made her want to know him more—a lot more. Her hair bounced around her face as she shook the inappropriate feelings away. Years of tamping down unwanted feelings finally did something more than give her an ulcer. After following her heart that first time with Lucas, she only used her head when it came to matters of the heart. Craving Dr. Cooper was not in the plan.

Oblivious to her discomfort, the vet guided Cody onto the stainless steel table, using a foot pedal to operate the hydraulic pump. The lift hissed as the dog glided to the doctor's waist level.

He finally extended a hand to her. "I'm Dr. Ben Cooper." She shook it dumbly, suddenly embarrassed by the jangling bracelets that had seemed so cool this morning. She and Johnny Depp were too old for so much wrist jewelry. "Sorry there was no one upfront. Doris left early to pick up her sick grandson from school."

Dr. Cooper was too much to take in all at once. He had longish, brown wavy hair, broad shoulders, deep bass voice, and eyes blue gray like the winter ocean. If she could draw, this was the dream man she would have rendered. Until now, the idea of a soul mate had been a cliché. In a few seconds, that cliché had become a very real possibility. The sense that she needed to touch this man was spilling over her again like an ocean wave. Hannah tried shaking her head again like a dog with a flea, but it didn't work a second time to clear her head. Maybe if she could think of something inconsequential to say, she would stop feeling so awkward.

"Um, the dog seems to be under the weather." Forget Oregon, her next stop should be 'Obvious Anonymous.'

Dr. Cooper looked at her like she was someone's doddering old aunt. Sympathetic smile lines crinkled around his eyes. He started speaking while checking the dog's ears, eyes, and gums. "Let me guess. This guy is Max? Jake?"

She shook her head, a small smile starting to crease her full lips. He could guess until the cows came home. He would never figure out the unique name she'd given her dog.

"Bailey?" She shook her head again, smiling broadly now. "Cody?"

Hannah gasped in surprise. "Fuck." She clapped her hands over her potty mouth. "Sorry. How did you know?" She'd removed the dog's tags at the same time she'd stashed her rings. The constant clinking of metal against metal would have driven her crazy for two long days in the car.

Dr. Cooper paused in his examination of the dog, moving around the table to close the door behind her. Her whole body tingled in the very small exam room. He gently touched her shoulder, directing her to look at the back of the door. Affixed to the wood door, with yellowing tape, was a ragged page, torn from a magazine. On it was a chart – one column pink, the other blue.

"The most popular dog names in the English speaking world," he said. The deep timber of his voice seemed to vibrate in her own chest with his body mere inches from hers.

"Oh." *Oh?* Was that the best she could come up with? It was rare that fate, or God, or the universe or whatever plopped a man like this right down in front of a woman—and the best she could come up with was, 'Oh?'

He walked back around the table, pulling the stethoscope from his neck. Placing the metal disk against the dog's chest, he listened.

"Is he going to be okay?" she asked, suddenly finding her full speaking voice.

"Cody is going to be fine," he pronounced, winding the stethoscope back around his neck, finished with his cursory examination. Surely, they had blood tests and x-ray machines up here.

"What's wrong with him?" she asked, genuinely perplexed. "He's always seemed so happy."

"Motion sickness," he said matter-of-factly.

Who knew? "Is there some kind of doggy Dramamine I can give him?"

He looked offended by the question. "Well, there are tranquilizers that we can prescribe for necessary travel. In your case, I'd recommend not driving long distances with the dog."

"That's going to be difficult," she said, Oregon's plains beckoning.

"Are you from San Francisco or Marin?" he asked, giving her no time to answer. "You can turn around and take him home, maybe fly to wherever you're going," he said as if she were driving the dog to the gallows, not the next state.

"I've driven all the way from the O.C. Turning around would probably take twice as long as getting to where I'm going."

Something seemed to close in him. His open manner and friendliness vanished. "Figures. You have that kind of vibe," he said.

What in the hell had happened? "What kind of vibe is that?" Did she sound as offended as she felt? Hannah wanted to be on Dr. Ben Cooper's good side. "I was planning on heading to Oregon." That had to be a more acceptable *vibe* than Newport Beach.

"What's up there? If you don't mind my asking." His nice-guy tone was back, and she was pushed off kilter again. This was why relationships based on the head worked better than those based on the heart. She hated that damned push/pull feeling when a guy really got to her.

"Nothing, I hope. I need some time to reevaluate my life. Thought I'd head up to a ranch in Bly, maybe Ashland. See where things go from there." Struck dumb one minute, diarrhea of the mouth the next. Well, this was going badly on all counts. It was time to pay, leave, and figure it out for herself.

"So you're not going to see anything or anyone in particular?"

"Does that make a difference?" Were his questions out of concern for the dog or had he gone stalker on her? That was one way to kill the romantic feeling.

"Well, since your dog is sick and all, have you considered stopping here for a while? This is a very nice, low-key resort area, you know."

"And where is 'here' exactly?" This little hamlet did not scream tourist mecca by any means. On her quick drive along the main drag, it had looked any small town in California – dotted with wood frame and stucco buildings, a couple of cafes, a movie theater, and a lot of free parking. No spas. No luxury bed and breakfasts with smartly painted signs. Sausalito, it was not.

"*Here* is Garberville, population nine hundred, give or take. But twenty five miles to the west is Shelter Cove." He paused as if she should know what that was. "Have you heard of The Lost Coast?" He paused again, and this time she shook her head with lack of recognition.

"No," she finally said aloud, probably sounding full of southern California snobbery. "Do you think Cody will get better over the next couple of days?"

"As long as he stays put," Ben said. "He's going to get a little worse, before he gets better."

"Why?"

"The road to the coast is a little windy," he said.

She was vacillating. Perhaps a stay in Shelter Cove would involve a little more get to know Ben Cooper time. Making major life decisions *could* involve meeting a new man, right? Maybe her new path should be a little more heart centered. Relying on her head had landed her Michael, after all.

Sensing her indecision, he went in for the kill. "My parents rent their house for vacations. It happens to be vacant right now. I'm sure they wouldn't mind you staying. Plus, they're one of only a few rentals that allow pets."

Message received. If she were any kind of good dog owner, then she'd stop the driving, camp out in Shelter Cove, and get her shit together. She looked into those sweet brown eyes, and gave Cody the thumbs up. She'd do it.

"Okay, I'm in—for Cody's sake."

Ben Cooper looked at the large stainless steel watch on his wrist. "I'll tell you what. I can close up shop here. Let me check on a couple of things, then you can follow me."

"Do you need to give your parents a call?"

"Nah, I'll do it later tonight. There's no hurry. No one is beating down the door. Tourism slows down in September. Coastal winter trips aren't very popular."

Hannah watched Ben's back as he retreated somewhere into the recesses of the clinic. She showed herself back to the waiting room, where a young blond girl had taken over counter duty. She paid the bill, glad they'd taken her platinum card, and grabbed a spot on a bench outside. Cody seemed happier out of the car. His nose was upturned taking in the scents moving on the air currents. She sighed, feeling more settled, knowing that she'd have a chance to unpack and think about the decisions she had to make. She had to figure out how to tell Michael she was leaving, once and for all. And she needed to make a plan, sooner, rather than later.

Dr. Ben Cooper took off his lab coat and hung it on the hook on the back of his office door exchanging it for his favorite leather jacket. What in the hell was he doing? His parents had closed up their vacation house for the winter. They no longer bothered with the sporadic rentals they got late in the year. And pets? He didn't know their pet policy. They liked dogs as much as the next person, but he wasn't sure they wanted a fifty-pound puppy roaming around their house and yard. His key was for *emergencies*. A nauseated dog did not qualify as any kind of emergency.

Ben zipped the close-fitting jacket, and ran a hand through his too-long hair, then glanced in the large rectangular mirror a previous vet, a rather vain southern California transplant, had affixed to the wall. He smoothed down the hair he'd ruffled. No reason for his hair to be standing on end when he went back to the waiting room.

Why was he doing this? He'd sworn off this kind of woman. Two long years with perpetual shopper Samara had weaned him from flashy women. O.C. Hannah was cut from the same mold. Her BMW, Louis Vuitton purse, Juicy sweats and gold bangles told him all he needed to know about her. It was no matter that her tall, lithe form had awakened his libido from hibernation.

Despite all the warning signs of her shallow, flighty nature, his heart sank when he came up front. One of his veterinary assistants, Joy, was behind the counter. Other than her female presence, the vast room was empty save for the smell of disinfectant layered over stale urine. He gave Joy instructions on the one cat who was going to be hospitalized overnight, and strode outside, relieved that Hannah had probably made the decision for him.

But there she was, sitting on the bench, long legs outstretched, frowning at her phone.

"So?" she asked, pursing her full lips. "Which car is yours?"

He pointed to the plain vanilla, none too clean, Ford Explorer in the lot. Ben looked at her, waiting for her look of disappointment that he wasn't driving something more her speed. It didn't come.

"I'll follow you, then?" she said, gathering up the dog's leash.

Ben stepped in her path. He kept his arms at his sides, resisting the urge to touch her—one time. "Why don't I take Cody? I have a harness and gated area set up in the back for carrying animals. He'll be more stable this way, and less likely to get sick on the ride." He looked at her dubious expression. "You okay with that?"

"I guess so." She took out her phone, again, tapping the screen. The damned thing was encased in rhinestones. Nothing escaped her universe of bling. "Give me your number in case we get separated."

Ben held up his hands in supplication. "I don't have a phone."

"Well it's nice to meet you, Mr. Twentieth Century." Hannah held out her hand again in mock greeting. He clasped it, even though her gesture was rhetorical. She pulled back like he'd burned her. "I guess I'll follow you then." She stalked off to her car, hopped in and started the engine. The waistband of her cropped jacket and the cut low-rise pants revealed a strip of warm looking tawny skin that he watched rabidly before his eyes skidded lower. He snatched a baseball cap from the passenger side of the car and pulled the brim low. Why was he looking at her ass? Why was he thinking about her in any way other than a dog owner?

Ben strapped Cody in, careful to ensure the dog's movement would be minimal in the car. He took a few seconds to massage the dog between the last few ribs, an acupressure point known to relieve nausea. Hannah had started her car, and was tapping incessantly at the phone again. This was why he didn't have one of the blasted things anymore. It took over a person's life.

A cell phone had put him at everyone's beck and call, mostly Samara's. He had received a never-ending stream of texts from his wife asking where he was, and what he was doing. It had been maddening. Then there were the assistants at his old Mill Valley office who viewed every flea and tick as life or death, and had to call him or text him about it. He was glad to be rid of the albatross.

He pulled out onto the road, signaling well before turns and making sure the BMW was always in his rearview mirror. It was hard to miss the car with the rhinestone license plate holder, glinting in the late afternoon sun. A few turns later, they'd passed through Redway, the last populated area before they reached the cove. Without much traffic going in either direction, he focused less on making sure Hannah was behind him. With nothing but open road and fifty minutes in front of him, Ben's thoughts closed in on him.

Ben's hand scraped against late afternoon stubble. Checking to make sure Hannah was behind him, he caught a glance at his forty-year-old face in the rearview mirror. Meeting his own eyes told him what he already knew. He was too old for this. Despite all his vows of celibacy and abstinence, and his dedication to the solitary life, he was attracted to Hannah. Why, was what he needed to ask himself? What was he doing having this woman set up house less than a stone's throw away from his fortress of solitude?

After his divorce from Samara, he'd quit the rat race. He'd sold the fancy house in Tiburon, and his share of the gold plated Marin County practice catering to the toy dogs of the wealthy. When his parents bought a retirement home in Shelter Cove, he followed right behind them, like a rudderless teenager. He never suspected they'd be gone a year later, missing the collegiality of

Davis, where they'd lived for much of his life. But once he'd settled in, he found he craved, no needed the isolation that the Lost Coast provided.

Celibacy hadn't been kind to Ben. As he steered into a brief straightaway, his hand drifted from the steering wheel toward his cock, already semi-hard with the thought of touching that smooth swath of skin Hannah had exposed. Just as he got close enough to his zipper to ease some of his suffering, he lost control of the truck, swerving into and out of a particularly curvy section of the road. Hannah slammed on her brakes, missing his chrome bumper by inches.

Great. The last thing he needed was a rollover. This could be a dangerous road, even to the familiar. He raised a hand in apology, and he focused on putting both hands back on the wheel for the duration of the drive. If Cody got sick all over his car, he'd look like an even bigger fool than he already felt.

With his mind focused solely on driving, the remainder of the trip went more smoothly. He pulled up to the driveway of his parents' wood-sided house, its blue paint weathered gray from constant sea exposure. Only a garage door and narrow front door faced the street. This side of the house was no more than an undignified entryway into a house dedicated to its view of the ocean. Hannah pulled up next to him. She swiped at her phone, making no move to get out. Ben shook his head in resignation. Maybe she really did need a vacation.

He leaned down and fumbled under the seat until he located the extra remote control and house keys. Squeaking and rumbling, the heavy wood door opened, revealing a large empty space. Hannah eased her SUV into the garage. She met him by the front door, no less alluring than she'd been an hour before. Only this time, instead of being overwhelmed by the glitz and noise of her jewelry, he actually looked at her, trying to figure out what about her was making him crazy.

Hannah's actual ethnic makeup was ambiguous, not that it mattered. Her smooth skin was a lovely golden hue. She was tall and slender, her head reaching his shoulders. Her hair came a little past her own shoulders. It was light brown and curly with blond highlights. He suspected the color wasn't real, but didn't care. She was getting under his skin. Maybe if he touched her once, or kissed her twice, he would have enough to take to bed and fantasize about. Kissing or a little making out did not mean he'd have to walk down the aisle.

Ben's problem was that he'd always taken dating and relationships too seriously. After his divorce his friends had urged him to take advantage of the hot and cold running women who were impressed with the 'Dr.' before his name, no matter that his patients were of the four-legged variety. But he didn't like casual sex and liked gold diggers even less. He had to admit his friends from college and vet school sure looked like they were having a lot more fun with a lot less heartache. Seeking solo satisfaction was boring him to death. Hannah was only here for a week at the most. Maybe he could get her to drop her phone long enough to consider a little fun. After all, a little bit of fun did not equal commitment.

"So, this is it," Ben said gesturing at the nondescript house on Sea Court.

"Are you sure this will be okay with your parents?" Hannah asked. "When Cody feels a little better, he will be an energetic adolescent."

Ben nodded, sorting through a few keys before finding the right one to open the front door. Chivalrously, he gestured for her to enter first. Being so near, and smelling the faint lingering odor of his soap and something else she was certain was unique to Ben, threw her for a loop. She urged Cody in first, and then stepped into the foyer. The street side of the house didn't do it justice. There were few walls downstairs or up, and sunlight flooded in from the huge windows facing the ocean. The house was directly on the beach. The smallest strip of land separated the wood floors, glass windows, and teak deck from the churning waters of the Pacific Ocean.

"Wow, this is so cool. This is exactly what I need. Please let me know how much I'm going to owe your parents."

"I'll get your bags."

Hannah hesitated, hating to use him like this without any recompense. Vets weren't supposed to be tipped, were they? "They're in the back."

The picture windows drew her to them. They set at forty-five degree angles to maximize the light spilling into the house. She lived very near the ocean in Newport, but it was nothing compared to this. Here the shore was all dark and imposing. The waves pounded their way to shore washing over the smooth rocks, before making their way back to the deeper ocean. It would be easy sleeping with the constant drumbeat of the ocean to drown out her sorrows.

Hannah started when the door slammed, the ocean having lulled her into some sort of meditative state. Ben bustled in carrying her two duffel bags and her tote.

"You don't travel light."

"There is dog food in there. I didn't know if they'd have his grain-free brand in Oregon, and I didn't want Cody to get sick."

"I'll take these upstairs and show you the rest of the house." She followed him up the staircase. The landing was all railing on one side, the cathedral ceiling soaring even up here. Three doors faced them. Ben opened the third, and plopped her bags on the bed. "This is the master." He pointed to a richly stained wood door to the right of the bed. "That's the bathroom. There's a Jacuzzi in there."

She opened one of the bags and took out a ceramic bowl and the large bag of dog food. He stopped moving and looked at her for a second. He came closer, blatant attraction in his eyes. Despite the fact that she was in a strange house with a man she'd only met hours ago, she wasn't the least bit afraid of him. She was scared of herself. Frightened by the feelings he so quickly and easily roused in her. The kind of feelings a married woman should ignore.

He cupped her cheek with his open palm. If he leaned in to kiss her, she'd let him. She would. Why not? It wasn't often in life that instant chemistry came along. It was too rare a feeling to dismiss. To her disappointment, his hand fell away and he took a step back.

"Should I put some food down?"

"No. Dogs are meant to fast every once in a while. He'll be fine until tomorrow. Give him some time to get his system on an even keel."

"What about us humans?" She didn't want him to leave.

"Mom is careful to empty the fridge. You won't be able to shop until tomorrow."

"So?" she prompted.

"There are two restaurants in town, The Cove on Seal, and the Chart Room on Wave."

Some developer had taken the cutesy names a little too far. "I've already forgotten what I saw on the street sign. Are we on Sea or Sail?"

His smile was reluctant. "We're on Sea Court. Anyway, neither one is open every day." He looked at his watch. "It's Friday, The Cove is open. They have pretty good seafood."

The phone almost vibrated itself out of Hannah's jacket pocket. She ignored it. "Are you going to let me go alone?" Why beat around the bush? She wanted his company for a couple of hours more.

Hannah could see the vacillation in the way Ben's jaw muscles worked. She was used to that push-pull with men, but she always got her way. Dr. Ben Cooper was no different. The power of the pussy, whether women admitted to it or not, worked nearly one hundred percent of the time. Men could never resist the idea that sex may be dessert.

He blew out a breath, then threw his keys up in the air and caught them. "I'll drive."

"Will the dog be okay here?"

"As long as he's house trained, he should be fine. Do you have something for him to chew?"

Hannah fished through one of her bags and pulled out a bigger ceramic bowl, and a hard rubber chew toy.

She trotted down the stairs into the kitchen as if she owned the place, and filled the bowl with water. Confidence was one of her greatest assets. Cody drank thirstily. She sprayed some kind of peanut butter concoction into the toy, and the Cody happily grabbed it and flopped down in front of one of the picture windows. He'd be fine.

With nothing more to do, she followed Ben to the front door. He opened the door of his car for her, and she hefted herself in as gracefully as was possible with a running board and high-heeled wedges involved.

It felt like they'd pulled into the inn's parking lot before she'd finished buckling her seat belt. The town was miniscule.

"Wow, I didn't realize it was so close. We could have walked."

Helping her out of the car, he looked pointedly at the four inch sandals.

"I do have other shoes." She looked at her hand. He hadn't let go even as he awkwardly locked the car with the other hand. She didn't say anything. She didn't want to let go either.

"I thought nobody walked in Southern California."

She looked in his eyes, and saw that he'd made a joke. Slowly but surely, he was thawing. "We don't want to risk our lives walking along a six lane road to get from one strip mall to the next."

A chuckle escaped his lips. He held the door open. An older gray-haired woman with a smart haircut greeted Ben warmly, and led them to an ocean side table. Their table was the quietest in the place. Ben watched the water beat against the rocks, though the view wasn't very different from the one at his parent's house. Ben spoke, eyes turned toward the foam on the jetty. "It's always amazed me how water can wear out anything on earth. It's absolutely necessary for animal physiology. Neither we nor our dogs or cats could survive without it. But it can take away life in a heartbeat."

He finally tore his eyes away from a view he must have seen nearly every day of his life. "What are you running away from?"

The owner made a special trip to their table, leaning in, saving her from answering. She spoke softly. "Dr. Cooper, I'm sorry to say we're putting out a fire in the kitchen."

"Literally?"

"Yes. An actual fire."

"Georgia," Ben said, halfway out of his seat. "Anything I can do to help?" Georgia waved him down.

"Sit, sit. Can we come back to you guys in twenty minutes? I only ask because you're a regular." She gestured at the rest of the room. "The tourists wouldn't understand."

"Take your time."

Georgia blew out a breath, relieved. "Wine's on the house." The owner darted away to have whispered conversations with another table.

"You're a regular?" Hannah asked.

"I don't have the dexterity to cook on surgery days," he said, flexing his capable looking hands. "You didn't answer my question."

Michael came unbidden to her mind. She pushed thoughts of her husband away. "I, uh, made a few missteps. I'm not where I thought I'd be."

He raised a single perfectly arched eyebrow. "Which was?" Eyes the color of a stormy ocean zeroed in on her like lasers. Hannah tried not to squirm in her chair. She wished he'd turn back to the ocean. She needed that free wine, now.

"Art. I used to have a photography studio in L.A."

"What did you take pictures of?"

"I shot faces." A scene of them alone on the beach, him, her and her camera unspooled in her mind. "I'd love to shoot yours," she said, lowering her voice deliberately.

"This ancient mug?" Ben scratched at his cheeks self-consciously. Didn't he know how good looking he was?

"I've done a thousand pretty boys and even more beautiful women." She searched his face with her eyes, instead of giving in to her desire to trace his features. "You have character, *and* good looks. It's a rare combination." Nerves shot through her like adrenaline. Where was that wine?

"Why are we here?" When she didn't answer, he prompted further. "Together?"

Her hold on him was slipping. She wanted nothing more than to tie him to his seat. Make him see her. "I wanted dinner, remember?" she said lightly. When he didn't respond, she went for the truth. Hannah was too old to mince words. She didn't want to play games. "I'm not going to beat around the bush. I'm attracted to you." Her brown eyes caught his gray.

"Everything you want is not something you should have," he said, cryptic.

"Does that mean dinner is off-limits? I wasn't proposing marriage, here."

"Can I be frank?" He said in a tone that told her she probably wanted anything other than barefaced honesty from him. She lifted her hands in an 'if you must' gesture. "You're not my type. I've been on this ride before and I'd rather not do it again."

Hannah had never thought of herself as anything but attractive. But, she'd been on *this ride* herself. It was time to pull the plug. She gathered her purse. She could find her way back on foot, even if they were shod in four-inch cork sandals. "Got it. You don't date black women."

2

Hannah was out the door before the waitress made it to their table with the much needed wine. Stomping all the way to his parents' house, she chided herself for the foolish behavior. Her attraction to Dr. Ben Cooper withered like a leaf of a neglected plant. Just when she thought the world had advanced. Just when she thought the election of America's first biracial president had opened people's hearts, here she was flying in the face good old fashioned prejudice. Living in liberal southern California had made her careless. Lessons she'd learned growing up on the east coast came back to her like a slap in the face.

The phone buzzed again in her pocket after she closed the front door of the house behind her. She turned it off and threw it on one of the room's easy chairs. No Michael. Not now. If she talked to him, she knew she'd be lured right back into the marriage trap. Granted, his infertility announcement had come at a really bad time. And she didn't want him to think she was leaving him because he couldn't get her pregnant. But Hannah didn't have it in her to soothe his wounded pride, with her own in tatters.

She took off her jacket, and curled up on the couch pulling a hand-knitted throw around her suddenly chilled body. Cody, sensing her disquiet, stopped his gnawing, and jumped up next to her, resting his chin on her lap. She looked into his soulful brown eyes and thanked God that not every creature on earth judged her based on her looks.

The hypnotic sound of the ocean must have lulled her into a doze. Hannah grasped her stomach as it growled, assuming that was what had awoken her. She stood up and stretched, taking a mental inventory of what edible non-canine food she might have stashed in her luggage, when she heard the door jiggle. Cody raised an ear, but nary a hackle.

Ben stepped in, carrying a large paper bag in each hand.

"What...?" her voice faltered.

"Geez, Hannah, you got me all wrong." He dropped the bags, and pulled her forward, kissing her full on the mouth. It was what she'd wanted a few hours before: warm hands pulling her face to his, hot breath scented with cloves, soft lips against hers. She wanted to melt into this embrace, and then remembered what had happened less than a mile from here.

She pushed hard against his chest, breaking off a kiss. *"Hvad fanden?* I wasn't looking for a consolation prize." Attraction and desire warred with anger within her. The sound of ripping paper filled the empty room.

He stepped back, looked down, and snatched the bags from the dog's nosey investigation.

"What did you say?"

"I said I am not anyone's experiment. If you don't want me, that's fine. I'm not a child." She'd meant to say *like,* but that *want* thing had slipped out of her mouth entirely on its own.

"No, the other thing."

"Sorry," she paused, and shook her head, off kilter again. Hannah wanted to slap herself. She had a rule about apologizing. Not wanting to appear weak, she never did it. She hated that he tossed her off her usually even keel. She made a point of being the most self-assured and confident person in any room. Then it hit her, he must be talking about her language choice. "I sometimes swear in Danish." She often lapsed into her mother's tongue under stress.

He stacked the bags on the counter far from the dog's seeking nose.

"I think we need to start over." He thrust out his hand. "I'm Dr. Ben Cooper, vet, Shelter Cove resident, and a guy who's really attracted to you."

Her stomach did a flip-flop. The awkwardness between them evaporated. Like two oddly shaped puzzle pieces, they snapped into place together. "I thought you said back there..." She needed to be sure.

"Ignore what I said. It's not what I meant." He walked around the kitchen island, unpacking bags, getting plates, and utensils. She watched his muscles bunch and release under his jacket. She wanted to die from his smell alone. The soap and cloves and leather came together in a heady cologne. She was itching to touch him again. "Why don't we have a civilized discussion over wine and food?"

Hannah uncorked the wine bottle he produced, and poured a healthy amount of the clear golden liquid into each glass. Something told her she was going to need it. He brought two delectable looking plates to the table. Not more delectable than him, but she was hungry...for food.

"Do you want the shrimp scampi or Alfredo?" He held out the plates—an offering.

Hannah sensed that now wasn't the time to ask if the shrimp was sustainably raised, farmed or wild, or packed with artificial preservatives. "I'll take the shrimp, thanks."

He laid both plates on the table and went back for cloth napkins and cutlery. "Glad you're not a vegan."

She laughed. "Nope, red blooded, red meat eating American, here."

Hannah tucked into her food, unselfconscious for once, too hungry to care. The only thing she'd had, before her frolic and detour to the Lost Coast, was acidic coffee and an unseasonably early pumpkin muffin. Halfway through her entree, she put down her fork, and looked at Ben. He'd hardly touched his food. Sipping his wine, he looked like he was turning something repeatedly in his head.

He was more handsome than she'd first thought. He wasn't conventionally appealing in that classic movie star way. He wasn't Robert Redford or Brad Pitt. He wasn't even George Clooney. And he wasn't Michael with his blond hair, blue-eyed surfer good looks. He was Ben Cooper. She fought the urge to squeeze her thighs together to relieve the pressure building there.

"You speak Danish?" The deep timbre of his voice broke into her silent contemplation of him.

"My mom is from Copenhagen." Then she corrected herself. Her mom's stay in New York City was the aberration. "Actually, she's back there now with her second husband."

"And your dad?"

"My black half? He lives in New York, City that is." She paused to sip some of the cool white wine, glad for something to do other than speak. "So, if I'm not your type, why are you here?"

"I divorced a woman like you a few years ago." The matter-of-fact words felt like a slap in the face. The only worse comment would have been if he'd said she reminded him of his father's mistress. A home wrecker beat out an ex-wife every time. Astroland's Cyclone had nothing on this roller coaster ride of an evening.

"So I remind you of your ex-wife. Wow, that's not a come on line, is it?"

He ate a few bites, then gestured toward her, taking in her whole body. "Is all of this, necessary?"

"What do you mean by, *all of this?*" She couldn't get a read on this man. He alternated between smooth talking stranger and snarker in chief. "I am who I am, and not looking to change for anyone."

"Samara spent every waking moment, planning to shop, shopping, or planning to shop some more. She had more logos on her than a Louis Vuitton purse. It was Burberry this, Gucci that, or whatever was being hawked at Neiman Marcus that week during the lunch fashion parade."

"Let's see, you've insulted me, and talked about your ex-wife. We should go ahead and have sex to make this a triumvirate of first date no-no's." She took another large sip of wine. Really, she was kidding, she told herself.

"Touché." His laugh was low and sexy. "I could make the last happen," he said. She couldn't tell if he was serious or mocking. She put down her wine and looked into his eyes. She didn't think he was kidding. Hannah abruptly pushed herself back from the dining room table, sending the padded leather chair skidding in her wake.

Hell, he didn't mean to scare her, but she wasn't a naïve twenty year old. She must know what a man in lust looked like. He heard scraping and running water, and assumed she was disposing of the remains of her dinner. He wanted to turn and watch her so badly, but played it cool.

She came back, grabbed her wine glass, and headed for a small settee backed against those massive windows that sold his parents the house. Hannah was rightfully putting some distance between them. He wanted to close that distance. He hadn't turned on the recessed lights in the living room and the weak light from the kitchen and dining room didn't quite reach her. Ben could see the reflection of the moon on the water, but none of that weak and distant sunlight reached the house. He couldn't see Hannah.

Ben bussed the table, and turned out the kitchen lights, thrusting them into darkness. She didn't say a word. He wanted to drag her off that leather seat and cover her body with his. He wanted to feel her breasts against his chest, and the rush of her breath as the shock of his actions caught her off guard. He wanted to rip off those damned velour pants and panties, feel her tight little ass in his hands. It had been too damn long. Pushing the fantasies from his mind, he kept up the gentlemanly facade.

Not wanting to lose the intimacy of sunset, Ben turned the royal marine tripod lamp to its lowest setting. Nor did he want her to see how hard he was getting thinking about all the ways he could touch her smooth golden skin. He was glad that the lamp's burlap covered shade kept most of the room in shadows. He placed his wineglass on the floor, and joined her on the small leather couch. Ben imagined she'd picked that particular piece of furniture to increase the distance between them. If he were a polite guy, he'd have sat opposite her on the plush couch that probably still held her scent, or on one of the wingback chairs his mother had swathed in nautical print. But he didn't want to be that far away.

He heard, rather than saw the wine disappear from that glass into her luscious mouth. He looked at her in time to see her tongue darting out to lick her full lips. That tiny movement alone nearly pushed him past control. The feeling he'd tried to ignore in his car was back with a vengeance. A low buzz sounded in the morgue quiet room, breaking the sexual tension. It was Hannah's phone again.

"Are you really a CIA agent? I don't think I've heard anyone's cell ring that much." To his ears, he didn't sound like the wolf he was hiding under the civilized clothing.

The husky sound of her laughter shot straight to his groin. It matched the timbre of her voice, low for a woman and sexy as hell.

"Undercover agent? No, I'm really an ex-Realtor. In this down market, my clients won't let me go, expecting me to work the same miracles I did in a better market."

It all clicked into place; the luxury SUV, the designer clothes, the incessantly ringing phone. He felt like a colossal ass for misjudging her. Even in college towns like Ithaca or Davis, every real estate agent drove a long, elegant Mercedes or wood appointed Lexus. Even when the families were only looking at modest track houses to call home. He assumed all the excesses of real estate agents were fueled by the belief that if people thought they were successful, that would bring them success. For some reason, people didn't want to buy a house from someone who drove a Hyundai or Kia. Guiltily, he had to admit, he probably wouldn't either.

"I think I misjudged you," he finally said aloud.

He pulled the wineglass from her hands, and set it on the windowsill behind them. This time when Ben leaned in to kiss Hannah, she didn't push him away. He settled himself in for a slow exploration. He slid one hand into that thick, glorious hair, so unlike his own, and put the other hand against that swath of skin that had been tempting him all night.

As her open mouth accepted his willing tongue, Ben realized how much he'd missed this. He hadn't kissed or touched another person in such a long time. This kiss, this slanting of his mouth over hers, this dueling of tongues, made him want to jump out of his skin with the anticipation of seeing and touching her golden brown body. He slid his hand up, so glad she'd removed the jacket, and unerringly found her nipple, erect. He changed the angle of their mouths as he grazed his thumb across the peak of her right breast. He swallowed Hannah's gasp of pleasure. He moved even closer on the small couch, pulling his hand from her hair to slide it down her back and over her small, firm ass. It was better than he had imagined.

Hannah broke the kiss, glad for the twilight invading the room, even with the lamp's weak light. The darkness hid any shred of guilt. Her relationship with Michael was over the minute she'd closed the door of the Newport Beach house. She was a thousand percent sure this was where she wanted to be right now. But, she desperately needed to take a minute to be as sure of him as she was of herself. Her heart couldn't handle another mistake.

"Ben," she said, pushing against his chest again. She needed some space to think—to make sure that he was thinking with his big head. She hadn't reached the ripe old age of thirty-seven without knowing who she was and what she wanted. The last few years had reinforced her decision to go with her gut with every future decision. Relying on her brain had wasted the last years of her life. Sure, with age one lost perky breasts, and the ability to stay up all night. But what she gained in wisdom was worth the loss. What she knew now, was that she wanted this man, no matter how brief their acquaintance. "Are you sure you want this? Now? With me? I'm not interested in you using me to work out issues with your ex-wife."

He grabbed her hand and pushed it against the hardness under his slacks. It was a crude but deadly accurate barometer of what he was feeling in the moment. Hannah molded her hands to the shape and length of him even though she knew it would be wiser to pull away. Ben had the wisdom to lift her hand from his zipper, and shifted his body back toward other end of the settee. "I don't know what in the hell I'm doing," he admitted, his voice hoarse with want. "You tempt me, Hannah. You really tempt me."

"Were you planning the ascetic life of a monk?"

"I moved here to give myself time and space to work things out. I don't want to repeat the same mistake again."

Neither do I. She pushed up from the small couch. Hannah extended her hand and he grabbed it. She tugged gently and he rose. For a moment, she thought of pulling him to the master bedroom that he'd shown her earlier, but her good sense won out.

"You need to go home, Ben."

Reluctantly, he walked to the kitchen and grabbed his leather jacket from the back of one of the barstools. "I didn't mean for any of this to happen like it did."

"Cody's vet said he needs a break from driving." She lifted the corners of her lips in a half-smile. "I'm not going anywhere."

"Can I have the keys?" Hannah held her hand out. "No more surprise visits." He dropped the keys, heavy with a small anchor keychain, into her outstretched palm.

"I'll be sure to keep the spare keys at home. I promise I won't come in again without your invitation." She heard both meanings in his words. As if all this artifice of keys, and locks, and doors would keep them apart.

He grabbed his own keys and headed toward the door. She followed him, ready to lock it in his wake. The kiss he planted on her forehead was unexpected and sweet all at the same time, disarming her.

"Good night, Ben." She lightly touched his leather clad back.

"This isn't goodbye, Hannah."

3

Ben didn't even bother to pull into his garage. He didn't have the wherewithal to struggle with the door between the garage and the kitchen, swollen shut in its frame. Instead, he slammed his way from the car through the front door of his house. Sometimes he hated living between the mountains and the rocky pacific shore. He had no place to go when he needed to drive and work out the crap in his head without risking his life if he didn't keep his full attention on the road.

More doors slammed in his wake. He couldn't figure out if he was angry, frustrated, or horny. What had he done back there with that woman? He knew better than that. Just because she looked good and smelled good, didn't mean Hannah would be good for him. How could he trust her not to use him and hurt him when she was done working out whatever was going on in her life? He didn't even trust his own judgment when he'd come up the fool more times than not.

Ben couldn't believe he was on the verge of blue balls. God knew that hadn't happened since he was a teenager. When he got to the end of the short hallway that connected the open living area with the back of his single-story home, he stalked into his bedroom and threw his jacket down on the mussed duvet. Why on earth did he have this huge king size bed? On nights like this one, its massive size reminded him how empty it was.

He seesawed between the idea of a cold shower and jerking off. Neither seemed satisfactory. Even thinking of the upcoming municipal election wasn't enough to ease the tightness in his pants. He thought back to his teenage years when this kind of problem had been constant. Back then, worries of his mother catching him with porno magazines was enough to cool any erection.

Snapping his fingers, he decided to call his parents. Now would be a good time to let them know about Hannah, and Cody. The distant ringing of their old style landline cooled him off quicker than a winter ice storm on the Finger Lakes. His mother answered. Her heavy

Brooklyn accent, which hadn't lessened one iota over the sixty or so years she'd spent outside of New York City, immediately identified her.

"Hello."

"Ma, it's me, Ben."

"You're the only son I have. How could I not recognize your voice?"

"It's about the Shelter Cove house."

"Is something wrong?" She had that worried tone she always got during a phone call. Elaine Cooper was always wringing her hands about something. "Walter!" she cried out. He heard his father's shout from somewhere else in their house. "You better come here. Ben says there's something wrong with the house."

As his father got closer, Ben could hear his dad's murmurs of regret about not installing a security system.

"Mom," he called out, trying to get her attention. "There's nothing wrong with the house. I'm calling to let you know that I've rented it out short term."

"What's that?" He could never figure out if she was losing her hearing or had never gotten the knack of a cord free phone.

"There was a woman who came into the practice. Her dog was sick, and I thought it would best if the dog recouped there a couple of weeks. Is that going to be okay?"

Ben heard a lot of noise as his father's glasses hit the earpiece, and the click of the extension hanging up. Why did his parents have to share the phone? He'd seen them do it hundreds of times over the last forty years. They acted like it was 1965 and extension phone lines weren't popular yet. They'd installed extra phone jacks when his sister was a teenager, but they still shared the hard-wired wall phone in the kitchen for the length of any conversation.

He repeated the whole spiel, waiting for their consent. They gave it, of course. He was their only son, and they found it hard to say no to him.

Ben knew, when his father got off the phone claiming a need for ice cream, and his mother paused a minute too long, that he was in for it. He should have claimed a pet emergency, and set off his own pager. Age did not equal wisdom, at least where one's parents were concerned.

"So, how well do you know this woman?"

"Ma, she's a client in need."

"Is she single? Do you plan to get to know her better?"

"Ma!" What was it about parents of children of a certain age? Why did they feel the need to pair them up?

"Are you going to ask her out on a date?" A date. His parents truly were a throwback to another era. If he explained the world of hook-ups, one-night stands, and online dating to them— they'd be rightly horrified. They still expected him to call a woman up, pick her up in his car, and pay for dinner *and* some form of entertainment, be it a movie or local theater.

No matter that they lived in a college town with free Wi-Fi everywhere. In some ways, it would always be the 1950s for them.

"Ma, you know that I'm not looking to date right now." He broke the news the same way he had dozens of times in the last two years. "I'm not getting married again, Mom." Abbe, his older sister by eighteen months was the fecund one in his little family of four. She'd married right out of graduate school, and quit her job as a therapist as soon as she had her first child. As far as he could tell, she was a happy stay-at-home mother of three. "You have Abbe and the kids to dote on."

"And there's Marty, too. You haven't met their new little one. He's a real cutie."

Static broke the minute long silence. He didn't talk about Marty. Ever. His mother heaved a deep sigh. In it, he heard her disappointment, but on the issue of Marty, he wasn't going to budge.

"You know, we never did think Samara was your type. You should have married someone more like you, more down to earth. Whatever happened to that girl you dated in Ithaca? What was her name?"

For ten more minutes, he trudged down his dating memory lane with his mother, reminding her that she didn't like the ones who were now perfect, and how they'd loved Samara until the divorce. His father asked his mother something and her response was muffled by her hand over the mouthpiece.

"Ben, I have to go. Don't worry about charging this woman anything. I wouldn't want money to come between you two. It's not every day a single woman wanders into your life."

"Ma, her being single is not her only redeemable characteristic. She's pretty, too." He could have slapped himself for falling right into that trap.

"Well, Benji honey, I'm glad you're taking a look at her other traits."

He flushed, glad she couldn't see the embarrassment now emblazoned high on his cheeks.

"Is she Jewish?"

"Samara's Jewish."

"*Touché.*" Mercifully, she let him off the hook. "Maybe she could leave a check for a few dollars for the utilities and housekeeper? But please keep an eye on the dog. We've had a no pet policy and there are quite a few breakables there. She doesn't have a lab, does she?"

"It's a Shepherd mix, Ma," he answered, purposefully leaving out the Labrador part of Cody's genetic equation. Labs had busy tails. They were legendary about knocking things over. He'd be sure to stop by in the morning and move anything precious Cody could unintentionally destroy.

"I'm glad you'll be there to keep an eye on things. She ended calls as she always did, quickly and without ceremony. "Okay, bye-bye, Benji, honey. We have to go now."

He looked at the silent receiver in his hand. For a moment there, he suspected his mother was doing anything she could to push him and *single* Hannah together. When had a woman's availability become the only thing parents needed to know before shoving their son in her direction? Either way, he had an excuse to see Hannah tomorrow.

Ben probably felt even more lost than Cody did as he sat on Hannah's single front step the next morning. He'd knocked, but there'd been no answer. He'd peered through the garage's tiny windows. The black SUV was still there. He stretched out his long legs on the tiny strip of pavement between the front door and the street, feeling ridiculous.

Now he wished he had a phone. Fiddling with the tiny computer surely made one look more busy and important than they were. His parents' neighbors were probably wondering if he was locked out, or taking the most uncomfortable break ever. He was saved by

Hannah coming around the corner, Cody in tow and plastic bag in hand. Today she wore slim jeans that didn't taper at the ankle in today's replication of the unfortunate 80's trend, and leather boots. He looked up from his low vantage point and took in the form-fitting sweater. It was a mess of uneven tan and white stripes, expanding over her generous breasts. Even though she was covered from neck to toe, his imagination was on fire. It was only when she got closer that Ben realized Hannah was on the phone.

Hannah had slid her finger across the screen, accepting Michael's call when his face lit up the screen. She kept the other hand tight on Cody's leash.

"You didn't answer your phone last night," he said without preamble.

"I was driving. I needed time to work through what you said."

She could hear pain in his voice. "I wish you were here," he said. A better wife would be with him now. A year ago she would have been that wife. But for better or worse, their marriage was over.

"I really need this time and space to get my head together."

"I still don't understand why you can't think down here—at home. We have the beach. I wouldn't have bothered you. You could have had your solitude."

That wasn't exactly true. Michael had turned out to be a much needier husband than she anticipated. He'd seemed so self-possessed, so self-assured all those years they'd been friends in New York. Two independent people coming together for companionship, occasional sex, and child rearing had been the tacit understanding. But, he had taken their vows so very seriously. He wanted and expected a wife with a capital 'W.' Michael needed the reassurance of a wife who loved him totally. It had exhausted her trying to be all of that. She needed space to acquire the courage to tell him it was over. If she'd stayed within his gravitational pull, she would never escape his orbit.

"I know, Michael," she lied. "I wanted to get away for a while. I'll be back soon enough."

There was long pause. "I still want to create a family with you. We can talk about a sperm donor or maybe even adoption. I did some research on the internet last night..."

"Stop, Michael. Stop. I think we should talk about all of this, about us, when I come back."

"Where are you, anyway?"

"I'm in some place called Shelter Cove, on the Lost Coast or something like that. Cody was carsick, so I decided to stop here." She could hear him at his desk, probably searching for her location on his computer.

"It says here that there's an airport there. I can probably make arrangements to join you for the weekend."

She turned back on Sea Court and could see Ben's long legs stretched out on her front walk.

"I don't think that's a good idea."

Hannah let Michael talk more. He was probably trying to persuade her that they'd be better off together, but she couldn't hear him. She had eyes and ears only for Ben.

Sandwiching the phone between her shoulder and face, her eyes met Ben's. With one hand, she pitched the plastic bag in the garbage bin his parents had sheltered with a little wooden fence. She handed Cody's leash to him.

"Good morning. Glad I didn't wake you," Ben said.

"Who is that?" Michael asked in her ear.

"It's Ben."

"Ben?"

"Dr. Ben Cooper. He helped Cody out yesterday. I have to go." Hannah ended the call with a tap of her finger.

She stuffed the phone in her back pocket and continued their conversation as if she'd never been on the phone.

"I slept like a rock after all that driving, the wine, the waves." Hannah gestured to the front door. "Let me wash my hands."

"Can I come in?" he asked. Though they'd had some intimate moments, he didn't want to assume he'd be welcome. Being married and *not* being married had taught him that he liked his space, and he was sure she liked hers. Her car hadn't been filled with a gaggle of spa-seeking girlfriends, so alone time was probably a premium.

She waved him in, and he trailed in her wake, her light scent beckoning him. "I think we're beyond formalities." Hannah excused herself and he heard the taps go on and off upstairs. Cody lay on the third step keeping a keen eye on him. This time, she came only partway down the stairs, sitting on an upper step, rubbing cream into her palms. He could understand her desire to keep some distance between them until they could get a better handle on what was going on between them. Sex, lust, and desire had a way of confusing things.

"So," she said, gesturing expansively.

"I'm off this morning, so I thought I'd help you get some groceries, coffee—you drink coffee, right?" When she nodded, he continued. "Maybe we could even share a little breakfast."

"Oh," she hesitated for a long time, and he thought he'd be out on his ass any minute. "I guess that's okay."

"I also thought I'd check Cody out too, though he seems to be doing fine."

Although Hannah had agreed to his morning outing, and goodness knows she was jonesing for some caffeine; she didn't budge from her place on the stairs. In the dark of night, she'd been so sure of her actions. She wanted him, she could have him. In the light of day, nothing looked the same. It wasn't Ben. Her hand longed to touch the curls still damp at the nape of his neck. His long sleeved Henley clung to his taut frame. She admired the sprinkling of hair on his chest, peeking out between the buttons. His broad shoulders tapered into faded brown corduroys. Low cut suede boots molded to his feet.

Ben leaned over to pet the dog, examining his eyes and ears. Cody opened one eye lazily, happily accepting what he viewed as affection.

"So where does one shop around here?" She'd taken Cody for a pretty long walk and she hadn't passed much that wasn't residential. She'd spied a general store—a quaint looking place that she'd considered stopping at— but it was closed until well into the morning.

"Warehouse store or health food?" he asked.

"Can we do both? I eat healthy when I can, but I don't need organic paper towels. If you don't have the time for that, I understand," she added quickly. Ben seemed unsure of women, in general, and her in partic- ular, and she didn't want to make him uncomfortable. Maybe he was being nice, and last night had been an aberration. Because she was wildly attracted to him, didn't mean he returned the sentiment. He could have been horny last night. It looked like it could get lonely up here in the sticks. "You can point me in the right direction. The car's navigation can do the rest." She was giving him an out. She wanted more between them. She wanted to see what would happen if they spent time together.

With a few words, he could push the reset button. She could spend the next week or so in retreat, and he could splint the broken wings of sparrows, or do whatever he did out here by the ocean. Hannah's attraction to him had hit her upside the head like a cartoon anvil. She needed time for the stars to fade. Ben paused and looked at his hands a long moment, before gazing out at the magnificent ocean view. She followed his gaze, watching the waves crash against the weathered stones. He turned that intense and contemplative gaze on her. Ben was making some decision more weighty than whether to drive to the store or not.

"I'll drive. You ready to go?"

Hannah stood, and turned to walk up the stairs. "Let me get something for Cody and my wallet." Coming back down with bag in hand, she threw the extra-large rope toy into the living room and the dog, who had previously looked dead to the world, jumped up, eager for the new treat. The path cleared, Hannah descended the steps, ready to join Ben wherever he wanted to take them.

Ben was surprised again at how tall she was, merely half a head shorter than he. He'd always dated small, curvy women—kind of like his mom. He paused, blinking at that little revelation. He'd probably need ten years of therapy to figure that one out.

Despite her height, or because of it, he felt very comfortable with Hannah. It felt more like she was his equal—that she wasn't expecting him to take care of her. He was more than ready for a woman who could take care of herself. A relationship of equals was right at this phase of his life.

Because she wasn't tiny, did not mean she wasn't all woman. As he was always taught, he opened her car door and helped her in. They reached for the seat belt at the same time, their hands meeting. He held hers for a moment too long, enchanted with her long slim fingers and plainly, but perfectly manicured nails. When she buckled herself in, Ben noticed Hannah jingled a lot less than yesterday. She was wearing only one bracelet today, a wide enameled bangle, instead of the gold collection she'd had the day before. Elegant simplicity suited her.

As soon as they turned onto Shelter Cove Road, Hannah's phone rang, a distinctive proprietary ringtone. It rang again, unanswered in her lap.

"You can answer it. I don't mind." All right, he did mind. Who was calling her all times of day and night? Was she really single, or here trying to get out of some relationship? He wanted to talk to her, find out who she was, without the distractions from her other life.

"You know what, I'm done with this for now." She flicked off the ringer, opened his glove compartment and shoved it behind the maps and box of syringes jammed in there. "Why do you have syringes?"

He sighed. It was for the crappiest part of his job. "I offer home euthanasia for clients."

She sucked air through her teeth. "Cody is my first dog. I can't imagine that his life is going to end one day. Tell me dogs die in their sleep like people."

He looked over at her, the car rounding a curve. She shaded her hands over her eyes as the strong morning sun lit up the highlights in her curly hair. The ends shone gold in the autumn light. One day he would tell her, it was all the gold she needed. "Dying in our sleep, it's a myth. Most people die in the hospital and most dogs are euthanized."

Hannah looked genuinely aggrieved. "So, do you have any pets? I always imagine that vets live on farms with armies of rescued pets, from iguanas to horses."

Ben had to laugh. He'd met a lot of veterinarians like that himself.

"I bought the practice from a woman like that. She started with horse rescue. Pretty soon people would drop animals off. She ended up with llamas and emus among the bunch. Oh, and she had a lot of rabbits. And they bred like rabbits. It's good thing she has those forty acres up north."

"No rabbit rescue at your house?"

He shook his head, embarrassed at his answer. "I don't have any dogs or cats, either."

"Don't you like pets?"

He could feel his face redden. Ben had always wanted a dog like Cody, a big goofy companion. "My ex-wife got custody of the dog in the divorce."

"Oh. Sorry," she said, contrite.

"No, it was actually for the best. I worked all the time, and Toffee was really her dog."

She laughed that husky laugh he was learning to like. "I'll assume, for the sake of argument, that Toffee wasn't your name choice."

"Um, no. And I'll tell you a little secret." He lowered his voice conspiratorially. As he'd hoped, she leaned in closer, her scent wafting over the gearbox. "I'm no fan of toy dogs. People assume vets love all animals equally. We don't. At least, I don't. It was a little dachshund with the most annoying bark ever. Let's say, I didn't retain visitation rights."

Hannah's phone buzzed again, pulling her back upright in her seat. It vibrated loudly against the box of needles. She opened the glove box, turning it off all the way, and shoved it farther back into its recesses.

"Sorry."

"Are you the only agent in Orange County? I can't imagine that your clients can't find anyone else."

"It's not them," she said, sobering.

So there was a guy. There had to be a guy. "Does it have to do with this 'retreat' you're on?"

"Are we close to coffee? I'm not much good without a morning jolt." Was Hannah caffeine deprived or changing the subject?

He glanced at his watch. "Maybe twenty minutes more."

She reached into the bottomless pit of her designer tote and pulled out sunglasses with lenses the size of Frisbees. The rhinestone logo on the stem cast starbursts of light in the car. Every tourist was wearing the same thing this summer. He tried not to fault her for lack of originality. It wasn't exactly like he was down on the farm sewing his own clothes.

They drove in silence for a while. He stole a look at her profile every once in a while, taking her in. Her curly flyaway hair, her full lips, the upturned, but proportioned nose. When he glanced at her this time, her brow was furrowed.

"I have no secrets," he told her plainly. Ben was too old to play games. He need honesty and openness between them if there was ever to be anything more. "Just ask."

"Since we've already done this the wrong way," she prefaced, "can I ask why you and your wife broke up?"

A sharp pain came and went in his gut. Samara's betrayal still stung, physically.

"I found out she was cheating," he said matter-of-factly.

4

"Oh!" Hannah sucked in a breath, and let it out slowly. She leaned back in her seat and closed her eyes, glad that the huge dark lenses hid them from his scrutiny. She looked at Ben from under her frames. Ben didn't have any lenses shielding his stormy gray eyes from the bright morning sun. Hurt still lingered there.

She wasn't cheating. She and Ben had not slept together. It was *over* with Michael. It had been over the minute she'd backed out of the garage of their Newport Beach home. There was nothing left between them but the details—selling the house, splitting their assets, getting a divorce. Seeking out a relationship with Ben was part of 'moving on.' The phrase every talk show guest and reality show star used must have some merit.

"I'm sorry," she continued finally, hoping he attributed the delay in her response to tact. "That must have been rough. Did you walk in on them or something?"

"Nothing as awful as that. I was on the computer in the den one night checking on some lab tests and an instant message thing popped up. I clicked on it... All downhill from there."

"How long had it been going on?" Maybe this Samara had been cheating for years. Long-term deception was unforgivable. A short break between one relationship and another happened all of the time. Almost every boyfriend she'd ever broken up with had had another girlfriend within weeks, if not days. She'd never thought they were cheating—but expedient.

"Whether it was one day or several years, I didn't need to know. I didn't ask a lot of questions. I didn't go all detective on her or the computer. The fact that she broke our marriage vows and was having a relationship with another man was enough for me," Ben said, banging a palm against the dashboard for emphasis.

"Had your marriage been okay before that?" Women didn't cheat for no reason. The both of them were probably unfulfilled. She knew that feeling well by now. Maybe he would understand why her marriage to Michael was ending even with no bad behavior on anyone's part.

"In retrospect, no. I'd sold out. Got the big house even though I didn't want it. Joined the gold plated practice even though I never planned to cater to the dogs of the rich and famous. Turned out to be all status and no substance."

She stuck her toe in the water. "Then maybe the best thing that could have happened is that you found out she was with someone else."

Ben slammed the steering wheel angrily. "Deceit is never the answer. Honesty would have worked. It would have been hard. I would have been hurt either way. But if Samara had told the truth, we could have ended things the right way." Hannah agreed with his sentiment. It was exactly what she was trying to do with Michael—end things the right way. All she needed was the guts, the courage to tell the man that had always been a true friend, that it was time to end the marriage part of their relationship.

After a pause, Ben continued, "The best thing is that we didn't bring any kids into it. Would have been a mistake."

"Did you want kids?" She immediately hated herself for the eager, pleading tone in her question. Hannah knew from talking to her single male friends that men of a certain age hated being asked about kids. They wanted women to want them, not be sized up for their father potential.

"Probably too late for me. Should have done it when I was a younger man, but Samara was never willing to give up her lifestyle for it. You can't go to Pilates in the morning, lunch with girlfriends, and shopping in the afternoon with a toddler on your hip." She held back her sigh of relief. Thank goodness they were at least on the same page about that. She'd finally met a man who set her insides on fire and wanted what she wanted.

"That's probably true," she said. "Parenting takes a lot of sacrifice." She was willing to make that sacrifice.

"And I didn't see us being a family that hired a nanny to raise our children. My mom raised my sister and me without help. She eventually worked full time. But we were always well cared for and knew we were loved. I think that's the only kind of environment I'd want to bring a kid into. It's the main reason we had *that* house and I had *that* job."

They drove the rest of the way in relative silence. From time to time, Ben pointed out different aspects of the beautiful landscape, the tall pines, the dramatic mountains, and the ever-present wildlife. Hannah looked at nature on display, and the compelling man beside her. She loved his outside, the hound dog eyes she wanted to see smile again. She admired his thick brown hair beginning to show a few silver threads. But she was starting to like his inside as well. He was a traditional man with a big heart and a gentle soul. She let her eyes drift shut and began to imagine a quiet life up here with Ben, and their babies.

Ben pulled into the lot of the warehouse store first. "If you're not picky, they have coffee here while we shop."

She hopped out of the car before he could turn off the engine and open her door for her. She wasn't a woman used to being taken care of and it rankled with him a little. He wanted a woman who could stand on her own two feet. Samara's need to have him chime in on every decision had been cloying. But he wanted her to need him, a little. He already felt a need for her that driving, and shopping, a little kissing wasn't slaking. Hannah strode forward, grabbed a cart and sailed through the automatic doors. He could do no more than follow her.

For the next two hours, Ben watched Hannah shop, and against her protests, carried everything for her. He hauled a sack of food for Cody, paper products, and fresh meat and produce in paper bags. The ride back was quiet and he fished in the cup holder for his MP3 player, plugging it into the auxiliary jack on the stereo.

"So you're not a Luddite?"

"No, Hannah." Ben shook his head ruefully. "The phone is a personal thing. Maybe I'll get one again someday. For now, I'm enjoying my solitude. My tunes, I have to have."

He was surprised when she sang along with R.E.M. and U2, with one of those whisky soaked voices that brought sex to the mind of any straight man. It wasn't difficult to imagine her in a smoky club, scantily clad, drawing in her audience. The scantily clad part of that fantasy had him shifting in his seat. The corduroys that had seemed so comfortable this morning suddenly constricted his movements. The closer Ben got to the house, the less he wanted to leave Hannah. He didn't have any etchings to show her, but he could cook for her. One or two late night cable movies he'd seen with hot sex on the kitchen counter sprang to mind.

"Let me make you breakfast," he said pulling into his parents' driveway.

"You've got it," she said easily. "Cooking isn't really my thing."

Hannah bustled into the kitchen, putting stuff away while he donned his mother's frilly checked apron and got to work. When Hannah left to put away the rest of her things, the room lost a little of its warmth. He put down the wooden spoon he'd been holding, and patted the amiable dog on the head. Cody was not a substitute for female companionship.

About twenty minutes later, Ben put steaming pancakes and bacon on the counter along with more coffee and called her to the kitchen. Sitting side by side at the counter in the light of day was more intimate than dinner by twilight.

They ate in silence for a while, except when Hannah complimented him on the food.

"Aren't you a little young for a mid-life crisis?" Ben was probing, he knew. He hoped she wasn't considering celibacy after a bad breakup or something like that.

"I turned thirty-seven this year, and I'm not where I thought I'd be." Ben was surprised her age was so close to his own. He'd assumed she was much closer to thirty. Her reason for getting away wasn't much different from his own, minus the cheating spouse, of course.

"And where is that?"

"In a long term relationship, maybe married, with a couple of kids. Living in New York. Pursuing a career more tangible than real estate."

"Real estate is a fall back career for a lot of wives I've met."

Hannah blinked, looking startled. "Yeah, I kind of fell into it, too. I thought it would be enough to make up for what I gave up."

"Do you sing? I really liked your voice back there in the car." That was an understatement. That voice made his cock twitch.

"I majored in music in college."

"Where was that?"

"New York." Hannah didn't offer more.

"What brought you out here to California? You don't strike me as a native." He gave her a disarming half smile, but she didn't return it.

"Taking pictures."

"Did you bring a camera with you?"

"Always. I got some great ocean shots on the One," she said, effusive once again. "I can't wait to do some sunsets from the deck here. They'll be incredible." She looked at him for a long moment. Her intense scrutiny literally had him squirming in his seat. "I still want to photograph you."

"Really?" At forty, he was grateful that he had all his hair—on his head.

She turned on the kitchen stool, her knees bumping his hip. She reached out her hands toward his face. "Can I?"

Could she touch him? God, yes. Speechless, he turned fully towards her. He intertwined his knees with hers so the barstool wouldn't swing him back toward the counter.

Her hands smoothed over the cowlick he determinedly beat down every morning, pushing his hair back from his brow. Her fingers tunneled through his hair and she stroked his scalp. She smoothed her manicured fingers over his brow, down his nose, and across his lips. He resisted the urge to take her fingertips into his mouth. She ran her hands along his neck, and he hoped that she couldn't feel the strain of keeping his hands to himself. The fact that Hannah kept her hands on the outside of his clothing was probably his saving grace. When she'd satisfied herself, she put her hands back in her lap.

Did he pass muster? It was stupid to crave something so much. Something he hadn't known he wanted a few days earlier.

"Tomorrow night around six? The light should be right."

He nodded, not caring that he was being led around by his dick. At this point, his penis could call all the shots.

After Ben left, Hannah cleaned up the morning dishes. She dragged a couple of heavy Adirondack chairs from the shed and got comfortable on the broad, weathered deck. As the ocean breeze picked up, she wrapped her sweater more tightly around her. Then she made sure the dog was comfortable on a rough wool blanket she'd found in a chest upstairs. Turning on the phone in her lap, Hannah propped her feet up on the second chair. It lit up like a Christmas tree, lights flashing as it displayed all her missed calls, voicemails and texts. She cleared the notifications without looking at them. Before she could put the phone down on the chair's arm, it rang.

"Hannah, why has your phone been off?" Michael asked in a mildly reproving tone.

"I had to get some supplies, and I turned it off while I was driving." The difference between driving and riding was a distinction without a difference. She didn't want to complicate their conversation by mentioning that Ben had been in the car with her.

"Isn't that why we paid for Bluetooth in this car? You said it would be easier to have a completely hands free call."

"Michael. Hands free driving may be safer, but it's not safe. The road into town winds through some steep mountain terrain. I needed to concentrate." Little white lies rolled off her tongue.

"Oh," he said, deflated. He was a bit of a safety nut, always buckling and snapping, and following the speed limit. The belligerent tone was quickly replaced by a wheedling one she'd always found annoying. "Why can't I come up there? I won't get in your way. If you're thinking about your future, don't you think your husband should be there?"

No, she didn't think he should be there. Hannah would readily admit that Michael was a smart man with good ideas. He'd helped her in the past when she'd closed her photography business and opened one in real estate instead. He'd helped her pick her car, pick her clothes, and make all her decisions. She didn't know when she'd gone from self-sufficient to reliant on him, but it was time to put it all to a halt.

"Michael. I'm going to say this only one more time. I need this time alone." Hannah spelled it out in case he didn't understand. "A-L-O-N-E."

Michael sighed, changing tactics. He was ignoring her as he always did when she didn't give in. Most of the time, she went along because it was easier than arguing. He could verbally outlast her every single time. "I know you're going through a lot. It's clear that moving down to Orange County maybe wasn't the best idea. But I'm going through something here, too. I'm still processing what Dr. Stern said." He'd thrown a left hook. She was on the ropes, but felt a last surge of self-protective energy.

"Michael, this isn't a good idea. I need to be selfish for a little while."

"Is this because I couldn't get you pregnant? There are other ways we can be a family." He'd gone from bullying, to persuasion, to guilt in less than ten minutes. She looked out at the dark water. She felt bad for Michael, really bad. But she also felt bad for herself. And them being together for twenty-four hours a day wasn't going to fix any of their problems.

"Michael, I've told you time and again over the last few weeks that I feel like I'm losing my artistic spirit." It was about the baby, but it was about these other things too.

"But you didn't give up art or photography, Hannah. I was looking at your website, and you're brilliant. You're doing so well in such a short time because your unique stamp is all over every house you sell. You do a beautiful job staging the homes, and making them really inviting. Your listings always look better than the other brokers around here."

"A wide angle lens and ample light is not art, Michael."

This was the problem with Michael. He actually thought decorating and taking pictures of other people's homes would fill her artist's soul. It wasn't that he didn't love her. He didn't understand her. They had known each other for years before Michael actually asked about her singing. Ben had picked up on it in less than twenty-four hours.

"Michael, you don't get it. Can't we leave it for me to figure out—on my own?"

"But I want to get it. That's what marriage is about. You can't expect me to read your mind. Talk to me. Tell me what you're thinking, what you need out of life."

Hannah resisted the urge to hurl the phone into the ocean. Something told her there wasn't an Apple shop around the corner. The last thing she needed was to be stranded up here in a town of five people without a phone. She put the phone back to her ear. Michael was still talking.

She interrupted him. "Michael." He wasn't listening. "Hear me out!" Finally, silence came from his end of the line. "Today is the last Saturday in September. Give me ten days. I'm going to turn off my phone now. I'll call you when I'm ready to get on the road for the trip back."

"What if there's an emergency?"

"Call 911."

"I'm serious, Hannah."

"So am I. In what emergency scenario would I be helpful?" She couldn't shoot a gun, give CPR, nor fight a fire.

"Okay, okay, you've got a point. Promise me you'll check your phone every night in case I or someone else needs to get in contact with you."

That was a fair compromise. "I'll do that, Michael."

"Please know that I love you, Hannah. I always have, and I always will."

"You too, Michael." She pressed 'end call.' The words had always felt uncomfortable. But she did love him in her own way. He was like the brother she'd never had. He'd been a friend when she needed one. But he was not Ben.

5

Ben Cooper stood naked in his bedroom. A draft from the open door pebbled his small nipples, and raised the gooseflesh on his skin. On the floor next to him were the torn t-shirt and cutoffs he'd worn that morning when he'd looked at a neighbor's horse, and worked on the sandy patch of dirt he called a yard. Caring for the horse had taken his mind off Hannah. This horse was fairly domesticated, but he'd learned in his many years of practice never to take his eyes off an animal— especially one that large. A moment of inattention and a shoed-horse hoof could kick him in the balls. He was on the fence about having children, but wanted to decide for himself.

Smooth black microfiber boxer briefs whispered against his skin as he pulled them in place. In spite of the adult looking underwear, he still felt as nervous as a thirteen-year-old going to his first middle school dance. He shook his whole body like a wet dog, trying to get rid of his nervousness. What should he wear? What would Hannah want to photograph him in? He looked at the paltry selection in his large walk in closet. He had two suits, still in their dry cleaner bags, and a few dress shirts, mostly for family occasions. The ten pairs of pants hanging from the otherwise empty rods did nothing to fill the small bedroom the previous owner had turned into a closet. His few pairs of shoes would have made Imelda Marcos feel like she was in a prison camp. Even the ten or twenty long sleeved shirts, that Ben preferred, were dwarfed in the large room, only occupying two of the many shelves. In the end, he picked clothes that weren't remarkably different from what he wore yesterday or what he would wear tomorrow.

Ben walked the mile from his house to hers. The damp, chilly air was what he needed to cool his libido. Even in his leather jacket, he shivered a little as the chill fog rolled in from the water. Fall had definitely arrived here in the Lost Coast. The scrubland leading to the water had greened a little, casting off its dry, brown summer look. The redwoods, spruces, and pines stood tall along the mountains. Their craggy peaks would soon be covered in snow.

Hannah met Ben at the door, black nylon Tamrac bag slung carelessly over her shoulder. She was as dressed down as he'd ever seen her in the few days of their acquaintance. Except for large silver hoop earrings, she didn't wear a lick of jewelry. She had on old jeans, worn at the knees and butt, a gray sweatshirt that covered everything. Her fingers poked out through a thumb and finger holes in the cuff. Even her sneakers looked like they'd seen a lot of miles. She'd never looked more beautiful to him.

"Do you mind if I bring Cody? He could use a little exercise," she said by way of greeting.

Ben shoved his quaking hands in his pockets. He'd never been more jittery with a woman. It had been a lot of years, but he knew the feeling. He really liked her and dreaded saying something or doing something that would scare her away. Something in her aloof nature suggested he wouldn't get many chances with Hannah. He watched as she grabbed the dog's leash, probably oblivious to his tension, and ushered them out of the house.

"I scouted out some locations this morning. I think we can catch the light if we hurry." She turned her back on him, and guided the dog down a narrow beach access path. Ben watched her walk away. Hannah had done nothing to restrain the golden brown hair that curled wildly around her head in the damp air. The baggy clothing did nothing to hide her slim figure, especially her small, round butt that he knew would fit perfectly in the palms of his hands if she rode him during lovemaking. She led them all to a small cove on the deserted beach. Off leash, Cody occupied himself picking up and discarding seaweed, small crabs, and running back and forth from the water.

Hannah busied herself choosing a lens and fiddling with controls on the camera. Despite years of having one Canon or another as the extension of her right hand, she fumbled with the dials. She gave up and watched him. Ben played with the dog, chasing him, and throwing some object Cody had found. He'd shrugged off his leather jacket, and dropped it carelessly on the beach. He looked so naturally athletic and in tune with the dog. He wore an off-white shirt and gray cords, and she could see the muscles of his shoulders and back move against the thin cotton. She couldn't help but notice that the shirt was a good contrast against his olive skin. He hadn't bothered to shave and the two day old stubble added a little bit of the rogue. This she observed with her photographer's eye.

She wanted to drop the camera, drop the pretense. Her fingers itched to grab his hand and pull him into a long embrace, and have his long, lean body warm her, warding off the chill. She wanted to look into those blue-gray eyes and see desire flare. She wanted him to bend his head and kiss her, blotting out the setting sun and darkening clouds looming to the north. If she were looking at him with the eye of a potential lover, she'd have dropped the guise of the camera and suggested they give sex on the beach a try. But she wasn't. She swung the camera back up to her eye, and the control knobs came as second nature to her again.

Hannah gave in to the impulse to release the shutter, snapping as many candid shots as the camera could handle. The pounding waves drowned out the snap of the shutter and the click of the lens. She hastily looked at a few of the shots on the viewfinder. This was going to be good. She was glad that she had lugged her MacBook with her. The satisfaction of looking at large scale images of Ben was waiting around the corner, even if she couldn't print anything to tack up on the walls. In her home office, the setup was perfect for making prints with the large printer she often used for house flyers. Thoughts of her home in Newport Beach rose like bile in her throat. She swallowed the unwanted feelings. Hannah closed her eyes for a long moment, willing thoughts of Michael and her Orange County life away. She made her one last candid shot, then caught Ben's eye.

"I discovered this afternoon that 'black sand' was a bit of a misnomer," she said hoping he didn't hear the quaver in her voice. "I'm sorry, I didn't think to bring something for you to sit on." Standing ten feet away from him fully clothed, she was more nervous than she had been halfway to naked on the small couch in the house.

"It's okay," he said, lowering himself onto his leather jacket on the pebble-strewn beach. "I'm used to it by now."

Hannah turned to aperture priority mode. She pressed the function button until her customized monochrome setting appeared on the screen. A wide-open aperture, black and white, and her favorite eighty-five millimeter portrait lens would suit Ben in this setting.

Hannah's hands felt sure and her stomach stopped roiling as she looked through the camera lens. This always happened when she lost herself in her craft. She asked him to try a myriad of poses. Whether he was sitting with his knees up, or squatting, or standing looking out into the distance, in every picture she made sure to focus on Ben's incredible eyes. He never once looked away from her. Somewhere in her mind, she knew, knew he was looking into her soul. She hoped the big black camera masked her deception.

Hannah lowered the shutter speed for the third time. The light was giving out on her. She'd shot on the beach countless times in Los Angeles, and evening fog had always been a godsend. The harsh California sunshine gave way to open shade as the marine layer pushed on shore. No matter how beautiful the subject, and there was no shortage of beautiful people in L.A., direct sunlight benefitted no one. But the fog here on the Lost Coast had come in thick and fast, bringing darkness. With regret, she realized her too-short session with Ben was over.

Hannah pulled the cap from her jeans front pocket and snapped it over her lens.

"That's it?" Ben asked.

She whistled for Cody and the canine came running. "There's no light left out here." A thought came to her, unbidden. Could she convince Ben to continue their session indoors? She thought she could adjust the light indoors to give her some great shots with a completely different mood.

"Did you get what you need?" His question gave her the opening she needed.

"I'd really like to get a few more. Would you be game?"

"Absolutely." Ben looked at the watch on his wrist.

"Do you have to be somewhere?"

"No, it's only seven." His eyes met hers. "I'm not quite ready to call it a night, if you're not." Her stomach bottomed out. Hannah opened the zip pouch of the camera bag and took out the nylon leash, trying and failing three times before hooking it to Cody's collar.

They made their way back with the sky darkening more quickly than she had ever seen it. She'd pulled the door closed only seconds before a first thunderclap sent Cody skidding under a wingback chair, tail between his legs.

"He'll be there the rest of the night." Ben's stomach rumbled in the too quiet house. "Are you hungry?" she asked.

He shrugged, and smiled sheepishly. "Maybe a little."

"I threw together some chicken salad. Help yourself. I'm going to set up some lighting." When she was focused on getting a great shot, all her hunger disappeared. Coupled with her attraction, she couldn't imagine ever eating again.

While he fiddled around in the kitchen, she grabbed the candelabra from the dining room table. The heavy pewter and silver piece that had seemed gaudy and overwrought before, was perfect now. She placed it on a small cherry table in the bedroom turned study, and lit the candles with matches she'd found earlier. Hannah moved a heavy leather club chair in front of the water-streaked window. The water trailed an irregular but fascinating pattern down the smooth glass. She wanted to capture that. She got her camera and tripod and made the necessary adjustments.

Ben's entry into the small study startled her. Flickering light from the lit tapers was the only illumination in the otherwise dark room.

"The chicken salad was good. You shouldn't..." Ben trailed off.

"Can you sit there?" Hannah asked, directing him to club chair. When he'd sat, she reached out to touch him, then pulled her hands back. "I'm sorry, do you mind if I..." she pantomimed arranging his limbs.

"You don't need to ask my permission to touch me."

Hannah didn't want to speculate on his meaning. She would love to have permission to touch him anytime she pleased. She put her nervousness, her feelings, her lust out of her mind as best she could. In the flickering light, she grasped his hands and arranged them on the table, propping his head up. She smoothed his hair, pulling it forward in a way that anyone who viewed the photograph on display would find sexy. Not able to help herself, Hannah smoothed her hands across the arches of his eyebrows, and prominent bones of his nose, and across his lips. She was startled when he broke his pose, grabbed her hand, and pulled her in for a kiss. It was awkward at first, with her standing. She felt every inch of her five ten height, like she had when she was a gawky teenager. He remedied that when he pulled her onto his lap, and deepened the kiss. All thoughts of her height and her clumsiness fled her mind.

Something akin to an electric current coursed through her veins. It was heaven feeling this again. Nothing had felt like this since Lucas almost twenty years ago. She avoided kissing Michael. How had she thought she could stay in a half-assed marriage with Michael? Guilt warred with desire. She broke the kiss with Ben. She wanted this man with a passion she hadn't felt in years. Was it fair to Ben or her to start something when she didn't have any idea where it could go?

Fuck fairness.

She stood, and reached for the camera she had set down on the daybed. "Let me get this shot."

Ben repositioned himself and looked where directed. She ditched the tripod and propped the camera on a *semanier* instead. Thirty shots in, she was satisfied she'd got what she wanted. Hannah put the lens cap back on one final time, and turned on the light switch near the door. Light would make sex less likely.

The harsh overhead light did nothing to make Ben less attractive or lessen her desire for him. She wanted nothing more than to pull him down on the scratchy daybed cover and have her way with him. Instead, she did something far more responsible.

"Don't you need to get home?"

"Can I ask you a favor?"

She knitted her brows questioningly. Of course, she'd probably give him anything he wanted right about now, even if that something was a blow job. She nodded. "Sure."

He grinned. Clearly he'd heard the quaver, the question in her answer. "I need a ride home. I walked over, but with the rain..."

"Oh. Of course." She shook the cobwebs and thoughts of pleasuring him, from her brain.

"Why didn't you drive over?" Hannah peered through the swirling rain and swishing wipers, trying to see where the street ended.

"Thinking about you, Hannah, made me so hard that I needed that mile to cool down," he said matter-of-factly. "I didn't want to go all caveman, drag you upstairs and do what we've both been thinking about."

She ground to a stop well past the red octagonal sign, jerking them both forward in the car. Maybe this was why the salesman had stressed the importance of antilock brakes. Ben directed her the rest of the short distance to his house. In the pouring rain, she couldn't see where he'd been holing up the last two years.

Hannah cut the engine. The steamy cabin of the car felt more intimate than a bedroom. The rain pelting the metal roof was muted, but made it feel like they were in a world of their own.

"Ben, what are we doing here? I don't live here. I mean I was only planning to be up here for a week or so. I really like you, but..."

He unbuckled himself, grabbed and held her hands awkwardly over the center console.

"This is not ideal. We have something here, something I want to explore. Let's see where it goes while you're here. Can we do that?"

She nodded, powerless to do anything else.

"I'll call you tomorrow before I leave the clinic. I want to have dinner with you again."

"Okay, but..." Why was she objecting? They wanted the same thing.

He let go of her hand and put his fingers to her lips. "Life is full of regrets, Hannah. You and I have our fair share. I don't want to add this to the list." He leaned in and kissed her soundly before jumping out of the car and sprinting toward his front door. She watched his figure disappear into the storm-muddled darkness.

6

Monday morning Ben called, as he'd promised, and for the next two weeks, Hannah and Ben dated like teenagers, albeit chaste 1950's teenagers. They'd spent every night together. He'd taken her back to the Cove for dinner—and this time she stayed through dessert. They'd gone to see the only movie playing in Garberville. It was easy not to argue about what to see when there weren't any choices. She was grateful that it hadn't been anything with too much sex in it. She didn't need any more ideas.

He called, picked her up, showed her a good time, and dropped her off at her front door with the briefest of kisses. But Hannah wanted more, a lot more. No matter how many times she'd pressed her mouth hard to his, or slid her hands under his clothes, or ground her pelvis against his in stark invitation, Ben didn't budge. He always set her back against the door, and said his goodbye.

Tonight, she was determined to get more from him. When he dropped her off after their date, she wanted her urgency to overwhelm him too. If anything was going to happen between them, it had to happen now.

Sunday, she'd start the trip back down the coast because Hannah couldn't put off going home any longer. Michael was getting antsy, texting her more than once that she'd stayed well beyond her original plan. He was right. It was time to go back to Orange County and put an end to that part of her life. She wanted to come back to Ben free to explore what they were building. But she needed a reason to return. She didn't want him to forget her.

The difference between driving on the north coast of California was that they actually covered miles in the car instead of marking time in gridlock. Sitting in the cab of the truck watching the acres of roads, farms, and trees go by, sex seemed more and more unlikely. They were moving too fast for sex in the car. Agitated, Hannah looked over at Ben in the confines of the vehicle and chastised herself for such a petty concern. She was really lucky.

She was exactly where she wanted to be and with the right person. Each night had been a surprise and a pleasure, even if it wasn't as much pleasure as she wanted. Tonight Ben had mentioned they were going to a club, so she ditched her casual shirts, and fished in the suitcase for her one stylish top. It wasn't dressy by any means, but at least it wasn't another shapeless Gap cotton shirt. The chocolate brown, off the shoulder sweater dotted with a few sequins complemented her skin tone.

Hannah was surprised when they pulled up to the Blue Monk jazz club in a town called Eureka. The tiny hamlet didn't look like it had more than a few thousand people. How could they support a jazz club? She was even more surprised that the place was packed with people of all different ages. Ben pulled out a chair for her, squeezing in next to her at the little round table. The waitress came right away, pressing for their order as the show was about to start. Hannah ordered a scratch margarita. Ben ordered a beer. If tonight's pattern followed the last few, Ben would nurse that beer much of the night before switching to water. He liked to be completely sober to navigate the roads that wound their way through the giant northern redwoods and sequoias. She admired his safety, but a sober man was hard to seduce.

The band assembled, and started to play. She recognized the first tune immediately. It was her dad's most popular song.

"Oh my God," Hannah exclaimed. She picked her bag up from the floor and rifled through the large tote looking for the program she'd been handed at the door. Her turned off phone, lipstick, Leica, Kelly green Kate Spade wallet, and several pens scattered on the table before she found the flimsy piece of blue paper.

"Do you like Shay Morrison?" Ben asked. "Something about your voice reminds me of his. When I saw they were doing a retrospective tonight—"

"Shay Morrison is my dad."

"What?" Ben said too loudly, leaning in closer and accidentally knocking her lip balm to the floor. He scraped the metal chair leg against the wood floor trying to chase it down, a discordant note in a mellifluous room. A nearby patron shushed them. Guilt flooded her. Noisy patrons were hell on musicians.

Hannah grabbed Ben's hand, stopping his movement. They could deal with all of this later. She held his hand, tapping it to the music as she tapped her own. She closed her eyes and swayed with the music. It was like being at home listening to her dad rehearse. She remembered the nights he'd defied her mom and took her to smoky clubs in Brooklyn and Manhattan—she being the only ten or eleven year old in the crowd. Those were some of her most cherished childhood memories. She'd felt so special – like the music was being performed just for her.

When the band broke for intermission, Ben turned to her.

"Your dad is Shay Morrison?" She nodded, still floating on a cloud of melody and memory, unable to pull her lips down from the huge smile she knew graced them. "Do you have your mother's last name, or is it a stage name?" he asked with innocent confusion.

Hannah crashed right back to earth. Keesling was Michael's last name. He and his family had been very pushy about the name change. After their "I dos," she'd no longer been Hannah Morrison, photographer. She wasn't Hannah Morrison, singer and songwriter, either. They'd insisted that she become Hannah Keesling, real estate agent. They'd been there for generations, after all. The Keesling name meant something in Orange County, they'd pointed out relentlessly. She'd given in without much of a fight. A name, she'd had to agree, was not an identity. The lie came to her lips before she could bite it back. "It was my married name."

Ben looked a little taken aback. "You never mentioned that you'd been married."

"It was more a youthful indiscretion, than a marriage," Hannah found herself saying. No way did she want to lie to Ben. He'd had enough lies for one lifetime. She needed to talk her way out of this. "My name is Hannah Caroline Morrison." Her words tumbled over each other. "Shay isn't really his first name, you know?" Her body hummed with nervous energy as she talked her way out of a corner.

Nothing in his bemused smile looked like he suspected her.

"It's Daniel," she continued on. She could hear herself speaking too rapidly—barely pausing to take a breath.

While chucking all her stuff back into her purse, she launched into the story she'd heard a million times herself.

"My dad was on tour in Ireland back in the late 60s or early 70s when he was just starting to get popular. Anyway, he was doing some sightseeing outside Galway and some guy they were hanging out with dared him to cliff dive." Ben looked at her astonished. "I know, crazy, right? Anyway, he dove off some cliff in Inis Mor," she said giving it the Gaelic flair her dad always did when telling the story. "It was like, a ninety foot dive into the Atlantic Ocean. Obviously, he lived to tell the story. I think the guy who dared him never expected him to do it. Anyway, after that the Irish guys they were traveling with called him Shea—which means 'hawk like,' or 'admirable,' or something like that depending on who's telling the story. It was Americanized when the whole episode was written up in Rolling Stone, and he's gone by it ever since."

Hannah was grateful to see the band reassembling on the stage. It would mean that Ben wouldn't probe her on her marriage, and she wouldn't have to make up any more lies or tell any more half-truths.

She had another couple of margaritas, hoping they would relax her. She had to put a period on the end of her relationship with Michael. While the band went back in time to the music of Miles Davis, Hannah made up her mind. She was definitely going back to Orange County on Sunday. No more delays. She started making lists of what she'd need to do: look for a divorce lawyer, talk to her parents and break the news to them, put the house on the market, look for her own place to live. She closed her eyes as her head swam. Whether it was the three tequila-heavy margaritas or the prospect of her future that caused her dizziness, she didn't know.

Ben grabbed her hand. The gentle and reassuring touch of his hand strengthened her resolve. "Are you okay?"

She wasn't. "Can we go home? I think I've had too much tequila."

She must have dozed off because Ben was pulling up to the house in what felt like minutes after they left Eureka.

"I'll walk you in," Ben said, his tone brooking no argument.

"Thanks," she said. There was no reason she couldn't trust him not to take advantage of her compromised state. Trusting herself was still something she was working on.

He led her up to the master bedroom, one strong arm around her waist.

"What do you wear to bed?"

She pointed to a large UCLA t-shirt, lying across the wicker chest at the end of the bed. Ben undressed her in the most clinical manner, pulled the soft cotton sleep shirt over her head. Drunkenly, she mused that all of his patients were naked. He was pretty good at dressing and undressing for someone whose only act of disrobing was likely shaving fur from dog's legs and cat's bellies. She laughed out loud, probably confirming for him her inebriated state. He stood to leave. She grabbed his hand, pulling him back down to the bed. The muddle in her head cleared out a bit. She needed to tell him this, now.

"Ben, I'm leaving on Sunday."

Ben knew it was coming, but that didn't mean those four little words didn't hit him like a punch in the gut. He had been pretending that Hannah was just a lady in town that he'd been dating. But this little time bomb had been ticking in the back of his mind for the last two weeks. And now it was exploding. He really liked her. He thought he could love her if he had the time to get to know her and find out if he could trust her. What was he going to do to get her to come back to the Lost Coast, and to him?

The chime of the doorbell started Hannah's heart racing. Ben. She banished the thought from her head. The small clock in the lower right hand of her laptop screen told her it was too early for Ben. It was one in the afternoon. Ben should be at work. It was the day he did scheduled surgeries. Who else would come knocking at her door now? It wasn't as if anyone knew her here. Her heart crashed to a stop. Maybe Michael hadn't heeded her request and had found his way up here.

Determined, she walked to the door. Only after she pulled it open did she consider that she should have peered through the glass and asked who it was. She was behaving like the worst too stupid to live horror movie heroine. But there wasn't an axe murderer on the threshold, just a smartly dressed older woman with a cap of carefully tamed curls.

"Hi," Hannah said, question in her voice. "Can I help you?"

The woman extended her hand assertively. Hannah felt compelled to grasp the small hand in a shake. "So you're Hannah," she said, Brooklyn accent as thick as if she'd run into her on Fulton Street. The diminutive woman nodded approvingly. "I'm Elaine Cooper, Benji's mom." Mrs. Cooper's voice transported her home for a fleeting moment. Ben had his mother's hair.

"Oh. Come on in." Hannah stepped back, extending a welcoming hand. She was in the woman's house after all. Of course, she should invite her in. She stood with this complete stranger for a long, awkward moment. "Did you drive up from Davis alone? Is Ben's father with you? I'm sorry I don't know your husband's name," she said filling the empty space with chatter.

"Dr. Walter Cooper. I dropped him off in town to have lunch with some friends."

Cody chose that moment to race into the room. He'd no doubt heard the doorbell ring, but had been working on nosing his way in through the partially closed sliding door. Hannah was quick to grab his collar to prevent him from jumping on Ben's mom. Paw prints on her tailored gray wool pants or fitted cream-colored linen jacket would make a bad first impression.

Clumsily, Mrs. Cooper patted the dog on the flank. She was not a dog person.

"Well, he looks like a nice dog," she said, stepping back out of Cody's orbit. "Is he a Lab mix?"

"Cody's half Lab, half Australian Shepherd. He's dog and people friendly," Hannah declared defensively. Cody was a nice dog in a world where people treated most of the canine persuasion like frothing pit bulls ready to attack.

They both stood in the front hall ill at ease for what felt like years. The only sounds in the room were the dog's panting and the seawater crashing against the shore. What was this woman expecting of her? Why was she here? Her years with Michael had made her adept at avoiding traps sprung by the older set. Adroitly, Hannah didn't voice her questions. It seemed extremely rude to make those kinds of inquiries when she was living in the woman's house and dating the woman's son. She towered over the pint-sized woman. Ben must have gotten his height from his father's side.

"Have you had lunch? I was going to throw together a salad for myself," Hannah said, her manners taking over.

Elaine's shoulders relaxed a little. "That would be great. Can you leave my dressing on the side?"

Hannah looked at Elaine's trim figure. She was in great shape for a woman who had to be in her mid-sixties, by all counts. She walked to the kitchen and got the salad fixings from the fridge. Nothing more than store bought lettuce, some canned corn, corn chips, chicken breast, and diced avocado. She tossed her own impromptu southwest salad with ranch and salsa. Careful not to sully Mrs. Cooper's leaves with gobs of oily dressing, she brought it all to the table, along with a bottle of ranch for Elaine.

It wasn't until she saw Mrs. Cooper carefully pressing keys on her laptop, that she realized it had been awful quiet when she was in the kitchen. His mom was looking at the photographs of Ben she'd taken on the beach, and in the upstairs guest room. Shit. What had happened between her and Ben was the kind of thing that happened between consenting adults, *in private*. The pictures were PG rated, but she was sure they revealed more than she'd want to disclose to any stranger.

"Wow. These are…something," Mrs. Cooper said, accepting the salad and dressing. Hannah went back to the kitchen to get linens and cutlery. "Do you love him?" Ben's mother did remind her of home. She had another annoying trait of New Yorkers, bluntness. Hannah and Elaine had grown up in a city where people asked questions that would be considered inappropriate anywhere else, and they expected an answer. New Yorkers also shared their opinions, tact be damned.

"I just met him, Mrs. Cooper."

"From these pictures, it looks like you and Ben know each other well," she said. "Why don't you call me Elaine? I think you and I are going to be seeing quite a bit of each other."

"Elaine then," she said, the name uncomfortable in her mouth. "Would you like something to drink? I have water, seltzer, maybe some lemonade..." She walked back into the kitchen, hoping the mini-cross examination was over.

"I'll have water, hon. Maybe a couple of cubes of ice."

Hannah brought back two tall glasses of ice water to the table, careful to keep each on a coaster. She didn't want Elaine to think she had no regard for her highly polished wood. She rolled one of the padded dining room chairs to the table. When Elaine picked up her fork, she pulled over the computer, and pushed the lid down.

"I'm a photographer. I'm thinking of updating my portfolio and Ben was kind enough to pose for me."

Elaine bit down on a small piece of grilled chicken breast and nodded. She didn't look like she believed a word Hannah blurted out.

"Where do you live, Hannah?"

"I have a house in Newport Beach—in Orange County." She didn't know why she added that. The woman lived in California. She knew where Newport was.

"What do you do down there that you can take time off to come up here for weeks?"

Hannah gave her the whole spiel about quitting life as a real estate agent and considering something different. Part of which was the truth.

"When did you get divorced?"

Hannah started. She didn't think Ben had talked to his mother about this. That would be weird for a forty-year-old man.

"How did you…"

Elaine gestured to the engagement ring and wedding band, Hannah had so carelessly tossed on the table. Shit. She'd thought the dining room a safer location than the car's glove box.

"Michael and I…" she trailed off. What in the heck had she told Ben? Lying wasn't as easy as it had seemed at first blush. She couldn't keep her 'facts' straight. "I'm not rich by any means, and I was thinking of…wondering if I could sell these. I don't need to keep them around for sentimental value or anything."

Elaine chewed a leaf thoughtfully. "You sound like you're from New York."

"I grew up in Brooklyn Heights." Hannah had worked to make her accent less obvious than Elaine's.

"Ben went to vet school in New York, but I'm sure you already knew that."

She didn't know that. This woman was piercing through her carefully constructed belief that she knew Ben.

She didn't want to talk about Michael or Ben. She knew too much about the former, and too little about the latter. "So what brings you up here? Ben said that you'd decided against using this as a second home."

"Walter and I are only here for the night. I wanted to check out the house and make sure you were doing okay. We'd closed the house for the winter, and I didn't know if Ben had turned on everything. But, it looks like you're doing fine."

"It's a lovely house. You guys have done a great job decorating—and that view is spectacular." No mother ever shrank from a little 'Eddie Haskell' treatment. Elaine was no different. She beamed with pride.

"I tried to do my best to incorporate a nautical theme with some of our best antiques. Came off well, I think."

They ate in silence for a few minutes. Elaine cleared her throat, expectantly. "So you said you grew up in Brooklyn Heights?" Hannah nodded. "That's not a very diverse neighborhood, is it?"

"It was pretty white when I grew up, but everyone was very nice to my parents."

"How did they come to live there? What did your parents do?"

There? Why not Bed Stuy, Brownsville, or East New York instead of Brooklyn Heights? Hannah debated between putting the woman out of her misery, or stringing out the torture. After all these years, she was very used to people's curiosity about her background. If she was in a good mood, she put them out of their misery. If they were unreasonably rude, she drew them out until they said something offensive and walked away. As she only seemed to be asking out of curiosity, Hannah let Ben's mom off the hook.

"My dad is a jazz musician. You may have heard of him—Shay Morrison? He met my mom in Copenhagen. She's Danish."

Understanding dawned on her face. When people found out her father was famous or her mother was European, they suddenly felt more comfortable being able to put her into a box. Her dad being a minor celebrity also disabused them of the notion that she somehow didn't belong in the tony Brooklyn neighborhood.

Elaine looked at her with a critical eye. "So you're..."

"My dad is black and my mother is white—like the president."

"Ah, okay," Elaine said. "I was born in Bensonhurst, myself. But I grew up mainly on the Upper East Side."

With one sentence, Elaine had communicated that she was descended from European immigrants who had struck it rich and moved to one of the toniest neighborhoods in Manhattan. Hannah was downtown, no Brooklyn eclectic, but it would do.

"What do you know about the ex-wife?" Elaine asked.

"Samara?" Trap set and sprung. "Ben gave me the high-lights. They were married, lived in Marin. She found someone else. They got divorced," Hannah answered mechanically.

"Is that what Benji told you?" Elaine asked rhetorically, cleared her throat, and pushed her empty plate and napkin forward. "I don't want you to underestimate the devastation that woman caused."

"How so?" Hannah asked, trying to hide her morbid curiosity about Ben's past.

"Ben has always been very loyal. He only had one girlfriend in high school, one during college, and so on—then Samara," Elaine said. "I always knew he'd be the kind of man who met someone, settled down, and stayed married forever. He's not one of those guys I see so much of in Davis who have to bed every girl that passes them by."

"Oh," Hannah interjected into the monologue—for lack something more to say.

"So when Samara started dating her Pilates instructor—of all the clichéd things—we were so sorry for Ben. Two years it went on before Ben left her."

"I thought he didn't know."

"Ben can turn a blind eye to the most obvious things, if he has half a mind. We didn't know if maybe they were in coun-seling or something. I've been around long enough to know you can never really know what goes on in anyone else's mar-riage."

Hannah shrugged at a loss for words.

"I'm telling you this because I don't want anyone to hurt him like that again. I don't know anything about you, really, or your past—but if you're still mooning over your wedding jewelry—maybe you're not ready. I don't think he could take another heartbreak."

"Mrs. Cooper," Hanna started, stacking the dishes on the dining room table. "I would never do anything to intentionally hurt him. And I'm not going to poison this with the crap from my past." At least she didn't intend to. But who knew where things were going? Moving from the past to the future may be messy, but she was going to do her best to make a life for herself that she wanted. Hannah finished gathering up the empty dishes and started to retreat to the sink, when Elaine spoke to her back. "So, Walter and I are planning on taking Ben out for dinner at the Cove and would love for you to join us."

Seven hours later, Hannah strode into the little restaurant trying to exude a confidence she didn't feel. She'd put on black pants, a black sweater, and sequined ballet flats. The jewelry that she'd abandoned for much of the trip was back in full force. Brushing by the hostess, she walked to the four top that held Ben's family. Walter stood up at her approach. Ben looked up from his menu, surprise written all over his handsome face.

"I didn't know you were invited," he said, pointedly looking at his mother. He rose slowly, matching his father's manners.

She wanted to tell him if he'd had a goddamn cell phone, she would have texted him like a civilized person. But that wasn't an option. By the time his mom had left, he'd already left work, and she had no way to warn him.

"Benji, I taught you better than that. Walter and I wanted to get to know your girlfriend a little better. That's all. Now be a love and pull out her chair, please."

He did as he was told, and she sat. When they were all in their seats, she extended a hand to Walter. "It's nice to meet you, Dr. Cooper."

"Call me Walter. My son here is the Dr. Cooper in the family. I only have a Ph.D. in biomedical ethics. I'm one of the few non-doctors teaching at the medical school."

Elaine, no shrinking violet, was quick to take over the conversation. "Ben, we're going to Marty's house next weekend. Can't you make time and come see his little boy? He's already two months old and you haven't met him."

Hannah struggled to pull names from her mind. Ben had mentioned a sister Abbe something, not Cooper. Had she had a baby?

"I'm so sorry for butting in. Did your daughter Abbe have a baby? I thought..." she trailed off. For someone who was supposed to be his girlfriend, she was feeling woefully ignorant.

"Oh, no dear. We're talking about Marty's baby. Marty is Ben's brother."

Hannah knew she hadn't heard of any brother. She was one hundred percent sure he'd talked about having only one sister. Her confusion must have shown on her face.

The waiter chose that moment to get their drink orders. She ordered a glass of wine. Before the waiter left the table, she snagged him and asked for a bottle of seltzer as well. Dinner could go either way. When the drinks got there, she'd decide if she needed lubrication to help with the parents, or water to remain as sober as a judge.

Ben's now cold eyes penetrated Elaine with a steely gaze Hannah had never seen before. His eyes had always held warmth when looking at Hannah. Michael's eyes, on the other hand could drop from warm sky blue to frozen tundra in a second. "Mom, you know I don't talk about this. Drop it."

"I'm not going to *drop it* Ben. You're forty years old. Quit acting like a child. I expected this when you were seventeen, not now. If I could get over it, so can you."

"Ma." Ben shook his head, a not so subtle warning written all over his stone-like face.

"Little baby Logan hasn't done a damn thing to you. He's innocent in all this. So are Marty, and Hallie for that matter," Elaine said in a voice best suited for a seven year old.

Ben started to rise from the table. "I'm leaving, Ma."

"Benjamin Aaron Cooper. Sit down." Her small hand smacked the table with force, the liquid sloshed in their glasses.

Walter finally spoke. "Listen to your mother." Ben sat back in the chair, though he pushed himself a few inches away from the table like a petulant child.

The waiter came back to a tenser table than before, this time looking for orders. Walter and Ben ordered steak and creamed spinach without looking at the menu. Elaine ordered fish, and Hannah held up two fingers to the waiter, in a gesture indicating she'd have the same as his mom. Sensing the disquiet, their waiter didn't linger.

"I didn't think you'd act like this way around Hannah," his mother said reproachfully.

"Is that why you invited her?" He turned to Hannah. Ben's eyes had gone from chilly to downright arctic, causing a shiver to run down her body. "If you must know, Marty is my *half*-brother. My dear father, Dr. Cooper, had an affair with his secretary. That little indiscretion produced a child: Marty."

Hannah lifted her butt halfway from the chair. Was she going to have to walk out of this restaurant for a second time? "I should go. I'm intruding on a family discussion here."

Hannah felt like she'd been caught in a bear trap a second time today. All that song and dance from Elaine about *her* breaking Ben's heart and his father had been walking the line of duplicity way further back than Samara. He'd grown up being lied to. Why would he want to think the worst of his ex-wife, when he'd already survived one emotional disaster? Ben grabbed her hand. She felt electricity run up and down her arm. Attraction to him felt so inappropriate in this setting. He looked her in the eye, his at once cool and pleading. Hannah lowered herself back into the chair. No matter how thorny this moment, she'd stay because he wanted her, no, needed her, to stay here.

Ben wanted to give Hannah an explanation. He'd left his parents at his house, and had driven straight to her. She'd poured them much needed glasses of wine, and they sat on the long couch sipping in silence.

"You didn't drink your wine at dinner," he said. His conversational tone belied the churning in his stomach.

"I needed a clear head to keep up with your parents," she said. Hannah put down the glass and got up to take the dog out for a quick pee. The cool air cut right through Ben. He was never so glad to see someone come back into a room. He wanted this woman coming back to him repeatedly no matter how far away she ventured. She kicked off her shoes and curled her feet under a throw his parents kept under the coffee table.

"Tell me about Marty."

Maybe ignoring the request would cause her to drop it. He stood up, got wood from the pile outside and stacked it neatly in the iron belly of the stove. He shoved some newspaper in, and lit it with a gas lighter. He kicked off his own shoes, and stretched out his legs on the opposite ends of the couch, helping himself to some of the anchor-patterned blanket.

"Tell me."

Ben took a deep breath. He had never told anyone this story, even Samara. Before Marty's wife had given birth to the baby, his parents had not really bothered him about the whole issue, and he'd thought it was something he'd put behind him. But in the last few months of Hallie's pregnancy and since the little guy's birth, his mother had suddenly ratcheted up the pressure.

"My parents were never a passionate couple. They made an excellent team. My father published his way to tenure, and my mother faithfully researched and assisted him." He paused. "I'm not explaining this right. I don't know where to start." He held his hands out in supplication. Hannah nudged his leg with one of hers, toasty under the blanket.

"The beginning."

He took a moment to gather the long-buried memories. "My sister and I were in high school over at Sacramento Day. Occasionally, I'd get ribbing from the guys on the cross country team or on Lacrosse that there was this guy at Davis who looked a lot like Abbe and me. Everyone supposedly has a double, right?" Hannah nodded. "I never thought much of it. Then one day this girl comes up to me with the Davis Senior High yearbook, and opens the page to this kid, Marty Wexler, who was on the wrestling team there. She thought he looked a lot like me and wanted to show me.

"A doppelganger in England or Australia was one thing, but a kid who looked like my little brother living across town was another." He paused, bringing the glass to his lips. His throat felt dry even after the swallow of wine. "I told the girl she was being silly, but the picture sort of tickled something in my brain, so I kept the yearbook. I showed the picture to Abbe. She put two and two together and said that Dad had had a secretary named Minnie Wexler. She remembered it because the woman had taken her home one day when Dad couldn't pick her up or something.

"So we got out the phone book." He nodded at her bemused look. "We looked her up, and there she was: Minnie Wexler right there in South Davis. We biked from West Manor Park, where my parents live, across Lincoln Highway, and through town.

"But we didn't know what to do once we got there. It was one of a whole bunch of copycat apartment complexes in Davis. We found a pay phone and called her, pretending to be Marty's classmates. She invited us in, but our pretense didn't last for a second. Of course, she knew who we were. Marty came into the room with a lot of bluster, acting like the man of the house when he was all of..." Ben counted backward on his hand, "fifteen, I guess. He asked what we were doing there.

"Abbe asked flat out if he was our brother. He looked at his mother uncertainly, and they both nodded. Minnie tried to pawn us off by telling us we should talk to our father. I would have gone home. Abbe was pushy though, and asked Minnie to make us some tea. All four of us ended up sitting around her little kitchen table, and Minnie sketched out what had happened. Then she answered all of Abbe's questions. Yes, our father knew about them, and saw Marty regularly. Yes, she was pretty sure our mother knew as well.

"It took us a couple of weeks to work up to confronting our parents. But one night during Sunday dinner, Abbe said that we knew about Marty. Our dad took us to the study and explained that he and Mom had some bumps in their marriage after I was born. Mom's attention, rightly so, I think, was focused on us, and he was on his own.

"We all know the birds and the bees so what happened next is that he had an indiscretion, she got pregnant, she wanted to keep the child, and that was that. Mom found out later, I'm not sure how much later, but she stayed with Dad. She said that she'd always married Walter for better or worse, and if this was the worst, it wasn't so bad."

Hannah was quiet for a long moment. How could she judge him for his inflexibility? "Other than that one time, have you seen Marty?" she asked.

"A few years ago Dad had a heart scare."

"Is he okay?"

"He was fine. He *is* fine. He has an arrhythmia—an irregular heartbeat. There had been some damage to his heart muscle from an undetected heart attack. He's on medication that controls it. When he complained of chest pains, the whole family rushed to the hospital. We didn't know if it was life or death and Mom thought he should have his family around.

"Mom called Marty. Maybe Dad saw God or something. After that, he didn't hide his relationship with Marty any more. Minnie retired and moved to be nearer to her family in Tennessee, but Marty stayed in town. Whenever they invited him over, I wasn't there."

"How do Marty and Abbe get along?"

"Abbe was always Dad's favorite. She was quick to forgive him."

"Have you forgiven your dad?"

Ben laid his head back on the armrest. That was a much more complicated question. "My mom has forgiven him. She acts like Marty was always there."

"I asked about you."

"I've made my peace with it. People lie. First, my mom and dad kept this huge secret for all of these years. Then Samara does the same thing." They were quiet for some time. Ben stood. Then he knelt next to Hannah on her side of the couch. "You're the first person who hasn't lied to me."

He cupped her face, the smooth skin silk against his palms. She looked so beautiful in the weak light of the room. Her full lips parted, and she accepted his kiss of gratitude. Lost in their kiss he forgot about lies, and half-truths and betrayal. Finally, he could put this all behind him and start again. Hope burgeoned in his chest. Maybe for once, he could get this right.

Arms pushed against his chest. "Don't think I don't want you here, now, doing this. But you need to go back to your house with your parents."

He pulled back and looked at her brown eyes smoky with desire. "You're right." He cupped her cheeks, kissing her softly with something other than passion.

7

Thank God for Federal Express. Ben had seen every stitch of clothing she'd brought with her. She'd done some quick on-line shopping at Bloomingdales because she wanted this last night with him to be special. Though priority overnight meant 4:30 in the afternoon by Lost Coast standards. That should give her time to pull out all the stops.

Blowing her hair straight was something she'd rarely done after her twenties, but the end result was worth the shoulder strain. Her light brown hair with its natural blonde highlights shimmered. Although Hannah had grown to love her curly, frizzy, and frankly unruly hair after years of trying to make it something it was not, she wanted Ben to know that she'd done something special for him.

Tearing open the newly arrived packages, she cut off tags, and peeled off innumerable stickers. Shimmying into new forest green skinny jeans, and a white cashmere sweater gave her confidence. The two colors looked good against her tan skin. She dug through her luggage and pulled out the worn-soft brown calfskin ankle high boots that she loved. The stacked heel gave her three additional inches of height. Ben was one man who didn't seem to care that they could see eye to eye.

Hannah willed Cody to keep from barfing during the mile long trip to Ben's house. Vomit wasn't sexy. Anticipation slowed Hannah's driving. This was the first time she'd be invited inside. In many ways, Ben had kept his distance from her. Whether it was because he'd been hurt or because he was naturally reticent, she didn't know. Tonight was her last night, and she wanted to peel back those layers and creep under his skin. She needed him to want her as much as she wanted him. Lopsided relationships—even for the one who was loved more—didn't work. She'd learned that lesson the hard way, twice. Hannah needed to know he still wanted her as much as that first night.

Ben greeted her at the door with a chaste kiss on the cheek. He wore no apron this time, and took the proffered wine politely. He looked down at the dog, eyebrows raised in question.

"I didn't want to leave Cody alone," she said defensively. Hoping she'd be there late into the night, she didn't want the dog to pee in the house or destroy something in his boredom. Was her new outfit, smooth hair and dog in tow too obvious?

Ben knelt for a second, giving the dog a few pets. "Come out back."

Like Elaine and Walter's, his view was stunning. That's where the similarities ended. While his parent's house was decorated in early 'sedate retiree' décor, Ben's deck screamed bachelor pad. Calling all the stainless steel that greeted her a grill didn't do it justice. It was better outfitted than the rustic wood paneled kitchen she'd glanced at on her way outside. The outdoor kitchen built onto the side of the house wasn't vastly different from hundreds she'd seen in upscale Orange County houses. She wondered if Ben had built it—somehow it seemed out of character, though he'd made himself right at home. In the chill air, she could feel the heat emanating from the coals, and rubbed her arms with her hands.

"Now that you're here, I'm going to throw a couple of steaks on the grill. That okay?"

She nodded. She wasn't here for the food. Her stomach had been tied up in knots thinking about Ben. Hannah hadn't been anything close to hungry in nearly two weeks. These days, she ate to survive. To be polite, she'd make an effort to eat something. But it could be Cody's dinner for all she cared.

Ben, the perfect host, poured her a glass of wine as she sat in one of the padded wicker chairs. Hannah pulled the blue cloth napkin from the zinc top table and spread it in her lap. Instinctively, she rubbed her thumb against her ring finger, momentarily startled to find it empty. She cursed herself for the mindless habit she'd gotten into as a child when her mother had given her a silver ring from Denmark that she loved. A friend who had admired the ring, casually told her a story about pickpockets who routinely stole rings from unsuspecting girls who were often less conscious of their left hands. She always felt the diamond turned toward her palm every few hours or so. Though she had no fear of crime here or in Orange County, for that matter, it was a habit she couldn't shake. She pulled her thumb from her ring finger, and picked up her wineglass with two hands. The absence of the rings was deliberate. Michael was her past.

The steaks were done in a matter of minutes, and Ben pulled creamed spinach off the warming rack. Despite her lack of hunger, she polished off much of the food.

"You really know how to cook."

"My mother insisted on it."

"I bet her 'insistence' didn't leave you much room for choice."

A smile flitted across his lips, but disappeared as quickly as it came. He probably still smarted from the whole half-brother discussion from last night.

Changing the subject, he reached across the table, and lightly touched a few strands of Hannah's hair. "Your hair is different." With that small intimacy, involuntary shivers raced down Hannah's arms. "Are you cold?"

Hannah was anything but cold. She nodded nonetheless. She had no plans to have sex out here on the deck. Getting as close to a bed as possible was first on her agenda.

"Let me help you with the plates." Surreptitiously slipping the dog the remainder of her steak, Hannah collected the dinner plates. Washing up the few dishes in the kitchen sink, Hannah heard Ben in the living room throwing heavy logs, and balling up newspaper.

Shaking her damp hands dry, she wandered into the living room. Ben was sitting on the couch, denim-clad thighs spread wide. Small blue flames licked at the newspaper. "I don't have great heating in this place. I've been meaning to have the HVAC system overhauled." Her face warmed at the thought of running her hands between those thighs. The last thing she needed was more heat.

Taking off her boots, she got comfortable on the cowhide rug between the couch and the fireplace. She leaned back against the couch, ensconcing herself between his knees. He absently stroked her hair. For all the passion in his touch, she could have been the dog. They sat in companionable silence for some time watching the fire catch on the tinder and spread to the larger logs. The odd combination of arousal and melancholy made her limbs feel heavy.

She turned and looked up at him. Here goes nothing. "Are you attracted to me?" The light from the fire reflected in his blue gray eyes. The sun had set rapidly, casting the room in shadows.

Large, heavy hands gripped her shoulders. "Jesus Christ, Hannah. Why would you ask me something like that?"

"It's that you haven't..." She trailed off. He hadn't what? This had to be the worst come on, ever. She wanted him, but didn't know how to say it.

"Haven't what? Jumped all over you like a salivating teen-ager? I'm forty, Hannah, not fourteen." Maneuvering off the couch, Ben knelt beside her on the black and white rug. "I've spent nearly every night with you. On the nights I didn't, I was wishing I had."

"I'm leaving tomorrow. I want..." She quieted, unable to figure out why it was so difficult to articulate that she needed him to make the guilt go away.

"I know what you want, Hannah. It's what I want too."

"Then why... You always go home after our dates."

"Why should I stay, Hannah? You're leaving. I don't know if you're coming back. I don't want a one-night stand."

She wanted more than one night. After Michael, she'd be back. "I want more, Ben."

"How can we? You don't live here. You have to deal with whatever relationship you're leaving behind, the life you have to go back to in Orange County."

"My relationship is over. I only want you, Ben." That was the unvarnished truth. She laid her want and need bare before him. "Please..."

"My dear, Hannah," he began, then cupped her face and kissed her.

Past and future merged in a kiss that was both what she remembered and what she wanted it to be. Ben kissed her slowly as if they had all the time in the world. The merest touch of his lips on hers and she already felt like she wanted to crawl out of her own skin. How could he go so slowly, when she could practically feel the sand filling the bottom of the hourglass? She slid her hands under his shirt, across the warm plane of his belly, and up the hot skin of his broad back, and still he didn't move.

To be ravished is what she wanted from Ben. If she didn't initiate it, she could blame it on him or blame it on the passion.

And then he did. He gently urged her mouth open, and thrust his tongue inside. Tasting like charcoal and wine, Ben's tongue tied with hers, and the intimacy of their kiss flooded her with want. This was it. This was perfect. Sex without reservation or trepidation.

Ben broke the kiss and looked at her, his eyes grounding her. He rubbed a thumb over her still tingling bottom lip. "It's been hell, Hannah. Every night I dropped you off, I wanted nothing more than to take you to bed."

"They why didn't you?"

"Because I needed to trust that you were done with whatever you'd left down south. After this, there's no going back."

Ben was giving her one last chance to bolt. One last chance to go home and forget they'd ever met. Passion rooted her to the rug.

After a long pause, he tugged her gently. More than willing, Hannah went with him. Prone on the rug, Ben's large body covered hers. Muscles of his hard chest pressed against her, an insistent erection pressing against her leg. He smelled of fire, and something muskier, intoxicating her. She wanted to move, rub against him, pull his clothes off, something. But she was pinned to the floor by the directness of his gaze. He hadn't used many words tonight, but the desire in his eyes said enough. Ben leaned down to kiss her again. The first touch was feather light, an exploration.

Thrusting her hands into the hair that curled wildly at the nape of his neck, Hannah urged him closer to blot out thinking and drown in desire. Ben could not be moved. He continued his lazy exploration.

"Ben," she whispered against his lips. "I'm leaving in the morning." The last two weeks had been hell. Did he feel one ounce of the urgency that clawed at her?

Hollow inside, she needed to fill the empty space. The dam broke then. He plied her with hot openmouthed kisses that stoked the fire in her belly. Finally. She stopped thinking and started feeling. The only thing that could fulfill her, fill her fierce need was him.

Ben pulled away and stood, dragging her up with him. "Bedroom."

"Will we be cold?" Hannah asked, the now roaring fire having warmed her body.

"We'll be anything but cold," he said, pulling her against him for another kiss that curled her toes into the rug.

His large hand enveloped hers. They walked to the bedroom. She stood by the door awkwardly while Ben bent to turn on a bedside lamp. Sex with Michael was never like this. This wanting, this waiting, this needing, this craving was unique to Ben. After tonight there would be no turning back. Rarely were the forks in the road of life so clear.

The warm hand that cupped her face, its thumb brushing against her lower lip, brought her back to the present. "Hannah, I lost you there. You okay?"

She nodded, enraptured by those smoldering blue gray eyes, and spoke another truth. "I've wanted you since the first moment I saw you."

Ben didn't speak then. He closed the minute distance remaining between them and placed an openmouthed kiss on her exposed neck. All pretense of restraint was gone. Ben was doing what she'd always needed during sex, he took control. His mouth was everywhere. Soft kisses glanced off her eyebrows and half-closed lids. His seeking mouth found first her lips and tongue, then the sensitive spot on her neck. Wanting to hold onto this feeling, she clamped her thighs together afraid she'd come from his kisses. She wanted to feel his hands and mouth on her breasts and in the most intimate of caresses. Hannah slid her hands under his shirt, smoothing them along the hot skin of his back, sculpting the clenching muscles of his back and shoulders. She pulled the shirt over his head, and initiated another kiss. If kissing Ben made them this hot, she didn't think she'd live through the actual sex act without bursting into flame.

"Let's go to bed," Ben said, tugging her toward the California king that dominated the wood paneled room. She sat, but Ben remained standing in front of her. With his waist at eye level, there was no mistaking his arousal. Involuntarily, her hand reached out, caressing his length and hardness through the straining fabric. Hands stilled, eyes closed, Ben threw back his head and sucked in a swift breath. When he got control of himself, he pulled her hands away. Lifting her arms up, he pulled off the cashmere sweater she'd chosen so carefully. Ben's breath whooshed from his lungs, and suddenly she didn't regret one penny of the two hundred dollars she'd spent on the La Perla underwear. The caramel brown lace lingerie had shimmered against her tan skin that afternoon in the mirror.

Hannah leaned back on her elbows and let Ben undress her. Worshipfully, he knelt before her, unbuttoned the skinny corduroys and pulled them from her long legs.

"You're incredible," he whispered into the chill air. He parted her legs, running a hand up each calf, and along each thigh. His thumbs brushed against the thin silk covering her sex. Blood pooled in her belly, and the area between her legs pulsed with anticipation. Shamelessly, she pulled his hands to her sex. He obliged, slipping one thumb between the silk and her heat. She held her breath until Ben lightly brushed against her most sensitive nub of flesh, then panted as he did it repeatedly. Their eyes locked and held. His eyes darkened to the color of midnight.

Sensation replaced reality, and rational thought started slipping away from her. Oh, God, she was going to come. The thought came only seconds before the feeling. The low moan of satisfaction escaped her. Her elbows went out from under her, and she tumbled back on the bed.

"Ben, I," she started. He shushed her with a finger against her lips. He needed no explanation. "Always, ladies first," he said by way of understanding.

He pulled her fully up onto the bed, resting her head on the pillows. Hand thrown over her eyes to shade them from the light, she watched Ben fully undress while her breathing evened. His nude form did not disappoint. His broad shoulders narrowed into a taut waist. He had the right amount of dark hair on his chest that arrowed down to his penis, thick with arousal. He turned away for a moment to open a bedside drawer, and she was rewarded with a view of his taut backside. When he turned back, it was with a foil packet in hand.

Thank goodness he had enough brain for the both of them. She hadn't thought about birth control for years. The fated phone call from Michael came back to her. She shook her head, clearing out the wayward thoughts.

Eyes narrowed in concern, he said, "What are you thinking?"

"I have on too many clothes. Help me, Ben."

Expertly, he unhooked her bra and carelessly tossed aside the expensive frill. She lifted her hips obligingly, and he tugged at the sequined straps of her briefs, sliding the damp silk along her legs.

"We're even," he said in a voice made gravelly by passion. He ran a finger down the cords of her neck, along her collarbone, circling one straining nipple. "God, you're damn near perfect," Ben said before kissing her again. Their bodies came together in the age-old mating dance. He leaned over her, bracing his weight on his arms. Their legs intertwined. His cock pressed against her insistently. She couldn't resist the urge to grind against him like an out of control teenager. The friction of his erection against her sensitive flesh made sweat break out on her upper lip. Reluctantly leaving her mouth, Ben kissed his way down her body. After a few hot, sucking kisses on her neck, he molded her breasts in his hands and took each nipple in his mouth in turn. His tongue played against each peak, pushing her to rub against his erection, with each stroke of his tongue. The kisses continued down her stomach, and she shivered with anticipation as he came close to her core. One of Ben's hands remained on her breasts, flicking the turgid nipple. The other parted her nether lips before his exploring tongue and lips gave her the most intimate of kisses.

Her hips bucked of their own volition. "Ben, I..." Hannah didn't finish her thought as a second orgasm came over her as suddenly as the ocean waves that crashed outside.

Utterly spent, she laid back. Her chest rose and fell, mocking her. The movement did nothing to give her enough oxygen to catch her breath. But Ben wasn't done. She saw him ripping at the condom wrapper with his teeth and sheathing himself. As he rolled the thin latex over his erection, she realized she'd never been so turned on by a man protecting her.

He leaned down for one last kiss. "Can I...are you?"

God knows she was more than ready. Grabbing his penis at the base, Hannah urged their joining. With her invitation, her acquiescence, he plunged into her. He nearly pulled all the way out before sliding back in slowly. She didn't need slow. She wanted this quick and hard.

"Hannah, I want to go slow. I want to make this good for you." He had to be kidding. It couldn't be any better. She took control then, flipping him over on his back. Leaning her hand against the middle of his chest, she rose and fell against him, quickening their pace. When his breathing quickened, she leaned in and rubbed her lips against his as slowly as she could. She knew when he'd lost control and he lifted up to meet her every down stroke until he exploded. She continued until she met her own smaller release. Spent, she collapsed on his chest, their hot breath mingling in the air.

"Hannah, I have to…" Ben said, gesturing to the bathroom. She eased off him and laid on top of the soft duvet she'd scarcely noticed before. She hadn't really taken in much about the room, but it was all him. He'd successfully mixed the wood paneling that covered the lower half of every room in the house with a leather covered headboard, and a matching club chair. The duvet and pillows were charcoal and navy striped. She wondered if he realized that his bedding matched his stormy eyes. Ben came back, cleaned up, his flaccid penis no less impressive as it lay against its nest of chestnut brown hair. Her fingers itched to touch him, bring him to hardness again, and release with her hands, her mouth, her breasts, anything that would give him the pleasure he'd given her. Two months ago Hannah would have gladly never looked at, tasted, or touched another penis. What had she been thinking? She'd finally had the best sex of her life. She could do this again, and again, forever. She'd thought with age went passion. How could she have been so wrong?

Hannah made room for him, and Ben laid down on the linen duvet, throwing his hands over his eyes. Jesus. Fuck. Masturbation was way overrated. For a fleeting moment, he wished he were fourteen instead of forty. He wanted to do it again, right now. But he'd have to wait for the battery to recharge. No way was he giving up this woman. He needed to know everything he could about her. They had to make this thing work somehow, even with him up here and her in Orange County. He didn't want to talk logistics right now, though.

"Did you sing?" he asked instead of a question that could scare her away.

Hannah rolled onto her side, facing him, expectantly. Propping herself up on her elbow, she answered. "I did." She was completely unselfconscious. He hated to think of Samara, but his ex-wife constantly covered up. He liked Hannah's confidence in her body. He tried to be gentlemanly and not stare, but it was hard. Her parents' heritage had produced skin that looked permanently tanned. The swell of her breasts were tipped with small brown nipples that were still semi-erect. What little body hair she had was the lightest brown, like her hair. He settled for twining one long leg with his.

Instead of telling her how beautiful she was, and how much he wanted to run his hands up and down her lithe form, he shifted back to her music. "What did you sing?"

"I guess the best description would be blues or jazz. I've been described as Queen Latifah meets Bessie Smith."

"Why don't you sing anymore?"

Hannah propped two pillows behind her and leaned against the leather headboard. She finally became aware of her nudity or the chill in the air, and pulled the duvet over her bent knees, and tucked it under her arms. "I grew up wanting to be a singer and songwriter like my dad. I spent a lot of time in clubs with my father. He played piano and bass, but I was never much for playing an instrument. I admired the singers. They all had these smoky voices, beautiful dresses, and a way of holding an audience in the palm of their hands. My dad let me sing from time to time, and I loved it. My mom wanted me to go to college, though, and not right into the business after high school. So I compromised and majored in music. I did voice and piano."

He touched her shoulder gently. "You still haven't told me why you don't sing now. Photography and singing are both artistic, I guess, but worlds apart to me."

"My mom divorced my dad because he abandoned the marriage for his music. It would've hurt her too much for me to follow in Dad's footsteps. It was hard to watch the other night, fighting the urge to jump up on the stage." Hannah's voice got quiet. "Not that I would have been welcome."

Ben turned down the light a notch, and burrowed under the covers, gathering her in his arms. He wanted nothing more than to feel her skin against his. Eventually, Cody even made it into the room, sniffing around and intimating that he wanted to jump on the bed. Ben pointed to the floor where the dog curled reluctantly. He didn't want to share the bed with anyone other than Hannah.

He knew he probably shouldn't ask the question. All of the men's magazines he'd skimmed before they made it from the mailbox to the waiting room advised against it, but he couldn't help himself. After all, they'd already started this relationship ass backwards. She knew all about Samara, and she'd met his parents way too soon. Why would any man want to leave Hannah if they didn't have to?

"Why did you divorce your ex?"

Hannah went from soporific to alert in a few seconds. "Do you have a robe I can borrow? I want to take Cody out for a quick pee."

"You stay put. I'll do it." It was the least he could do for her. How did a guy thank a woman for the best sex he'd had in two years? He pulled a gray velour terry robe from the bathroom door, throwing it around himself, belting the waist. He hunted some flip-flops from the nearly empty closet, and ushered the dog out.

Irrationally, he feared that Hannah wouldn't be there when he got back in the house, trailing cool, damp air behind him. But after he gave the dog some water, he found her wrapped in a throw, the color of early morning fog, by the fire. Only her head with its muss of straightened hair and hot pink toenails were bared.

"Are you cold?"

She looked at him over her shoulder. The golden highlights of her hair shimmered in the dying firelight. And he had thought of passing up this woman because he was bitter about his ex? Afraid of trusting? He was never so glad to be pursued.

"It was chilly in there without you, Ben."

That husky voice made him want to rip off his robe and take her right there, but his body craved sleep. Good sex always did that to him. He banked the fire, and gathered her in his arms, the throw slipping unconsciously from her shoulders. He couldn't resist one kiss, which quickly became two or three. Before he knew it, he was walking her back against the wall. He slipped a hand down her back, and cupped her butt in his hand, lifting her leg to rest on his hip. The slickness he found there practically begged for his touch. Hannah was so responsive, he couldn't resist, sliding the pad of his thumb along her clit, using the moisture he found there as lubrication. As he knew they would, her husky moans quickly escalated until she was coming apart in his arms. Despite his exhaustion, he could feel himself flying at more than half-mast. He leaned her against the roughhewn wood and rocks that surrounded the fireplace. Without preamble, he pulled open his robe, and lifted her other leg, impaling her. He knew that having come earlier, he could ride her this way for a long time.

Hannah's head was thrown back. Her cheeks were flushed, her full lips open, her tongue darting out to wet her parched mouth. When he thought he could go on forever like this, he realized with a jolt than he'd forgotten to sheath himself. He pulled out abruptly.

"Hannah, hon, please look at me." Her unfocused eyes slowly cleared, looking at him with confusion. "I forgot to get a condom."

That sobered Hannah completely. "Ben, I'm not on anything. I wasn't planning..."

He looked down at his quickly deflating member. "I think we're okay, but maybe we should go to bed...and sleep."

She nodded, walking to the bedroom. "Do you have something I can sleep in?"

It was a good idea. If their bodies didn't touch, maybe they could prevent a repeat of what had almost happened back in the living room. He pulled his favorite vet school t-shirt from a dresser drawer. Threadbare, it was the shirt he liked the most. He fished out some novelty boxers he never wore – a tacky souvenir from a bachelor party – patterned with lipstick kisses and handed them both to her. She excused herself and went to the bathroom to change.

Scrubbed clean, and smelling of soap and minty toothpaste, with her hair scraped into some kind of braid, Hannah looked more attractive than she ever had with all the sparkly clothing, carefully coifed hair, and artfully applied makeup.

Before he turned out the light, he tugged at her braid. "You look beautiful like this." He snapped off the bedside lamp and spooned her from behind, cupping her soft breast in his hand. He missed sleeping like this against a warm, satisfied woman.

In the last throes of a deep sleep, Hannah felt a large hand shaking her awake.

"Michael?" What did he need now? Was her temperature up?

"Hannah?" She opened her eyes a tiny bit. Ben Cooper was in her bed. Instantly alert, she realized where she was—good, and what she'd said—bad.

She sat up. "What time is it?" Shocked by the cold air on her skin, Hannah slid back down and was about to pull the covers back up over her sleepy head when Ben stopped her.

"Do you want to go see the sunrise on the black sand beach? It's really special this time of year."

Peering closely at Ben, Hannah saw nothing but sincerity on his ruggedly handsome face. Maybe he hadn't heard her call Michael's name.

Shivers ran through her as she imagined rubbing her palms along his darkly stubbled jaw. The idea of curling up closely with this man anywhere was an unexpected treat.

"I'm game."

Realizing Ben was already dressed, she hauled her sleep heavy limbs out of bed. While he put on hiking boots, she put on the clothes from last night he'd neatly folded on a chair. Hannah happily took the down jacket proffered by Ben. In her attempt to be cute the night before a warm jacket hadn't seemed important.

While Ben drove, she pulled her braid apart. If her hair was going to go curly, she at least wanted it all to be the same. They pulled onto the side of the road and parked. This cove was much better than the one she'd found the other day. Instead of black pebbles of various sizes, this was actual fine black sand like she'd once walked on during her honeymoon in Maui. Ben laid out a waterproof blanket on a sand dune. She sat and he handed her the throw she'd been wrapped in last night. His own was a large white cable knit blanket that looked like it had been hand knit by a kindly relative.

They turned to face the grove of oak trees to the east, the ocean beating its timeless rhythm behind them.

Ben wrapped an arm around her and she put her head on his shoulder. She was going to miss this. But she couldn't stay.

Ben turned to her. "Your hair. It's all curly again."

Hannah put a tentative hand through her hair. Indeed, it was back to its natural state, tiny corkscrew curls rioting around her head and shoulders. She started to pull the elastic band from her wrist and twist a manageable ponytail when Ben stopped her.

"Don't. I like it." The intensity of his gaze made the insistent throb of arousal start between her legs. "Are you over Michael?" It was as if a tsunami-sized wave had swelled from the ocean and drenched them.

"Why…"

"I heard you call his name this morning." Ben ran a hand through his own unruly waves mussed by the wind. "You avoided my questions about him last night."

The doggy distraction hadn't worked. Itching for her absent camera, she gazed upwards. The sun had not yet risen over the horizon. If she'd brought her Canon, she could put the heavy machinery up to her eye, keeping Ben from seeing her face and asking too many questions.

"Hannah?" Ben asked insistently. She looked down at her hands; no camera, no cover.

"There really isn't much to say." Hannah paused a long time, trying to find the best way to tell most of the truth. "We were friends for a lot of years, decided to get married out of boredom more than anything else. After a couple of years, it wasn't working out." Hannah said in a rush. There, that was done. Every sentence she had uttered was the truth, even if Michael didn't know it yet.

"Are you over him?"

"Ben I couldn't have been with you in that way if I wasn't over him." The heat rose on her cheeks. Hannah had given herself to Ben in a way she hadn't with any other man. It had been at once deeply moving, and liberating. It was the first time she hadn't held anything back. He knew without a doubt how much she wanted him. She was sure it had been written all over her face every time she'd come. But she'd let down her guard because she had nothing to lose, and so much to gain.

She didn't want to answer any more questions about Michael. Banishment befitted the specter that kept rising between them. Hannah banished Michael and silenced Ben in the best way she knew how. She wrapped his blanket around the two of them, and threw her legs over his hips, wrapped her arms around his neck and kissed him.

When her kiss hit its intended target, Ben gave up asking questions. All at once, his hands were everywhere, smoothing her hair, unhooking her bra, unbuttoning her pants.

"Ben, do you....? Can we?"

"God, yes. I've never seen a soul out here in the morning."

One minute she had the upper hand, in the next, her pants and panties were down around her ankles, her shirt was pushed up under her neck, and Ben was sheathing himself, filling her with his hard, thick penis, and mercilessly teasing her nipples. This was their first so-called quickie. She wanted it to last forever. Ben was in complete control of the pace. With nothing more to do, Hannah threw her head back and enjoyed the ride. It was going to be the last time for them for some time. As she heard his breath hitch, and caught her own in her throat as she came apart, she opened her eyes to see the sun peeking through the mist on the horizon. Ben had been right. The sunrise was spectacular.

Ben drove her home in her car and puttered around his parents' house while she showered and packed. He helped her load all her stuff in the SUV. He put two pills in the palm of her hand, and delicately closed her fingers over her palm.

"In case you don't do the trip in one day. The dose of tranquilizer I gave Cody should be enough to get him through the long ride. He'll mostly sleep along the way. If you stop, for the night, he'll need one of these for tomorrow."

She wedged the pills in the change pocket of her jeans.

It was and it wasn't goodbye. Tears pricked at the back of her eyes. She willed them not to fall.

"I'll give you a call when I get home, okay?" She gave him one last kiss, and looked away from his intense gaze as she swung herself up into the SUV. She looked over her shoulder into the back seat and cargo area. Cody was secure, as was her luggage. She had water and a couple of granola bars at hand, but she didn't have Ben. It would be a long time and thirteen hundred miles before she would be with him again.

She looked back at Ben one last time. He was gesturing for her to roll down her window. She pushed the lever with one finger. The motor hummed as the glass glided down almost silently.

"Thank you," he said.

"For what?"

"For being the one person in my life that hasn't lied to me."

8

No way around it, Hannah had lied to Ben. During the unending drive back to Newport, she worked out how she was going to keep Ben from finding out the truth. It was easy. Two simple steps: wrap up life down here, and get back up there. It shouldn't take more than two weeks. Michael would realize their marriage was a mistake and be happy to divorce her. His family had never really liked her. Their worlds had never meshed. Hannah was confident that it would be an easy decision for him.

By the time she pulled up the driveway of the house she'd shared with Michael for more than a year, it was nearly nine o'clock. Wearily, she pushed the garage door opener on the roof of the car and drove the last few feet into the garage.

When the door reached the top and the light illuminated, she shouldn't have been surprised to see Michael standing there. He prided himself on always being her one man welcoming committee.

Ever the metrosexual, he stood, in his usual lounging clothes. The Hugo Boss drawstring pants and matching sweatshirt he dutifully bought from Nordstrom every fall. In every way he seemed the opposite of Ben. Where Ben was dark, he was light, with quintessential blond hair, blue-eyed, all-American good looks. Where Ben was tall and broad, Michael was slight. He was her height, and only outweighed her by a few pounds. She had always wished she could have been more physically attracted to him. Their marriage might have worked out better if she had.

The minute she stepped from the running board, he wrapped her in a weak hug. His head moved in for a kiss, but she turned her head, ostensibly to get the dog from the car.

"Can you help me get Cody out?"

Michael pulled open the door and looked at the groggy dog. "What's wrong with him?"

Could he not remember why she'd stopped on the Lost Coast? "The vet up there gave me some tranquilizers."

Lifting Cody out onto shaky legs, he looked at her skeptically. "Your north coast vet sounds like a quack. I hope he's better by tomorrow. I'd like to take him on a hike before work."

If Hannah had been a dog, her hackles would have risen. "He was not a quack. Ben was a very qualified veterinarian."

"Aww, it sounds like you have a soft spot for the old small town vet. I bet you charmed the socks off the old guy."

She did not want to talk about Ben with him. "Help me get him into the house."

They got Cody watered. Soon the dog was ensconced in his bed in her home office where he usually spent much of his day, curled up near her feet.

"Are you going to get your bags?"

That wasn't a backhanded offer of help. Hannah didn't give Michael that benefit of the doubt. Tonight she was thankful that he wasn't the kind of guy to offer to help her out because she didn't want him anywhere near her stuff. She wanted to unpack at her leisure, reliving the last two weeks with Ben. "No, it can all wait until tomorrow. I want to go to bed."

Michael waggled his eyebrows at her, Groucho Marx style. "So do I."

Hannah sighed inwardly. Of course she should have suspected that her husband would want to have sex with her. It had been more than two weeks for him, and he'd always had a healthy libido.

Turning out lights throughout the house, they walked to the master suite.

"Michael, I've been driving for like eleven or twelve hours. Cut me some slack. I want to sleep, okay?" She sagged onto one of the armchairs in front of the fireplace. She leaned down to take off her shoes and socks, tossing them aside carelessly.

"Okay, okay," Michael said, coming to squat beside her. He stroked her hair, pulling it back to kiss her neck. "I missed you." She shrugged him off and got up to walk into the closet. She deposited the rest of her clothes in the hamper and pulled on a t-shirt and old, stained sweats, hoping Michael would take the hint.

When she came back into the bedroom, Michael was in bed, under the covers, flicking away on his iPad. Suddenly she could see why Ben eschewed technology. Michael was always on his Blackberry or his laptop or this iPad, his latest gadget—checking stock prices, or sports scores, or weather. He didn't really need any of it.

He laid the tablet on the bed, screen side up. A quick glance revealed that he was looking at porn.

"I know you're tired. But can't you touch me a little?"

She'd been down this road before. If she said no, they'd end up wrestling with this for an hour. He'd whine that she wasn't sexual enough. She'd complain that he was selfish. Hannah needed to get out of this with the least fuss possible.

"What do you want?"

One beat too late, she realized her mistake too late. "I'd love a blow job." Michael pulled down the covers to reveal his nude form, erect penis twitching in anticipation. Before they started trying for a baby, this had been his preferred way to have sex. He liked fantasizing about other women, usually busty, barely legal blondes, while she licked and sucked his cock. He'd said time and again that their encounters were all about her. The women on the screen were extra, like sprinkles on an ice cream cone. She'd pretended to be placated, all the while growing more disgusted. Vindicated when he'd had to acquiesce to plain vanilla sex during the fertility treatments, he was back to his old ways now that there was zero possibility of a baby on the horizon.

"Can I touch you?"

A hand job was second best for him. Already painfully aroused, Michael didn't have the heart to put up a fight. Hannah opened the bedside table and filled her palm with the baby oil she kept for this purpose. As she'd done a thousand times before, she knelt between his legs and slicked both of her hands up and down his throbbing cock.

If Michael was inside her, he never lasted more than a few seconds. But he could go on forever like this. Tonight was no different. She shifted and reshifted her travel weary limbs as he moaned in delight. Seconds before he came, he asked her to lick her lips simulating fellatio. Hannah tried not to let humiliation shrivel her pride and did as she was told. He closed his eyes, spurting all over himself. She did as she always did, got up and made her way to the bathroom for tissue. Passing him the scented pink wad, she went back to wash her hands of the whole night.

"Are we going to talk about this?" Michael asked when she came back into the room, night cream in hand.

The elephant in the room had lifted its trunk and trumpeted. "I know that I went away at a really bad time," she started. The news that came from Dr. Stern should have been a game changer, but she'd made her decision before that little bomb had been dropped on her already decimated marriage. "I'm really sorry, Michael. I really am. But I think we need time to think about this. I don't know what I want to do yet, and I don't want to go rushing into anything we might regret."

Michael laid down and pulled the covers over his bare shoulder. "Okay, we'll talk about it tomorrow." She knew from his tone he wanted to say more. Hannah finished rubbing cream into her face and hands, and pulled her hair back into one thick braid. Out of things to do, she knew she was going to have to share her bed with her husband. Wishing she were anywhere but here, she pulled back the covers on her side, and lie in the bed she'd made for herself.

When Hannah woke up alone she was grateful, for once, that Michael worked in finance. He was always up and out of the house in time for the opening bell of the New York Stock Exchange. Cody was wagging his tail by the bedroom door, imploring her to let him in. She slapped the bedcovers and he jumped on the bed. Michael hated dog hair on the duvet, but what he didn't know wouldn't hurt him. After yesterday's marathon drive, the dog didn't seem any worse for wear. She was grateful for Ben's thoughtfulness in providing tranquilizers. She pulled a couple of foxtails from Cody's fur. Michael had obviously taken the dog out for an early morning run. He was zealous about making sure that he and the dog got exercise.

She showered, dressed, and with dog in tow, went to unload the car. Everything was as she'd left it, carefully packed in the SUV. In three trips, she brought it all to the bedroom. Opening her satchel, she was surprised to find Ben's t-shirt and boxers. She didn't remember taking them from his place. Unconsciously, she must have wanted to keep a tangible connection to him. Hannah brought the garments to her nose reveling in her and Ben's mingled scents. Senses on overload, all the intense feelings of the last weeks came flooding back in a rush. Hannah luxuriated in the feeling of burgeoning love. She folded the items carefully and tucked them in the back of her underwear drawer. One by one, she unpacked all the other things she'd taken for her retreat. Only when she heard the thud of mail in the box, and the mailman's truck rumble down the street did she realize that more than two hours had passed since she'd started her journey down memory lane.

Ignoring the growl of her stomach, Hannah slipped her computer bag over her shoulder and padded her way to the den. Her desk was as empty as when she'd left. Not one speck of dust marred the sheen of the recently polished wood. She plugged her laptop into the wall. When she lifted the lid, she ignored the pings signifying hundreds of e-mails she'd missed.

Instead, she moused over to her pictures and clicked the last folder she'd created. She was rewarded with fifteen diagonal inches of high resolution Ben. Tucking her legs under her, she took her time clicking first one shot, then another. The lighting on the beach had been perfect. Having used a wide open aperture, anything that could have detracted from Ben blurred into the background. In sharp focus were his eyes. She looked from one picture to another, searching for clues about his feelings. It wasn't until she got to the pictures that she'd taken by candlelight in his parents' guest room that she saw it. She couldn't remember if the kiss had come before or after, but in these pictures, she thought she saw fire reflected in his blue gray eyes. Whether from the candle's reflection or from the fire that burned within them that night, she didn't know.

The slam of the front door jolted Hannah. Her gaze snapped to the clock on the wall. It wasn't yet two in the afternoon.

"Michael is that you?"

"Yep," he said, whistling. She heard him toss his keys in the box by the garage door, and listened as his shoes clicked on the wood floor. He poked his head in the study. Heart pounding in her chest, she snapped the lid of the laptop shut.

"You're early." She was standing, with her hand firmly on her computer lid, when he strode into the room.

"The stock exchange is closed. I've done nothing but work while you were away. I missed you, baby." He came around to her side of the desk, his hand joining hers on the lid. "What were you working on?"

"Slogging through the backlog of e-mail. I didn't really have great internet up there. You know how it is."

Michael pulled her to him, and she hugged him dutifully, hoping he attributed her racing heart to him. When he pulled back, his eyes didn't meet hers. He started picking up random books and papers from her desk and examining them intently. She knew this deflection; he was hiding something. Her heart slowed.

"Did you hear something else from Dr. Stern's office?" Please, God, let a cure not have been found.

"No. But the good news is that my parents are expecting us this afternoon."

She wouldn't have called that good news. It wasn't that she didn't like Maggie and Drake. Her in-laws were well meaning people. She didn't like spending time with them because she couldn't forgive their casual racism. They were the opposite of everything she'd grown up with. They were suburban and conservative, and couldn't imagine a life outside of Orange County. They'd retired early and as far as she could tell, spent their days golfing, sailing, and watching Fox News.

"Did you tell them?" Michael didn't keep secrets from anyone in his family. Their marriage might as well be an open book. Maggie and Drake knew too much about their finances, their fertility problems, and their sex life. The lack of discretion with his parents had caused more than one rift in their relationship.

Michael nodded. "They're my parents, Hannah. They have the right to know that we may not be able to give them grandchildren." No doubt, the look on her face had prompted that explanation.

"When are we due?" she asked, buoyant. This would be the last obligatory family gatherings she'd ever have to attend with him.

Michael's eyes narrowed at her easy acquiescence. "I told them we'd be there around three."

Hannah looked down at the same sweats she'd armored herself in last night. "I guess I'd better get ready then."

A ping emanated from the dashboard before Hannah had driven to the end of Twenty-Third Street. At the first stop sign, she looked at all the indicator lights trying to remember what that particular chime alerted.

"It's the gas, Hannah," Michael said, exasperation in his voice.

"Gas?"

"You're out of it. Pull up to the 76 on the 55."

"The overpriced gas?" she asked.

"It's a total of two dollars, Hannah," Michael said looking at his watch. "Or we can drive all over creation looking to save five cents a gallon. Your choice."

Didn't really sound like her choice. She did what he'd requested, and pulled the car up to the pump. Then she waited. Michael looked at her expectantly. She huffed, opened the driver's door and walked around to the pump. She had to knock on the passenger door to get Michael to hand over her purse and wallet. She sucked her teeth in frustration. Why couldn't this man ever pump gas for her? Yes, she was a strong woman. And yes, she was self-sufficient. But did Michael think chivalry was dead? She waited while twenty-two gallons of fuel filled her tank.

"You smell like gas," he said when she got back into the car.

"I'll wash my hands at your parents' house."

Michael cracked his window. Her ears popped with the uneven cabin pressure throughout the forty-five minute drive to the Keeslings' Fullerton home. By the time they made their way through the gates of the new development and up to the cookie cutter house, the smell of food on the barbecue overwhelmed the lingering scent of gasoline.

She had helped Maggie and Drake buy this house, but had no idea why they'd picked it. It was one of those neighborhoods that had popped up on an old orange grove overnight. Every fourth house was exactly the same, each stucco box painted some shade of tan or brown that was supposed to complement the landscape, but stuck out like blight against once fertile fields. There were no trees to speak of, but plenty of vast green lawns that sucked up precious Colorado River water by the tens of thousands of gallons. She wouldn't have been able to tell their house from any other if it weren't for the twin Trojan and American flags flanking the entrance.

Without knocking, they opened the door to the vast two story entry way, past the zillion-inch built-in flat screen televisions, and past the kitchen with its wall to wall distressed country cabinets and ubiquitous stainless steel appliances. The Keeslings' home didn't much differ from the model a few streets over. But they loved the house and prided themselves on being able to pay for it outright. In their minds, they'd achieved the American dream. To her, it all looked rather hollow.

As Hannah had feared, their faces were the epitome of sympathy and concern. Maggie ushered them through the sliding glass doors, each hand rubbing motherly circles on their backs.

"We're so sorry to hear the news," she said as soon as they'd sat at the wood slatted outdoor dining table.

"It's okay," Hannah said automatically.

"But it's really not, is it?" Maggie said. "Matthew is never going to have kids, so Michael was our only hope." Matthew was Michael's older brother, and Hannah's favorite Keesling. She'd spent a lot of time with him and his partner when they'd been up in L.A. A bit awkward with their parents, he didn't come down much.

"Matthew and Kendall have talked about adopting, so you never know," Hannah said. Michael gave her a hard blue-eyed stare. Provoking them was a habit she'd promised to break. Only she'd wanted to throw the spotlight off herself for a while.

"It's not really the same, Hannah. You know that. Who knows what kind of child Matthew would get. And being raised up there in West Hollywood..." Drake said, grill side.

"Dad, we haven't ruled out adoption, ourselves," Michael said quietly. This was the most he'd ever challenge his parents. He talked a good game when they were by themselves, but he went from lion at home to pussycat when it came to his parents.

Drake stepped back from the grill, tongs still raised. "I told you, you need a second opinion. No man in our family has ever had a problem down there. I'm sure that someone at Hoag

Memorial could fix you right up—and you and Hannah could get back to the business of baby making." He gave them a broad wink, turning and basting the ribs.

Dr. Stern was one of the foremost experts and if he said it couldn't be done, then Hannah believed him. An image of Ben flashed across her mind. It was all a moot point anyway. Her days of trying to make a family with Michael, trying to make the Keeslings her family, were over.

Drake turned back, wiping sauce from his hands on the 'Kiss the Cook' apron that he favored. "Wow, nothing from you, Hannah. You usually disagree with everything I say." She'd spent too many hours over the past few years trying to convince Drake Keesling of the error of his ways. He wasn't going to vote Democrat, he wasn't going to drive a more reliable car, and he wasn't going to buy a house better suited for a retired couple. He was going to do what he wanted, and that was his right. She needed to move on to more like-minded people.

"I'm not in the mood to argue with you today."

Her response deflated him somehow. Until then, she'd never thought that her relationship with him thrived off their animosity.

"Dad, we trust the guys at the Pacific Center. Hannah's barely been home for twenty-four hours. We haven't yet discussed all the alternatives."

Her phone vibrated in her back pocket. Ben. She pulled it from her jeans, and there it was, his seven-zero-seven area code. Stepping away from the table, she tossed over her shoulder, "I have to take this." In less than three seconds, she went out the front door, and walked toward a bright green bench in the development's pocket park.

"Ben." His name on her breath was a prayer for salvation.

"I had a break from surgery." Hannah couldn't think of a thing to say. When she'd been a kid, she'd thought tangible objects could be sent through the holes in the heavy plastic telephone. She'd been disabused of the notion when she'd once unscrewed the receiver and all the food she'd sent her touring father fell out in a heap of stale crumbs. Knowing better, she still wanted to reach through the phone and touch him, pull him to her across the transmission lines. Every bone in her body ached for him. "How's Cody?"

"He came out like a champ. We even went for a hike this morning." It was a little fib.

"What are you up to now?"

"Some people I know put together a little barbecue welcoming me back. I couldn't really get out of it."

She heard the scratchy sound of something like an intercom in the background. It muted whatever he was saying to her. "...there's an emergency here, I have to go. I'll talk to you later." The call disconnected, ending as abruptly as it had begun. Hannah sat for as long as she reasonably could without being rude.

"What took you so long?" Maggie asked.

"Work call. Even though I turned over most of my listings to other agents, they still have a lot of questions." She had received several calls like that recently even if this call wasn't one of them.

"I think it's such a shame that you're giving up on this. Selling houses is the perfect job for raising children. It keeps your hand in the career world, but you can fit in time with your kids for all the mommy activities with young ones," Maggie said as if she hadn't said this time and again over the last six months as Hannah had wound down. Maggie had occasionally worked as a receptionist in a real estate brokerage and still saw herself as a career woman.

Hannah dropped her carefully applied mask of civility. "I fucking hate real estate, Maggie," she said emphatically.

Michael's mother covered her ears in horror.

"Oh, Maggie, please with the act. You have HBO. I'm sure you've heard a little cursing in your life."

"You know we don't like that kind of language in our house," Drake said as if she were thirteen, not thirty-seven.

"I'm sorry if I've offended you, but I'm tired of pretending. I hate selling tacky little boxes. I hate all the code about living in the 'right' neighborhood with the 'right' schools—when all they mean is that they *don't* want to live next door to someone like me."

Maggie's face turned red. "Oh, that's not true. We referred all of our friends to you. They sang your praises." Maggie and Drake had referred all their golf and yacht club friends. And she'd worked for them like a dog, yielding to their every whim. What had appeared generous at first, now felt no more than a means to control her. A way to keep Michael tethered to this life in Orange County.

"Sure they did. I did a great job for them, no matter how I felt personally. And it's absolutely one hundred percent true what they felt about me. I'm glad to have washed my hands of the whole damned thing."

"If you think that, then maybe it's best," Maggie's lips pressed into a thin crimson line.

"You know what I remembered about myself while I was up North? I remembered that I'm an artist. I can't tuck that away when it's inconvenient for you all. I want to take photos again. I want to sing."

"Don't you think you're a little old for that?" Drake asked. "Even Britney Spears is a little old for it, and she's got to be half your age."

They knew she was sensitive about her age. It was one of the reasons she'd felt such an urgency with the whole baby making thing. "I'm not planning on being a teeny bopper pop star doing acrobatics at the Pond. I'd like to write some songs, maybe get on stage once in a while. My dad still performs."

"Are you going to live off Michael then?" They'd always intimated that she'd married Michael for the money. Now that the gloves were off, their true feelings emerged.

"How we spend our money and conduct our marriage is our business." She'd waited years for Michael to say this to them. Today, she was taking the initiative.

"You've always acted like money didn't mean a thing. Especially with Michael making the bulk of it."

"I'm an artist, not a capitalist. Happiness and fulfillment are more important than money."

"That's easy to say when you don't have to put food on your own table," Drake said, gesturing toward the food he was taking off the barbecue. The cost of this dinner had gotten too high.

She held her hand up, Jerry Springer style. "You know what? I'm done." Hannah picked up her phone, purse, and walked through the patio door. "I've put up with this for years, and I'm done." If she was burning bridges, then so be it. Sparing Michael's feelings was no longer her top priority. "If there was one thing I learned in the last two weeks, it was that it's best to be honest."

She'd started up the car and was about to put it in gear when Michael came running out. He knocked on the passenger window. She put the car back in park. With one push of the button, Michael came into full angry view.

"What's up with you?"

"What's up with me? How many times have we had this conversation, Michael? Your parents treat me like the bastard stepchild, and I'm supposed to put up with it."

"I think you really hurt their feelings."

"Hurt *their* feelings? I'm... They... Forget it. I'm not going to bother with this argument. Are you getting in the car or not? I'm leaving. Now." Michael looked back at their house longingly before he opened the car door and got in.

She'd finally stood up for herself. It was too bad that Michael looked like a boat tossed around in a storm. She could see from the squint of his eyes and the set of his jaw that he was angry. But he didn't like confrontation and would never tell her that. Instead, he froze her out for the next week, and that was fine with her. Hannah had spent the time opening her own bank accounts, researching her legal options, and thinking about how she could get back to Ben.

After a week of silence, Hannah still tensed when she heard Michael come into the house. Instead of ignoring her and going right to the bedroom, he came into the family room. She'd been mindlessly flipping through the nine million satellite channels they subscribed to, plotting her escape.

"Truce," he said, sliding next to her on the couch so they sat hip to hip. She turned away from some celebrity chef who was doing more yelling than chopping on the Food Network, and looked at Michael. She wasn't mad at him. She was mad at herself for letting all of this—the fertility doctors, the move to Orange County, the real estate, his family—go too far.

Years ago when she was burned out from trying to make her mark in New York City, arranging her own marriage had seemed like a good idea. After all, families had been bringing together their progeny for generations and those marriages seemed no better or worse than those people chose for themselves. She'd thought choosing a man for whom she'd felt no passion, but for whom she'd had warm fraternal feelings would be the best way to go.

Because he couldn't break her heart. Because he didn't have it to begin with. He'd be a good father. She could build the kind of family she'd always craved—normal, happy...together.

"Truce," she said, holding out her hand. They shook like strangers. He fished the remote control from the linen upholstered couch cushions and turned off the TV, thrusting the room into silence and near darkness.

"I got you something."

A rush of guilt swarmed her body. "You didn't have to."

"I know I didn't have to. I wanted to."

"What is it?"

"It's in the bedroom."

Michael had dimmed the lights in the master, and lit a fire warding off the chill in the fall air. He wanted to go to bed with her. In a marriage as long as theirs, subtlety disappeared quickly. Until she'd met Ben, she'd assumed that her diminished libido had been a function of age. Now, she had to face the truth. She looked around the room for a trap door she could plunge through, like Lucy Pevensie slipped through C.S. Lewis' wardrobe.

Michael sat in a chair and produced a manila folder and a jewelry box. Hannah's unrealistic hopes were dashed. Neither of them were disappearing.

"Which should I open first?"

He paused to consider. "The box."

She lifted the lid of the midnight blue velvet box and a small charm bracelet sat atop a silk cushion. She lifted the delicate silver chain from its perch and two little charms jingled. She fingered them and realized they were a tiny old-fashioned camera and a small microphone, its head an onyx sphere. Tears gathered at the corners of her eyes. It was really thoughtful. Despite his family and all the downsides, this was why she had married Michael. He thought her dreams were worth pursuing, even if his parents didn't. He'd never once complained about her artistic nature or her ever-changing careers, working tirelessly for years at various brokerages and financial firms to make a very good living for them.

"Thank you," she said, using her finger to wipe away the tears.

"I know my parents can be a pain. Deep down they only want us to be happy. I've always supported you in whatever you wanted to do. I really thought that you'd enjoy real estate and it would be a good way for you to use your talents while we made a family. I'm sorry I was blind to your unhappiness." She could feel her resolve weakening. Ben felt more like a figment of her imagination than the real person she'd married right in front of her.

Hannah resisted the urge to massage her temples. "What's in the folder?"

He handed it to her. There were a couple of printed sheets inside. She moved by the lamp to read them more clearly. The first page was a receipt from a domain registration company. She had to read the words twice before it sunk into her brain. He'd gotten her two domain names, one for her music career, and the other for her photography. She'd foolishly abandoned these so long ago. The other paper was a receipt from a web designer. He'd prepaid someone a hefty sum to build two websites for her.

She sank into the other chair. "Wow. This is... I don't know what to say."

Michael looked directly at her, arousal clear in the breath flaring his nostrils like a bull in heat. "I have an idea of how you could thank me."

Hannah couldn't figure a way out of this. She could only delay the inevitable for so long. "Let me..." she gestured toward their bathroom. Escaping behind the bathroom door, she turned the fan on its highest setting. Hannah sat on the toilet lid, face in her hands. No matter how she racked her brain, she couldn't think of a way to get out of having sex with her husband.

She could do this one last time. Women had been through worse. Hannah pulled open the drawer next to the sink and pulled out a hermetically sealed tube of lubricant. The folks at the fertility center had given her a handful of sample Pre-Seed tubes to help Michael's sperm swim their way to her egg. She'd started using it every time they had sex because it made it hurt a lot less. She scrounged for scissors, snipped the top, and went to work.

By the time she got out of the bathroom, Michael was nude on the bed covers. Attempting to make the room more romantic, he'd lit a few candles. Lying propped against the pillows, naked as the day he was born, her husband's erection jutted from the curly blond thatch that surrounded it. He always did this preening display. Like she should be salivating at the sight of a nude man. He held out his hand and she let him grab hers, pulling her on the bed next to him.

Michael reared up. He positioned her in the middle of the bed, pillows propping up her head and rear. He always made love to her this way, as if she were a porn star on display for his pleasure. He pulled off her t-shirt and jeans, dropping them to the floor without a care.

"Lift up," he implored.

She did as he said and he unceremoniously unhooked her bra. He slid her panties down and off her legs. He thrust a hand between them, rubbing at her clit, his fingers like sandpaper against her most sensitive flesh. Hannah pulled his hand from between her legs and placed it on her hip hoping he'd get the message.

9

Eight days without Hannah and Ben was stir crazy. He couldn't fathom how he'd ever thought solitude was a good idea. So here he was in Eureka with Chase Edgerson, shooting pool in the local bar.

He missed an easy shot and Chase looked at him, coolly appraising. "What's wrong with you?"

Ben grunted, watching Chase sink ball after ball. The money he'd laid neatly on the side of the table quickly made its way into Chase's pocket.

"Woman trouble. How did someone find you up in your Lost Coast monastery?"

Ben ignored him, racking the balls and breaking again. Back into the groove, he made a few shots, then missed. He hadn't lost to Chase or anyone at Ragg's Rack Room in two years. His hand eye coordination was legendary up here. But for some reason he was having his ass handed to him tonight. Maybe too many small animal surgeries had blunted his accuracy. He flexed his fingers. Cracked his knuckles.

"She was a patient's owner."

Chase pocketed more of Ben's cash. "If this keeps up, I'm going to have the down payment for that sweet little Challenger I've got my eye on."

Ben quit when he got down to his last twenty. Out here in the country, he always kept a little something in his wallet in case of emergency. They moved to a booth on one side of the room, and ordered a couple of draught beers. The Sacramento Kings were playing silently on the big screen.

"What's her name?" Chase asked, his gaze trained on the screen.

"Hannah."

"Why are you with me instead of her?"

"She lives in Orange County."

Chase reluctantly tore his gaze from the heavily endowed twenty-year-old woman selling corn chips on the big TV screen. "Fess up."

Ben sketched in the story of how he'd met Hannah while she was up here figuring out life. "And she's single?" Ben nodded. "So was it a fuck and forget it, or are you angling for something more?"

"Don't know."

They were quiet, nursing the mediocre beer and neon or-ange corn snacks for the entire third quarter of the game. The Kings were losing badly.

"Look, I'm not sure what went down with your ex-wife, but for you to come out of retirement is a big fucking deal. You've got to figure out if it's worth pursuing. Buy a plane ticket and get down there. She's in Southern California, not Antarctica."

The hour-long drive home was cold without Hannah. She had radiated warmth and heat when she was in the car. Her body and hair crackled with life. Everything had appeared in Technicolor when she was here. Now that it was back to its muted sepia, he wasn't sure about his self-imposed isolation. His hands danced on the steering wheel, the gearshift, the dashboard. It was the first time he missed having a mobile phone. Right now, he craved an instant connection.

The small clock on his mantle struck eleven when he en-tered the dark house. Bypassing the living areas, he picked up the cordless handset from the kitchen and headed to the bed-room. Other than that one time between patients, he hadn't called Hannah. They'd made no promises to each other. He'd assumed that when she'd gotten her life situated she'd come back to him. In hindsight he could see, it was a stupid as-sumption. Because she was between careers, and exploring other aspects of her life, didn't mean she should or would drop everything and appear on his doorstep, dog and suitcase in hand. It was a ridiculous fantasy he'd harbored. He'd been burned pretty badly, but wanted to see where this would go. He'd waited long enough.

"Hannah Keesling's phone," a man said into the receiver.

Ben was a little taken aback. The phone had been with Hannah like another appendage. He couldn't guess who was answering her phone. Panic closed his throat, making speech difficult. Had he waited too long? She was an attractive single woman. He couldn't be the only man interested in pursuing her.

"I'm Ben Cooper," he said, finding his voice. "I'm the vet who helped Cody when Hannah was in Shelter Cove." He hoped that sounded like a plausible explanation. After all, didn't vets call for follow up at ten o'clock on a Tuesday night?

"She's in the shower. Can I give her a message?"

How could she be naked in such close proximity to another man? He unballed his fist and loosened his death grip on the plastic phone. "No message." Ben pressed the 'end' button. Had he missed the boat? All his worry about getting hurt, dating another woman like Samara seemed foolish. He wanted Hannah. All he had to figure out was how he was going to get her.

He was groggy with sleep when the phone rang. The clock confirmed that it only been an hour since he called Hannah. He'd been so worked up, he never thought he'd fall into a deep dreamless slumber.

The phone bleated again. Was that the second time or the seventh? He snatched it from the cradle.

"Ben?" the familiar husky voice said hesitantly. Hannah.

Sleep lowered his inhibitions. "Come back to me."

"I will," she said

"Who's with you?" She hesitated. "A guy answered your phone earlier."

"A friend helping me out."

"Get here soon."

"I'll be there as soon as I can," she said. Then Hannah disconnected the call.

When he awoke in the morning, he wondered if he had dreamt all of it.

Her bags packed, Hannah walked through the Newport house one last time. She'd fallen in love with the place the minute it had gone on the market. She'd envisioned bringing babies back here from the hospital, though not much beyond that. Lack of foresight was starkly evident now. But none of that mattered. As soon as Michael came home from work, she was going to break the news to him that she was leaving. Looking around at all the perfectly decorated rooms, she knew in her gut that she would never be back way again.

Leather bottomed ballet flats slid along the gleaming hardwood floors as Hannah looked at the perfect molding, the custom arches and woodwork of the great room. She'd miss the acres of black granite that topped custom white cabinets. She'd never cooked much but the sixty inch stainless steel stove and vast number of Viking appliances had always invited her into the kitchen—even if it was only to microwave dinner. The built-in bar and huge family room had always begged for entertaining, but she'd never gotten around to it. She walked through the four bedrooms that she'd planned to fill with a couple of children and all their stuff. The travertine baths that she never used gleamed. She stood by the saltwater pool, and looked over the perfectly manicured lawn and watched the calm waters of Upper Newport Bay lap at the shore.

She heard the garage rumble open, and swallowed the lump in her throat. It was time.

"Hannah," Michael shouted.

"I'm out back," she responded. Cody wiggled, jumped and licked at Michael. He leaned down and patted the dog before pushing him away with his knee. He didn't like dog hair on his custom tailored clothes.

A sheaf of glossy papers fluttered in his outstretched hand.

"What's that?"

"I saw Dr. Stern today, and he gave me a list of pamphlets on surrogacy and private adoption."

Hannah closed her eyes, solidifying her resolve. "I don't think that's a good idea."

"What? Surrogacy? Adoption? I know there are pros and cons to each, but if we want to have children someday soon, I think we're going to have to be willing to compromise."

"Michael." She paused to get his attention. "Listen to me." Hannah took a much longer pause this time. "I'm sorry."

He dropped the papers onto a stone table, determined to get his way.

"Look, I know it was a devastating blow. But I'm ready to move on. We want the same things. I don't see any reason to wait."

"Stop." She put her right index finger on Michael's determined lips. "Please stop."

"Why?"

"I'm leaving."

"Where are you going?"

"I want..." Hannah faltered. "I want a divorce."

"Oh my God. You're leaving me. Because of the infertility?" His face shone with incredulity, hurt and anger.

"No, it's not that," she assured him. "I decided this while I was away. Before...well, before..."

"You met someone else." Michael's volume was increasing. It was unlike him to display anger, especially where others could see or hear. He'd always been concerned with what the neighbors thought of them.

She averted her eyes. "That's not why. We're not right for each other. I don't want you to think..."

"Think what?"

"The fire's not there. I thought I could live without it, but I can't. I want... I want my life back."

"What's his name?"

"Who?" Hannah tried for innocence.

"Who is he?" Michael saw right through her.

"I met him *after* I made my decision Michael, after. Who he is isn't important. I'd be doing this either way."

"Are you leaving here and driving straight to him?" he asked, raking his hands through his hair. She'd rarely seen him muss his carefully waxed hair.

"You're not being fair," she said softly, hoping he'd match her tone.

"I'm not being fair," Michael shouted. Cody cowered by the French doors. "After all these years together, that's it. You're pulling out. No warning, no marriage counseling, no talking this over. *You're* done—so *it's* done? Is that it? Correct me if I'm wrong here. I'm supposed to—what—bow out gracefully so that you can drive off into the sunset with someone new—someone who *fires* you up?"

She wanted to protest—to say it wasn't that simple. But in reality, it *was* that simple. "Yes."

With one word she cut him to the quick. He crumpled onto a brightly striped chair cushion. Actions warred within her. Should she comfort the man who used to feel like her best friend, try to make him feel better, or leave him in the chair oozing like an open wound under a prematurely torn off bandage? She shook her head clear. There wasn't anything *she* could do. His parents could give him solace. She patted her thigh, ushered Cody through the house into the garage, and into the car. If she left now, she could be in Shelter Cove by tomorrow morning.

Hannah only made it as far as Tustin before she had to pull off the road. Had she lost her mind? What had she done? She'd left her husband for a guy she'd only met a month ago. She had done irrevocable damage to her marriage...to Michael. They would never be friends again. She'd never live in that house or have that life. Yawning unknown stretched before her. She didn't know when or if she'd ever work again, whether it was real estate, photography, or music. She didn't know if she'd ever have the children that she'd so desperately wanted only a month ago.

Pulling her phone from the charger, Hannah dialed her mother even though it was nearly midnight in Copenhagen.

"Mor." She cried when the achingly familiar voice answered.

"Honey, what's wrong?" Her mother spoke to her in Danish. Growing up it had always been an intimate way of speaking—a language only the two of them shared.

She switched to her mother's native tongue. "I left Michael."

The phone clattered to the floor, sounding a discordant note in her ear. She heard mumbling, between her mother and her stepfather, before her mother came onto the line again. She could hear the familiar sound of water filling the kettle, and knew her mother was putting up coffee.

"Are you okay?"

Hannah nodded. "I think so."

"Why now?" The question jarred Hannah.

"Now? Did you think this would happen?" She heard her mother sigh. She knew that sound. It carried days, or months, or years of things gone unsaid. "Mor? Tell me."

Hannah could almost see her mother in her kitchen. It was very simple, very old, and very Scandinavian with its white IKEA cabinets, ancient wood stove, and light pine floors.

"I never thought Michael was right for you."

"You never said anything."

"That was not my place. You had made a decision. I wanted to support you in any way that I could."

"Why did you leave Dad?" She had never asked her mother that directly. They had talked around the topic in a hundred different ways, but she never knew why her parents broke up.

"I'm not sure if going over this will help you."

"I need to know, Mor."

That sigh again. The clink of the spoon against the porcelain sink, Mor had poured and stirred her coffee.

"I loved your father. I never regretted any moment we spent together." Her mother paused. "I will always be grateful that he gave me you, Hannah. In many ways, you are the love of my life."

Tears leaked from Hannah's eyes. Her mother was rarely sentimental. The Danish weren't like that, except when they were drunk.

"Shay, Daniel, was passionate, and hot tempered, and incredibly talented. I loved all those things about him. But, I spent nearly twenty years with a man who was more passionate about music than he was about me. He was happy to be on the road, singing, and performing with his band. Shay could spend weeks in the studio recording a new album, rarely coming out. When I toured with him, when I was working—this was all fine. But after I had a baby, the life of a jazz musician wasn't practical. I didn't see him at night, or on the weekends, or when he was touring, or making a record. I loved him, Hannah. He swept me off my feet. I never felt like I got off the whirlwind ride. But, I think he loved the music more."

"I met someone, Mor," Hannah said, scrambling for a tissue in the console. "I think I could love him, really love him. I never had that passion for Michael—and thought he was a safe choice."

"It was Lucas, wasn't it."

A feeling of long suppressed dread burbled up from her gut and lodged itself in Hannah's belly, like an immovable stone in a crevasse. This was her Achilles' heel. She nodded, looking at the small white church outside her passenger window. "It was Lucas."

"Sometimes I think he broke your spirit as well as your heart, honey."

"It hurt so much, Mor. I thought I would die when he left me." Mortification crept into her face. She was glad no one could see her. Hannah couldn't believe she was this damaged by something that happened nearly twenty years ago.

"It took you a long time to get over it. In some ways, I think you are still not over it."

It was true. She'd never quite gotten over the pain of that relationship. Instead, she'd worked to bury it as deep inside as possible. Hannah rarely allowed that pain of rejection come to the surface.

Lucas had been her first love and he had dumped her. It was the same story shared by millions of young girls. Hannah had showed up for her last year of college when Lucas had dropped the bomb. He'd met someone else. One day she was in love. The next day, she was alone.

After three years of hot and heavy romance, there hadn't been an inkling, a warning that her world was going to come crashing down that hot and humid day in August. She had trusted him with everything, and he had tossed it aside like so much detritus.

Hannah hadn't thought herself naïve, but in the back of her mind, she knew she was going to marry Lucas, that she was going to have his babies, and live happily ever after. She felt stupid even thinking about it now. Scores of people told her that no one married their college sweetheart. Ever cool and nonchalant on the surface, she'd agreed with them. Secretly, Hannah had thought it could happen. Why not? College sweethearts married all the time. The alumni magazine was packed with their announcements.

In the last twenty years, Hannah had never looked him up on Google or Facebook, fearful that she'd find him happily married with a bunch of darling moppets with his tawny hair and green eyes. She'd held out for a love like the one she shared with him. When she reached her mid thirties and it hadn't happened, she'd turned to Michael—compounding one huge life mistake with another.

"I never want to get hurt like that again, Mor," she whispered.

"What makes you think that this new man won't hurt you?"

"He's been hurt himself. I think Ben is the most honest man I've ever met. I want to take the risk this time. I've spent too many years being afraid."

"How are you going to handle a new relationship while getting out of the old one? What does your Ben make of this?" Six thousand miles of silence separated them. "Did you hear me? What does Ben make of this?"

"I haven't told him." Hannah rushed on, ignoring her mother's reproachful gasp. "I don't want to taint this new relationship with the old. I told Michael I want a divorce. We don't have any kids…"

Her mother misinterpreted Hannah's tone. "Are you pregnant?"

"Oh, no, Mor. Michael found out he's infertile. He can't have children."

"Did you tell him you wanted a divorce before or after he told you this?"

"After."

"Oh, honey. Michael must be devastated."

"I thought you said you didn't like him."

"I did not say that. He is not the right man for you. He has been a good husband, though, has he not?" Hannah didn't have a straight answer. Mor continued. "Honey, if it weren't for you, I sometimes wish I'd met someone like Axel first."

Now that she was an adult, she could see her mother as a woman with wants, desires, and passions. And maybe, maybe her parents weren't perfect for each other, and maybe her mom's new husband *was* a better match, but it still stung a little to think about that. "We had all the passion and the fighting and the making up and the heartache, and I do not know if it was worth it. In the end, after all that, we did not even make it."

"Are you saying I should stay with Michael?"

"In many ways, I think he's good for you. He's balanced. He loves you. You know he would never leave you."

"I want more," Hannah said.

"You always did, honey. I want you to know that passion isn't everything."

"I want to make a clean break from Michael and try to build something with Ben."

"It's not going to be that easy, my darling daughter. I think you better tell Ben about Michael."

"Why?"

"Because I don't think Michael is going to let you go."

10

Ben couldn't keep the ear-to-ear grin from his face. He wanted to do the Snoopy happy dance, but feared he'd fall and incapacitate himself before Hannah got here. And he couldn't make love to her if he were in traction. The corners of his lips quirked up again. His Hannah was coming back to him. The hour and minute hands on his watch had finally made the slow journey to noon. Ben stood up and grabbed his keys. In less than ten minutes, he was at his parent's house. When Hannah had called announcing her return, he wished for once he weren't unfailingly honest. If he'd told her that the Sea Court house were booked, then she would have had nowhere to stay except at his place.

The mere idea of waking up to her every morning had given Ben a semi-permanent hard on for two days. But he hadn't told the lie that had nearly tripped off his lips, because Hannah's decision was the right one, the mature one. They needed to take this slow—see if there was any more to their relationship other than mutual attraction and smoking hot sex. He wanted to do this right this time. The two weeks Hannah had been gone had been torture. Going from celibate to one spectacularly hot night and morning of earth-moving sex with Hannah had been like taking a vintage sports car out of storage. It was slow starting, but now it wanted to race its engine.

He started when he heard a car pull up to the driveway. Ben pulled on an old oilskin jacket from the closet by the front door, and zipped it halfway—not to ward off the cold—but to hide the erection that had gone from half to full mast at the sound of the engine. Adjusting the coat, he took two deep breaths to calm his rapidly beating heart. He was not a caveman and should probably help her unload and get Cody situated before he dragged her to the bedroom.

But the car in the driveway was not Hannah's big, black luxury SUV. It looked like his parents' much more practical Toyota Camry. Ben's ardor cooled like an Ithaca winter. He tilted his head to make sure it was Walter and Elaine, but even with intense scrutiny, he couldn't tell if this car was a new one or an old one. Loyal Toyota owners, they replaced one red or maroon Camry with another every few years. He squinted. It was them. His mom's blow-dried head was out of the car before he could open the door for her. His mother had always hated her curly hair, and had paid to have it professionally blown into smooth waves each and every week for as long as he could remember.

The Camry's engine tick, tick, ticked its way to cool, as his father sat unmoving in the driver's seat. No doubt, he was caught up in some long-winded NPR broadcast. His dad never came into the house before a National Public Radio segment ended. God forbid his dad got home at the beginning of This American Life. He could be in the car, in the darkened garage, for forty-five minutes. His mother pointed out time and again, they could easily turn on the radio in the house—but for his Dad, it wasn't the same. He refused to budge.

"What are you doing here, Mom?" He hoped he didn't sound ungracious.

"Ben Cooper, I'm here to help our guest settle in. If that's okay with you." Apparently, he didn't sound congenial.

"Mom, I'm right down the street. I told you I was more than happy to do it."

"I'm sure you were, Benji." Gesturing toward the car, she said, "Dad and I had some time and thought we'd take a road trip. We miss you, honey." She patted his stubbled face gently. "I remember when you were a boy and wanted to shave every day like your daddy. I used to rub your smooth skin knowing you'd end up shaving for more years than you didn't."

Oh, damn. His mom had that faraway look in her eyes. That look always made him feel like a little boy in a man's body. Before Ben could remind his mother that he was a grown man, his mother enlisted him to pull some groceries out of their car. "You brought groceries?"

"You know how isolated it is out here. We always start our guests off with something. A lot of times, they arrive at night after a long drive. The last thing they want to do is make that two-hour drive inland and back. It's not the best way to start a vacation."

As scheduled, Hannah's SUV pulled into the driveway a few minutes after noon. Her eyes locked with his, then glanced at the red sedan. He made a tiny shrug. Distractedly, he realized that his parents had put more thought into their rental business than he realized. But he wanted to get to Hannah. He abandoned the paper bag inside the front door, damning the perishables to spoilage, and jogged toward his woman. Restraining himself, he gave Hannah the briefest of hugs. With his parents here, he couldn't grab her, swing her in the air, kiss her senseless, or ask her the question that he really wanted an answer to—how long she was going to stay this time. Even if he'd had the guts to accost Hannah in front of his parents, his mother had insinuated himself between them before he got the chance.

Elaine extended her hand. "Hannah, so nice to see you again. Walter and I thought we'd come and check you in. We didn't get the chance to welcome you last time with the impromptu nature of your stay."

"It's good to see you again, Mrs. Cooper." Hannah was gracious where he was not. "Ben, can you help me with Cody?" That husky voice grabbed at his balls and didn't let go. He was glad he hadn't abandoned the coat even though he was sweating in the heat of Indian summer.

Ben walked toward the back of the car and pulled open the door. The dog was still groggy from the tranquilizers and a little wobbly on his feet. Despite that, it was clear that Cody was glad to see him. The tail wag may have been slow, but was there. The dog nuzzled his hand. He hadn't realized until that moment that the dog had grown on him nearly as much as Hannah.

The radio segment must have reached a good stopping point because his father finally got out of the car, carried in the remaining groceries from their car, and then stopped to gather the half-dozen or so paper shopping bags Hannah had brought as well. The refrigerator and cabinets filled up quickly.

His mom and Hannah laughed in the kitchen, probably at their shared idea of stocking up. A New York accent he didn't know Hannah possessed, snuck out in conversation with his mom. His dad had disappeared with the dog, walking off Cody's tranquilizers. A few minutes later, Hannah and his mom brought an impromptu lunch of tuna salad to the table. Even though his hunger wasn't for food, he pulled the cloth napkin from the table and sat politely, counting the minutes until his parents would leave them alone. The anticipation of waiting for Hannah, had him feeling like a teenager wading through a interminable family dinner before a hot date.

"So Benji, Hallie is having a little 'hundred-day' party for Logan's *baek-il*," his mother said, stumbling a little over the

Korean phrase, "and we thought we'd invite you, since we're here. Hannah, you're more than welcome to come. I told Marty and Hallie about you, and they're looking forward to meeting you."

Check in, my ass. Ben shook his head. He couldn't believe he'd almost fallen for his mother's bullshit. Elaine Cooper was a New York hustler at heart. She always had an ulterior motive. They'd used Hannah as an excuse once. He should have known they'd do it again.

"I'd love to go meet Marty and his family as long as Ben is game," Hannah said sweetly. What the hell was that about? Didn't she understand he'd rather cut off his own hand than spend time pretending to be brothers with Marty? How had Hannah turned on him like that? If he said anything but yes at this point, he'd come across as the biggest asshole in the world.

"Fine, Mom, fine. You got me. I'll go to the party. That doesn't mean we're going to be blood brothers or something. As far as I'm concerned, I have only one sister."

Walter walked in the door at that moment, dog in tow. Cody looked refreshed, and almost sober. His father looked a little flushed from the exercise. He took off his doctor hat for a moment, not wanting to spend the remaining hour or so worrying about his father's health. "Good news, Walter. Ben and Hannah are coming to the party."

His father nodded as if Ben's acquiescence were no big deal, and came to the table, helping himself to the salad. Now, that his parents' work was done, they prattled on about the regular inanities—departmental politics at Davis, gossip about the neighbors, and what geniuses Abbe's offspring were.

It wasn't that he didn't love his parents, but after two hours of lunch, showing Hannah how every switch, dial and plug worked, and their meandering conversation, he was ready to bid them farewell. Now that he was going to the damned party, he'd see them in a couple of days. In between, he wanted to reacquaint himself with Hannah's body.

As they descended the stairs after a more than thorough explanation of the Jacuzzi's controls—and he tried to steer his mind away from all the things he'd like to do to Hannah in the whirlpool tub—his dad clutched at his chest.

"Dad? What's wrong?"

"I have a little tightness here," his dad said patting his chest, probably in time with his rapid heartbeat.

"Mr. Cooper, please lay down for a minute," Hannah implored. She jogged down the few remaining stairs and pulled the throw blanket off the couch. He and his mom helped his dad down the steps, and laid him down. Ben was immediately regretful that he'd been so ready to shoo off his ageing parents.

"Do we need to call your cardiologist back home?"

Walter waved away all the attention. "Ben, Elaine, I'm fine. This happens from time to time. I thought I told you that. The decaf I ordered at Starbuck's was probably switched with fully loaded coffee. My mistake for not double checking. Don't worry. The dysrhythmia makes me feel a little weird when my heart goes too fast. I'll be fine in a minute."

"Walter, I don't think we should drive home today. It's a long way back. I'm sure Ben won't mind us staying over at his place. Would you, honey?"

Every fantasy he'd had about this first real night with Hannah dissipated like smoke. Foiled for the time being, Ben tried not to sigh with frustration. He felt like a shitty son, thinking of sex when his father was hurting. "Mom, of course that's not a problem." Ben's dad had sipped some water, gotten to his feet, and announced he was ready to go. Elaine got him situated in the passenger seat of their sedan.

Ben looked pleadingly at Hannah. "Ben, go, I understand. I'm not going anywhere," she said when they were alone for a brief moment. Relief flooded his body.

His parents' one night rest stop turned into two. They all set out early Sunday for the four-hour drive to Davis. It was the first time he was alone with Hannah. And while it was not as horizontal as he might have preferred, it would have to do for now. Especially as his parents were following behind in their car.

"How was your time in Orange County?"

"Difficult," Hannah answered.

"How?"

"Putting your life on hold is impossible," she said. The phrase 'on hold' jerked him back to reality. But what did he expect? She wasn't going to sell her house, quit everything, to follow him after only knowing him a few days. "A two week hiatus to explore yourself is fine. Running away like Elizabeth

Gilbert, without an advance or a book deal, seems a little crazy."

"Did you tell anyone about me?" He swallowed. "Us?"

"My mom."

"How long can you stay this time?"

"As long as I need to."

It had taken some convincing from Hannah, but he'd finally relented and chosen her BMW for the drive down. Between the more comfortable amenities and navigation, it won out over Ben's more utilitarian vehicle. Halfway through the trip, he had to admit that it was a fun car to drive. And the navigation system saved them from consulting the map Ben kept in his glove compartment. The pinpoint directions led them right to the Wexler house. Ben didn't know what he'd expected from Marty Wexler, half brother, but the house they pulled up to several hours and hundreds of miles later, was a typical mid-century ranch with gabled roof and diamond paned front windows. He parked Hannah's car behind his parents' sedan.

Ben was grateful there was already a crowd when they got to the house. If it was this busy while they were there, it would save him from having to interact with the man who embodied the worst period in his parents' marriage.

Hannah pulled him toward the kitchen, pastel blue gift-wrapped box in hand. She'd insisted that they stop for a gift at Westlake Plaza before they got to the party. He didn't know why it was necessary when the parents themselves hadn't even invited him to the party. Hannah said it didn't matter how they'd come to be there, they should get a card and a gift. From the tall pyramid of multi-colored and ber-ibboned boxes towering on the dining room table, she'd been right. How any three month old could ever need so much stuff, he'd never know, but at least he hadn't embarrassed himself.

Ben's sister Abbe, two-year old glued to her hip, bore down on them like a tiger going for prey. His sister took after their mother. There wasn't a shy bone in her body.

"You must be Hannah?" She thrust out her free hand. "This is Vienna," she said, cocking her head toward the tired little girl, her eyes red, auburn Shirley Temple ringlets droop-ing. "And she's tired already. Why do people have parties at naptime?"

"I couldn't tell you," Hannah answered matter-of-factly. "I don't go to a lot of kids' parties."

Abbe smacked an open palm on her head, dramatically. "Of course, you and Ben are child-free. Enjoy it. Impromptu sex gets a lot harder with little ones running around. They never nap enough for you to get in more than a quickie."

"And this is my sister, Abbe, inappropriate as always," Ben said by way of formal introduction.

"Oh, hush Benji. You're forty and Hannah is a grown woman. I'll assume I haven't assaulted her virgin ears."

"Thanks for the advice. I'll keep it in mind," Hannah said diplomatically.

Ben looked away from the tight jeans cupping Hannah's cute little butt. A little impromptu sex wouldn't be half-bad. The last two nights had been torture. He was back to masturbating in the dark, as if he was fifteen years old again. For two torturous nights, he'd stroked his own penis under the covers, hoping his parents didn't walk in. Ben couldn't wait to get to the hotel room he'd reserved for them. No way was he going to try to make the trek home tonight. The party gave him the perfect excuse to get a little room service, and get Hannah alone without his parents or even Cody for a good chunk of time. His pants felt a little tight and he tried to think of anything but sex. Damn his sister for bringing it up at a kid's party.

Thankfully, the lights dimmed and the room grew quiet. His mom walked in with cake candles lit. A woman with wavy brown hair, pale skin, and Asian looking eyes came into the room, holding what must be baby Logan.

Abbe stage-whispered in his direction. "That's Hallie and Logan." Like he wouldn't have guessed. His mom had mentioned one too many times how cool it was that Marty had married a half Korean woman, and how cute the baby was with his straight black hair and blue eyes when Marty and Hallie's eyes were chocolate brown. His dad liked to say that the blue eyes came from his side of the family. Ben tried to banish that thought whenever possible.

An older Asian woman and tall Irish looking man, clearly a long married couple, followed. Hallie's parents. All the grandparents sang a song for the baby, in what he quickly realized was Korean, and blew out the candles. When had they gotten together to practice that? His mom did not know any Korean.

Then bright bursts of camera flash filled the room, temporarily blinding him as everyone cooed and fussed over Logan. The baby drooled in response. What was the big deal with babies? As he was thanking his lucky stars that he'd managed to get away child-free for so many years, he noticed Hannah rubbing her flat stomach and tearing up. Not her, too. She got weepy over babies? Was no one immune to the little germ carriers?

His mom took the cake back to the kitchen for slicing. The crowd in the dining room thinned out. Then he saw Marty. It was like looking in a fun house mirror. His half-brother looked like a soon to be middle-aged version of himself.

"Ben." Marty extended his hand. "Long time no see."

Ben reluctantly grabbed the hand that reminded him so much of his father's. "Marty. Happy one hundred days, is it?"

Marty nodded. "*Baek-il*, it's a Korean thing. Probably from back in the time when many babies didn't survive long after birth. I hear the *dol*, the first birthday, is even more elaborate. I'll probably need all nine months to prepare."

Ben didn't know what to say to this man. Two conversations in twenty-five years didn't make things any less awkward. He was infinitely grateful when Hannah intercepted.

She extended her own hand. "Hi, I'm Hannah Keesling, Ben's friend. Congratulations on your son. He's beautiful—but I'm partial to multi-racial babies myself."

Marty laughed, awkwardness dissipated. Ben watched Hannah ask all the right questions about nursing, sleep and baby milestones. She and Marty laughed about the baby unexpectedly rolling over the first time—almost off the changing table. They talked about whether Marty and Hallie were going to have more, and what their work schedules were going to be like now that Hallie's maternity leave was coming to an end.

This was a side of Hannah he'd never seen before—the domesticated side. The car, her clothes, and her attitude all spelled big city. He didn't think she'd be so much at home at a suburban baby party. When Hallie brought Logan back in, Hannah held him, cooed to him, and made all the appropriate noises. Rather than being scared, Logan was fascinated by all the bracelets adorning Hannah's wrists. His little fists looked like they were trying to open and grasp at her hammered copper earrings. When he looked sleepy she rocked him, and the tiny sleeping form curled against her shoulder, infinitely trustworthy.

His dad joined the circle. "I'm so happy to see my two boys together," he said extending his arms and clapping both heartily on the back.

The buzz of good vibes he'd had going disappeared in one hot second. Why did his dad have to go and say something stupid like that? He was gratified to see that Marty, shifting on his loafer clad feet, looked as uncomfortable as he felt.

"Mr. Cooper. I've only met Ben for the second time..."

"What's with this Mr. Cooper business? You haven't called me that for years. I've always been Walter, or even Dad."

The Mr. Cooper business had been for his benefit. Ben reeled back, realizing that the relationship between this Marty

Wexler kid and his father was probably closer than he'd thought. All those years his father had kept this relationship a secret, and even more years when this was an open secret— his dad and this guy, who was no longer the kid he remembered, had probably gotten close. He'd never heard that Marty's mother had married or anything, or that Marty had another father figure in his life. His own dad, the one he saw at breakfast, dinner and bedtime, was it.

He had the briefest flash of sympathy for this man who'd only ever had a part-time dad, but it was washed away with the notion of all the lies that had been told to obscure the truth from his mom, his sister and him.

Hannah gently handed the sleeping baby to Hallie, stood and stretched.

He didn't need this. Marty Wexler was not the person he needed to build a relationship with. That person was Hannah and he wanted to get to it.

"While I'd love to stay dad, Hannah and I have to make the long drive back."

Hannah looked at him questioningly, but fortunately didn't say anything. He'd mentioned his plans for the Woodland Inn to her before they'd left for the trip. She had smiled brazenly, looking as excited about the night ahead as he'd felt.

His dad looked crestfallen. "You won't stay for the night? With Hallie's parents here, I thought I'd take all my children out for dinner. On me."

Dad had put him between a rock and a hard place. He hadn't mentioned to his parents his plans with Hannah. Some things he liked to keep to himself. He closed his eyes for a second. If he didn't do some fancy footwork to extricate himself, it would be a long night with his family and the Wexlers.

As they slid into the largest booth at Osteria Fasulo, it was clear that Ben had lost his dancing shoes. With Logan's grandparents in town, it looked like Hallie and Marty were looking forward to a date night, but like Ben, they'd been shoehorned into tonight's festivities. Abbe and Dad seemed to be the only two people happy to celebrate this mini 'family reunion.'

All four couples took up quite a bit of space at the table for eight. Introductions were made. It had been some time since he'd seen Abbe's husband, Isaiah. He was a senior staffer in Sacramento. With California's perpetual slide toward bankruptcy, he was always there working out one budgetary problem or another well into the night. He'd been a good match for his sister. He was quiet and steadfast in the face of her ebullient effusiveness. Glad that at least he was seated next to Hannah, even if they couldn't be any closer right now, Ben grabbed her hand and pulled it to his thigh, lazily circling her soft palm with his thumb. In less than twenty-four hours, if nothing else went off the rails, he and Hannah would finally be alone.

Hannah looked around the table. This was one hundred and eighty degrees from where she'd been last week in the Keeslings' Fullerton backyard. A new man, a new family, and a new dynamic.

After everyone was seated and situated, Walter tapped the side of his water glass with his fork. Conversation paused.

"I want to thank you all for being here. This is the first time I've ever had all of my children with me." Ben shifted in his seat. He would never be a championship poker player. Although he looked like he was trying to hide them, Ben's emotions were written all over his face. Right now his features were shifting between discomfiture and latent anger. Hannah shifted uncomfortably in her own seat. She'd never want that anger directed at her.

"You okay?" Ben asked under his breath.

"Yeah," she said, trying to give a reassuring smile. She squeezed the hand on his leg. He was doing crazy things to her libido with his thumb. But that wasn't what was making her uncomfortable. His attitude toward his father made it clear that she needed to keep her past with Michael absolutely separate from her present, and hopeful future with Ben. She'd had years more practice hiding her emotions. Easily covering her trepidation, she said, "This is a little awkward."

"I know. I'm sorry that you got wrapped up in all this. I wanted to be with you this weekend."

"It's okay. We have nothing but time," Hannah said. She wanted to give this relationship time and space to grow. Whether that was two months or two years, she was in for the long haul.

After the food came, Walter tried to steer the conversation. "Ben, did you know that you and Marty have a lot in common?" Hannah looked from Ben to Marty and back again.

Both men looked pained at their father's attempts at creating camaraderie. "Marty's been talking about taking out his grass and going for something that doesn't suck up water from the aquifers like a sponge. I mentioned to him that you don't have grass in front of your house either."

"Dad," Ben started, "I live on the ocean. Nothing much grows on the seaside. The pines are what grow nearby. I figure they'd do as well at my house as they do in the national forest."

"Exactly what I was saying to Marty. He should take his cue from the national parks around here."

Walter went on like that for much of the meal, picking up little things that his 'boys' as he kept calling them, shared. He was grasping at straws.

"Dad. Stop it," Ben said, finally while they were finishing up tiramisu and coffee.

"Benji," Elaine said in a warning tone.

"Stop what, Ben?" Walter asked.

"Stop trying to push Marty and me together. We're related. I get that. You cheated on Mom, and now Marty's here." Elaine gasped, and put her hand in front of her mouth. When she recovered from the shock, she looked like there was plenty she wanted to say, but Ben plowed on. "I'm sure Marty's a swell guy, Dad, but I don't want to be friends with him, I don't want to become an instant family. I'm forty years old—too damn old to get a baby brother. You kept him a secret. You kept us all apart. You lied again and again. I've made my peace with that, mostly for Mom's sake. But we're not going to be the Brady Bunch. I've got one real sibling, and that's Abbe. No amount of pushing us all together is going to change that."

11

Walter rocked back in his seat. Hannah had no idea what had been said in the past between Ben or Abbe and their parents regarding Marty's existence. But she guessed from their reaction, this was the most explicit Ben had ever been in his dismissal of the family ties his parents were trying so hard to forge.

"Well, Ben, you may not like that you have not one sibling, but two. But Elaine and I have discussed this. We've made our minds up to bring Marty and Hallie and Logan, for that matter, into our lives. And you might as well get used to it, because we're changing everything. Your mother has forgiven me, I think it's time you did, too."

"Next thing you're going to tell me is that you've changed your will and left everything to Marty."

"Well, you're about one third right there, Benji. We did change our trusts, though I didn't plan to talk about it here. We're leaving a third to each of you." Walter pushed his chair back from the table and strode from the restaurant.

Ben looked at his sister. "Did you know about this?"

Abbe shook her head. "God damn it, Ben! Why did you have to do this now?" She got up from her chair, running after Walter.

Hannah watched the family drama unfolding before her. If she'd been anywhere but Davis, she'd have picked up her stuff and quietly slipped away. But she had nowhere to go.

She tugged at the hand in her lap. "Ben, maybe we should go."

"We'll meet you at home, Benji," Elaine said.

At home? Whose home? Their home? Now that would be awkward.

"Oh, Elaine, we will not put you out. Ben and I can..."

"Mom, I made arrangements to stay at the Woodland Inn," Ben interjected. Hannah's relief was short lived.

"Of course you'll stay with us. And you too," Elaine amended, not wanting to be misunderstood. "I think you and your father need to talk. You can't do that if you're across town."

The ride to Ben's parents' house was silent. With every streetlight they passed, she could see his jaw working.

"We don't have to go in," Hannah said.

"My mom puts up a good front," Ben said, putting the car in park. "She's not the type to ask for help, outright."

His parents weren't home yet, and he sifted through his keys to find the right one. After turning off the alarm, he turned on the lights in the living room. Hannah shouldn't have been surprised that the house looked a lot like the one in Shelter Cove minus the nautical touches. It was all wood, and leather, and flower patterned linen. On any other occasion, she might have thought it cozy and comfortable. Now she stood there with her overnight bag feeling awkward.

"Come on upstairs," Ben said taking her bag in one hand and his in the other.

"Do you have enough room?"

He stopped halfway up the carpeted stairs looking down at her. Despite their ages, she didn't feel comfortable sharing a room with Ben in his parents' house.

"We'll stay in my room. My parents made it into a guest room years ago. It has a queen bed, now."

"What about Abbe's room?"

"Abbe?" Ben looked at her questioningly. "You don't want to sleep with me?"

Hannah could feel heat rushing to her cheeks. "Ben, I missed you...a lot...but your parents are under...a lot of stress, and I don't want them to feel uncomfortable..."

"Hannah, we're consenting adults. You're sleeping with me."

He turned back to the stairs and ascended two at a time, turning right into a bedroom. She had no choice but to follow. A door slammed below. She could hear the murmur of voices.

"Ben, Hannah," Elaine's voice filtered upstairs. Hannah didn't get any more than a glimpse at the guest room before she turned to go back down.

Elaine poured the remaining group, Abbe, her husband, Ben and finally Walter, small glasses of port in the large study. The masculine room was obviously Walter's domain.

Hannah leaned toward Abbe. "Did Marty and Hallie go home?" she whispered.

"They said they had to relieve her parents of baby duty. Who knows? But I wouldn't be here if I didn't feel bad for Dad and Ben."

The room lapsed into silence. Hannah took a sip of the port. The sweet liquid burned a fiery path down her throat. It tasted like it was one hundred proof. She put the glass down. Anymore of that and she'd be useless in the morning.

Walter lifted his head from deep thought. "Ben, Abbe. I love you two. I always will. I know that accepting Marty like a brother is probably too much to ask of you. But I love him too. He's my child as much as you are. I refuse to shortchange him. Your mother and I agree on this, and won't hear any more argument."

"Dad, what you do with your money and your time is your business. Don't ambush me again. It's my choice as to what kind of relationship I want to have with him. If that's none, I want you to accept it."

"Can I ask you why, Benji?" His mother's voice took on a pleading tone. "You've always had the biggest heart."

"I can't start a relationship based on a lie."

Hannah tried not to reel back physically, though she felt like Ben had slapped her in the face.

"Marty didn't lie to you. He's the innocent one in all this," Elaine said.

"You're probably right, Ma. But the situation is so messed up. Every time I see him it brings up all the years Dad deceived us."

"Is this about Samara?"

Ben looked pointedly toward Hannah. "Ma, can we leave this for now? I've got to get to bed so we can leave for the North Coast first thing in the morning. I have to get back to work."

Ben put down his unfinished drink and left the room. Hannah wished everyone a good night, and followed Ben upstairs.

When she closed the door behind them, Ben grabbed her roughly and pulled her to him. The gentleness she'd come to associate with Ben was gone. In its place was a storm of pent up emotion. He claimed her mouth, opening hers without ceremony. His tongue boldly stroked hers. Ben's body vibrated with anger, desire, and passion. Where she would have gentled his movements, she took the punishment instead—overwhelmed with guilt for the lies she'd told him. Ben's hands shoved up her shirt, and released her breasts from her bra. He pushed her against the door and stroked between her legs over her jeans, while suckling first one nipple, then the next.

Hannah forgot his anger, forgot her guilt, but remembered the sensations he had aroused the last time they were together like this. Her fingers tangled with the leather of his belt. She itched to stroke him, bring him the same pleasure he'd brought her so many times a few weeks ago. A faraway knock sounded. Ben pulled back, disoriented. The knock sounded again.

"Ben, Hannah, I brought you some towels. The housekeeper doesn't leave them in here anymore."

Hannah swiftly pulled her shirt down over her bare breasts, and sat primly on the side of the bed.

Shoveling a hand through his hair, Ben pulled open the door a crack. He murmured something and closed the door, reappearing with a thick stack of towels in his hands. He dropped the linens in the adjoining bathroom and came to sit next to her on the bed.

"I'm sorry. I shouldn't..."

She pressed a finger to his full lips, ignoring the electricity shooting up her arm. "It's okay. A lot has happened tonight. Why don't we go to bed...to sleep. It's a long way back tomorrow."

Hours later, Hannah woke from a deep, dreamless sleep. Shielding the light of her phone from Ben, she checked the time. *2:30*. He was sleeping soundly. She lay awake flat on her back, forearm thrown over her eyes for half an hour, trying not to move or disturb the man next to her. Despite her best efforts to divert them elsewhere, she kept thinking about holding that precious little bundle, baby Logan.

She hated the hormones that made her want to have and hold a baby, a dream that was fading fast. She'd gone so many years not thinking much about children, then one day the empty womb feeling smacked her in the face. She'd been at Trader Joe's buying wine and cheese when a pregnant woman pushed a cart toward the register. In the little seat was a three-year-old girl whose untamed frizzy hair reminded her of dozens of childhood photos of herself. With a fierceness she'd never felt before, she wanted to be that woman. To feel the swell of pregnancy, to have a toddler to cuddle and hold. The feeling took hold that day in downtown Brooklyn and rarely let go.

Her desire to become pregnant and to have *this* man be the father, sent arousal thrumming in her veins. At 3:00, she tip-toed to the bathroom and relieved herself, hoping that would make sleep come, make her desire for consummation go away. It didn't. The more time passed, the more Hannah became aware of the living, breathing, sexy man next to her. He'd gone to bed in boxers. Against her better judgment, she shifted to her side and stroked Ben's broad back, bare to his waist. Michael had always hated when she touched him outside the boundaries of sex. Wary of Ben waking and swatting her hand away like a fly, her touch was light as a butterfly.

Instead, his large hand caught hers. Surprise made her gasp. Then her hand flew to her mouth, too late to cover the sound that escaped.

"Hey lady," Ben said in a sleep roughened voice.

"I'm sorry..."

"I love the feel of your hands on me." He turned, now flat on his back. She could see his outline in the faint moonlight filtering through the wooden blinds.

Emboldened, she continued to caress him, sliding the hair from his brow, tracing his prominent nose, his full lips. Her hand tangled briefly in the fine hairs that sprinkled on his chest, circling the flat nipples there—feeling the small protrusions harden. Sliding down his flat, hard belly, Hannah slipped her hand through the slit of his boxers, and eased his penis out. Hard pulsing flesh catching for a moment on the now restrictive fabric.

His chest rose and fell rapidly and his breath started coming harder and faster. She bit back a moan as his hand slid up her loose tank and a thumb slid back and forth across her nipple. Pulling away, she knelt between his legs, and took him full into her mouth. She wanted to do something for him. No more than two strokes in, he pulled her back up him so that they were face to face.

"Ben, I want to make you…"

"Hannah, that feels good. Really good, but I want to make love with you. I want this to be good for both of us. More than anything, I want to be inside you. I want us to be in this together."

As Ben eased her panties down and off, and leaned over to fish a condom from his shaving kit, she tried to push Michael from her mind. Her soon to be ex-husband, would have taken a blow job over intercourse every single time if he had a choice. If they weren't trying for a baby, she didn't think he'd ever want to have sex with her that way. It was unfathomably sexy that this man wanted both of them to share each and every experience.

Ben kissed her then, blotting out thoughts of years of selfish sex she'd subjected herself to. He tried to go slow, to make sure it was good for her. But his generosity alone made her wetter than she ever remembered.

She knew she should wait until they got home, but passion overwhelmed her common sense. "Ben, fuck me. I need you inside me."

And he did, first slow, then with increasing speed as they both got close to the edge. She stopped caring about concealing her moans, or keeping the bed from squeaking. She wanted the fulfillment that this man so easily gave her.

Hannah would never know if his parents heard them that night because Ben woke early, insisting they leave. She sensed that his anger hadn't fully dissipated despite the passion they'd shared.

The next few weeks were as close to perfect as Hannah had ever experienced. Ben was with her nearly every night that he wasn't working or she wasn't focused on her artistic endeavors. They still shared separate houses, but they came together for dinner, conversation, and the most passionate sex she'd ever had. Until she met Ben, she'd compared Michael's narcissistic lovemaking with the earnest adolescent fumblings of Lucas, and neither was particularly satisfying. Those men could not hold a candle to what she and Ben shared. He was the most giving partner she'd ever known. He insisted that sex was always good for men, and that his primary goal was to make sure she was sated and satisfied. She was definitely both.

Hannah had blossomed in a way she hadn't imagined up here on the North Coast. She'd had Michael's brother, Kendall—at least one Keesling was still speaking to her—ship her photographic catalog from storage. She'd scanned in all her best film work from the negatives she'd so carefully preserved, and touched up the digital files. Now she was putting together a spring show that contrasted portraits in urban New York and Los Angeles settings with rural portraits. During one of her day long excursions in the area, she'd found a gallery interested in the work she'd started here with Ben on the black sand beach.

Tonight she was going to surprise Ben, and hopefully not embarrass herself. She'd been doing some song writing, something she hadn't done in years. She was going to join the band that had covered her dad's music for a few songs. The band, Funk Fiesta, was one of four that rotated for the Wednesday night jazz spot. In exchange, they agreed to back her up on the two songs she was debuting tonight.

The taffeta gown she selected from the few clothes she'd brought was a little tight when she zipped the side. Fortunately, the ruching, and damned shininess of the dress, which was somewhere between silver and gold, depending on the lighting, hid the softening around her middle. Being a tall woman had few advantages, but this was one of them. Whenever she gained weight, it was distributed all over her five foot ten frame. Hannah chastised herself for her laziness, vowing to cut back on the dinners she'd been sharing with Ben. Going from takeout salads to fully satisfying home-cooked meals was playing havoc with her waistline, if this dress were any indication.

Satisfied that she didn't look like she was squeezed into sausage casing, she zipped herself into a full-length down coat, and set out for the Blue Monk. Tonight was going to be a surprise for Ben. She wanted him to get to know her in a way he never had. She had demurred anytime he'd asked about her singing. Tonight, she was going to sing her heart out for him.

Hannah had purposefully driven separately. She'd needed to spend some time warming up, and doing a sound check with the band, and there was no need for Ben to be there. But she also needed an out. If tonight went badly, she'd need that long drive back to Shelter Cove to lick her wounds. Leaving the band members on stage working out last minute kinks, she peeked into the parking lot and saw Ben's white truck pull up. He looked good enough to eat. She'd always thought clothes made the man, but it never mattered what this man wore. The sight of him got her going. She shook off the arousal that pooled in her belly and waited for him to come toward the door.

Ben looked perplexed. "This was the surprise? We came here before, together that first week. The band was playing your dad's music."

"Ben, that's not the surprise." She took him by the hand and led him into the club. A small table in front of the stage was empty, a tiny 'reserved' placard in the middle. She sat and pulled her Jimmy Choo 'fuck me' pumps from her over-sized handbag and slipped them on. Looking Ben in the eye, she unzipped the coat all the way and slid from its black mi-crofiber confines. His eyes almost popped out of his head at the sight of her in the dress. Relief washed over her. This wasn't going to be so bad. This man was still attracted to her, even with a few extra pounds. The band was ready and she joined them on stage. When she opened her mouth to sing, it was like all the years between her last performance and this one disappeared in a puff of smoke. For the next hour, she was in her element, belting out tunes she'd heard her mother prac-tice time and again. The band stayed backstage during the break. But she wanted to see what he'd thought. While she was performing, she didn't look at Ben. She was focused on making sure she hadn't missed her cues and was entertaining the entire crowd, not merely the one person most important to her.

"I had no idea," Ben said to her when she gulped some honeyed tea she'd asked the bartender to prepare. "You're amazing."

"Thanks. I'm planning on doing only one more song, after the break. Then we can go." Her hands shook a little as she placed the cup on the saucer. "You okay? You didn't look the least bit nervous up there."

"A little," she admitted. "I wrote the next song."

Before he could ask any more questions, she strode up on stage and conferred with the band. The house manager turned down the stereo system that had been playing CDs during the intermission.

Hannah wrapped her hands around the microphone, now sitting in its stand.

"Thank you so much for having me here tonight," she started and the crowd clapped. She introduced and thanked the band. "This last song of the night, I wrote." Hannah faltered. She was laying it all on the line. "This is for you, Ben Cooper."

The piano player started first, then the alto sax joined him in the slow melody. Then it was Hannah's turn. She blocked out the entire crowd, looked directly at Ben, and sang.

When you look at me
I wonder what you're seeing
Because I know what I'm seeing
When you smile at me
I wonder what you're thinking
Because I know what I'm thinking
When you touch me
I wonder what you're feeling
Because I know what I'm feeling
When you speak
I look for the meaning
beyond the words
Because I wonder
Is it the same for you
As it is for me

She sang a second verse, repeated the first and ended with the refrain:

Because I wonder
Is it the same for you
As it is for me

Hannah's voice trailed off as the sounds of the strings, woodwind, and brass instruments reverberated in the expectant club. There was a long moment before the audience erupted in applause. She swept her right arm in an arc encompassing the band, as each member stood and bowed. Then she exited the stage through a side door. The band members followed her off stage after taking their own bows. Turning down their offers to grab a drink now that they were done, she started the long walk down the hall back toward the well of the club. Able to peer around the door at Ben, she couldn't get a read on whether he returned the feelings she'd expressed on stage. He merely looked stunned.

Now, she was more than happy that they had driven separately. She looked in a mirror along the tiny corridor—probably for performers to do one last check before going on stage—and arranged her face into a pleasant mask, hiding all emotion.

He rose, his manners winning out over his confusion.

"I'm going to do some post show stuff with the band, so I don't know when I'll be home."

"Oh, okay. Hannah..." he broke off.

She leaned over, bussed his cheek and walked back to the stage door before he could say anything. She watched him gather his jacket and leave the club. The mask fell. She had told him that she loved him in so many words on stage, and he hadn't said them back. She honestly had no idea what he felt for her. She loved him. It was as plain as the nose on her face. After her performance on stage, there was no going back. He felt something for her. Of that, she was sure. But whether that was love, or if she was someone to fill the time in between the heartbreak of his divorce and his next real relationship, she didn't know. Whether he would ever have another relationship, she didn't know.

She waited ten minutes, changed her shoes, slipped back into her long coat, and took her leave.

Hannah settled in for the long drive, planning to feel sorry for herself the whole way. It was too early in the morning to try commiserating with her mom. Her parents hadn't had much in common, but neither of them was a morning person. She was going down a mental list of people she could call near midnight, rather than be alone with her thoughts, when her phone rang. For one long second, she hoped it was Ben, but then she remembered he didn't have a phone.

She glanced at the Caller ID on the dashboard. Michael.

"It's kind of late, Michael." There was little civility in her tone.

"Are you alone?"

"Yes, Michael, I'm alone. What do you want? I know it's not to talk about dissolution at this hour."

He ignored the dig. "I've given you a month, Hannah. When are you coming back?" Clearly, talking rationally to him wasn't going to get any easier anytime soon.

"I'm not coming back, Michael," she said baldly. No matter how many times she had said it to him over the phone or e-mail, he wasn't ready to let go. Her mother had hit this nail on the head.

"How could you do this to me? You picked up your stuff and left. We had five years together, Hannah. Are you willing to toss this aside on a whim? Following after some guy you've only known for a second?" Hannah didn't answer. That's exactly what she was willing to do. She'd proven it when she'd left Michael for Ben. "Okay, okay. I'm sorry. I didn't call to harass you. I wanted you to know that I've been seeing a counselor, Hannah. I've been talking to someone to try and work out what I could have done wrong. Will you go to counseling with me? Can you give us one more chance?"

Despite her behavior over the last two months, at heart Hannah was a nice girl. Her mother and father had raised her to be kind and considerate. She had been unkind and inconsiderate to Michael. "Maybe." She wanted to kick herself the minute that one small word left her mouth.

"When will you be home?"

"Maybe, I'll think about counseling, Michael. I can't up and come home, right now. Do you know where I was tonight?"

"With him?" Michael asked, unattractive petulance in his voice.

"Michael, I was singing on stage for the first time in years. I sang my dad's music with a local band. And they were kind enough to let me perform a song I wrote."

"Congratulations." Michael's sentiment sounded real. "That must have been really cool for you. I remember when you turned down that invitation to sing with that roots rock band that performed at Room 5 all the time. We were moving, and it really depressed you for a while."

"I probably should have done it then even with the driving."

"You're probably right." Michael paused. "See Hannah, during my sessions, I realized that the changes we made were probably too abrupt. Why did we think we had to go from Silver Lake to Newport to raise a child? It was stupidity on both our parts. We could live anywhere, you and I, Los Angeles, even Brooklyn. I liked New York. You loved it. We don't need to be in California. My brother's here if my parents need anything. There are airplanes that fly both ways."

If Michael had said any of this before she'd driven away in September, she may never have come here. In so many ways, that would have been simpler. Making the choice to leave her husband had been hard enough. Now she had two choices, whether she wanted to work it out with her husband or whether she wanted to throw in her lot with Ben.

Even with Michael's voice backgrounding her drive back to Shelter Cove. Even with the uncertainty coming from Ben, the choice was easy. She was going to choose love.

12

Ben wasn't the first thought on Hannah's mind when she awoke on the Thursday morning after the jazz fiasco. Michael wasn't the first thought either. Her first thought was about babies. All night, she'd been dreaming about babies. And she didn't think it was because of Logan's party. While she and Michael were trying to get pregnant, she'd scoured a million websites, cataloguing the signs of pregnancy. She'd ordered ninety-nine cent pregnancy tests by the boxfuls. Like so many women she'd seen posting on 'trying-to-conceive' boards, she'd gotten addicted to peeing on tiny sticks.

Following the rules faithfully, she always dug out the sticks on day ten after her ovulation cycle. Before she could freak out too much, Hannah leapt out of bed and turned on her

MacBook. Scrolling through the calendar, she realized with a sinking feeling that she hadn't had her period since September. She clicked on 'today.' It was November fourteenth.

Where were her pee sticks? She must have some, somewhere. She'd stashed them everywhere over the last year. Scaring the hell out of Cody as she ran downstairs, she rounded on her leather carryall and turned it upside down, not caring that the contents spilled everywhere.

There, in a Ziploc bag were about ten of the tiny little strips she'd ordered from earlypregnancytests.com. Some were blue, some were green. The discount tests didn't have much in the way of labeling. Hannah racked her brain trying to remember which were for pregnancy and which were for ovulation. Didn't matter. She'd throw both in a cup of pee. None of the 100 pack of Dixie cups she'd bought months ago were in the bag, though. It wasn't the kind of thing she'd have thought to pack.

Tearing through the upstairs bathrooms, she found a green plastic cup – probably for rinsing out her mouth – but she'd used it for her toothbrush. Grateful that she hadn't peed in the middle of the night, she did her best to hold the cup under her urine stream. She looked at the fluted cup, and thanked God that the dishwasher downstairs had a sanitizing cycle. What the Coopers or future guests didn't know wouldn't hurt them. Warm urine in hand, she realized she'd left the strips downstairs. Her progression down was slower this time, as she dodged Cody's big head, which could have easily caused a spill in the dog's eagerness to follow in front.

Hannah peeled back the tiny film covers on both the green and blue sticks and tossed them in. Then she set the timer on the microwave. It was the longest five minutes of her life. She let the dog out, fed him some kibble, and started to unload the dishwasher—then, ding! She ran to the cup.

Memories she'd repressed returned. It was the blue stick she needed. She tossed the green in the trash, and pulled out the blue. There were two lines on the strip, a dark pink line and a lighter one. These damned things hadn't come with instructions. Putting the stick on a paper towel to absorb the moisture, Hannah ran back upstairs in a flash. She searched her e-mail, banging the keys in frustration as the e-mail program slowly sifted through thousands of messages, none of which was as important as the one she needed. Finally. Hannah found the last order she'd placed for strips and lubricant, clicked on the website and surfed for the instructions.

She looked from the picture clinically labeled "interpretation of results," to the flimsy stick in her hand. No doubt about it, she was pregnant. Could Michael be the father? The thought flashed through her mind, and she dismissed it as quickly as it had come. Nope, wasn't possible. The computer clock said it was nearly nine o'clock in the morning. Ben would be at work already, elbow deep in furry pets. The local drugstore didn't open for an hour. Did she need a twenty-dollar test to confirm what she already knew? The truth was sinking deep into her bones. Did she need to go to a doctor? They used the same kind of tests women used at home. During their fertility consultations, she'd been surprised to learn that blood tests had gone the way of the dinosaur. She was no dinosaur.

She snapped the lid of the laptop closed. At least she wasn't just getting fat.

Ben wouldn't be back home for nine hours. It was time to call her mom, time difference be damned.

"Mor, are you working?"

"Not today, honey. Axel and I are planning a little weekend getaway to Malmo or thereabouts on the ferry. We're packing now and will leave first thing in the morning. How are things going with Ben? You've been up there for a few weeks."

"I sang last night." There was a long pause on the other end of the static free-line. It was nothing like the short, bank busting phone chats of her youth, when they spoke to Mor's parents. When her mother didn't speak, she sensed her mounting ambivalence to Hannah performing again. "I wrote a new song—basically telling him that I loved him."

"Oh, honey—it is so soon. What did he say?"

"Nothing," she said. Then blurted out, "I'm pregnant."

Her mother did nothing to hide her sharp intake of breath. "Who is the father?"

"Ben, of course, Mor."

"Are you sure?"

"Michael and I haven't been intimate like that for a while," Hannah said. It was a partial lie. The truth was far too humiliating to share.

"You never said. I thought with you trying for a baby..."
Mor let the sentence hang.

"Can I come see you?" The ache to see her mother,
pounded in her chest. A need to be loved and cared for unconditionally seared through her heart. Thoughts of people speaking in her native tongue, the sounds so familiar. She missed
the smoked fish, strong coffee, and even the cold weather with
an acuteness she hadn't felt in years. It would be perfect. She
could live with her mother, have the baby in a country with
great health care, her mom could help her watch the baby.
She could truly get a new start this time.

"I think you need to stay where you are," Mor said, sending
Hannah's burgeoning fantasy crashing back down to earth.
Her mother was right, of course. Hannah had already tried
running away from one problem, and she'd landed here. Flying
away would do no good.

"Any advice?"

"Tell him tonight about the baby, about Michael—all of
it." That the best relationships were built on truth went un-
spoken. She took half the advice.

During their short relationship, Ben had done all the cooking, because he was good at it and liked it. Except for chicken
or tuna salad, Hannah hadn't really cooked for him. In southern California, building big kitchens was a sport—actually using them for cooking—not so much. When times were lean,
when jazz wasn't very popular in the 1980s and when her Dad
finally left, her mom did all the cooking. Hannah had grown

up with lots of smoked fish, hard bread, and Danish meat-balls—which were much better than the Swedish ones.

She had no idea how Ben really felt about her, and no idea how he'd take this second punch in the one-two combination she was about to deliver. But she had to assume it would all be better with food and alcohol.

After leaving a message at his office asking him to join her for dinner at her place, she turned off her phone, opened the freezer, and got to work. When the doorbell rang that evening, she was putting the finishing touches on the simple dinner she'd prepared.

Suddenly shy, Hannah dried her sweaty palms on her jeans, and opened the door. "Hi." Ben fidgeted with his jacket. He looked almost as nervous as she felt. "Come on in. I made dinner—a real dinner."

Ben patted Cody and wrestled a little with the rambunc-tious adolescent on the floor. No matter how many walks she took the dog on, his energy seemed boundless. If the goofy doggy smile was any indication, he liked Ben's companionship as much as she did.

"Hope you're hungry," she said before returning to the kitchen.

"Hannah, I..."

"Ben, there's plenty of time for talking. Let me get this food on the table."

He opened the fridge and took out a bottle of red wine. "This okay?"

She stirred the sauce on the stove. "When I was a kid, no self respecting Dane would have had wine with dinner. It was beer all the way, but I think they've changed."

He left the kitchen with the uncorked wine and glasses in hand. She brought the food to the table.

"Wow, what's this?"

"It's *stegt flæsk*—fried pork slices," she translated. "It's boiled potatoes with *persille sovs*—um, parsley sauce, I guess."

Ben dug in as though he'd been down in the mines for twelve hours, instead of an office for eight. "This is really good." Hannah tried the food. It wasn't as good as her mom's cooking. Still, it reminded her of home.

"Thanks." They finished the simple dinner in record time. She'd planned to talk to him after dinner, and that time had come upon her like a speeding freight train. She jumped up from the table like she'd been bitten in the ass. "I made dessert, too. It's *æblekage*—apple crumble would be the best way to describe it." Hannah practically ran into the kitchen and poured them each a glass of wine, a German dessert white this time, and brought the fruit and cream filled mugs to the couch. As soon as she set it all on the coffee table and put the tray she'd used on the floor, Ben grabbed her hand.

"Stop running, Hannah," Ben said, his deep voice as serious and solemn as she'd ever heard. "I love you, too." That bass vibrated down her spine like it always did, resonating deep inside.

All the nerves fell away, and she fell back into the couch cushions. "You don't have to...I didn't mean for you to feel...The song..." Obligation is what she couldn't quite get out. She didn't want him to feel obligated to say he loved her. She loved him, and that for now was enough.

"I love you, Hannah Keesling," he said again. Michael's last name at the end of the declaration put a small chink in her buoyant mood.

"Ben, I need to tell you something." His face took on the same perplexed look she'd seen at the Blue Monk. She plowed on before he could say any more. Her courage screwed up, she plunged in. "The thing is...I'm pregnant."

Ben had learned about the birds and the bees when he was six and a half years old and a precocious eight-year-old Abbe had taken him aside and spilled the beans. He'd literally studied the mating habits of birds, bees, and other animals while in college and veterinary school at Cornell. But the idea that his own actions could result in an actual baby, floored him. Knowing something *could* happen and to have it *actually* happen were two completely different things.

"When was...do you think...probably the fireplace, huh?" He said, sounding clueless to his own ears.

Hannah didn't answer. She held her throat, like an entire frog had jumped in there. Her head went up and down in a nod.

Nothing that had happened in his life before today had prepared him for this moment. Somehow he suspected what happened right now would chart his future. He wanted to do the right thing. Ben didn't know what that was so he did the only thing he knew how.

"Come here." He pulled Hannah into his arms, holding her tight. He kissed the top of her curly hair, and her forehead, and her cheeks. Finally, he did the one thing he probably knew he shouldn't, the one thing that had gotten them into this predicament. He kissed her full on the mouth, deepening the kiss when she opened for him. She tasted like apples, and bacon, and the woman he loved.

She pulled back when their breathing became labored.

"Are you mad?" Hannah asked. Her husky voice was unusually tentative.

"Mad with wanting you," Ben said. Her announcement hadn't dampened the feeling he had for her by one iota. He wanted to get her upstairs and naked as fast as he could. Ben was done talking for now and leaned in to kiss this beautiful woman again and again. They were both breathing heavily and naked from the waist up before they made it upstairs. He worked as quickly as possible to get the rest of their clothes off. He wanted to possess her, brand her as his. He sucked her tongue. He sucked her very sensitive nipples. He sucked the ultra sensitive flesh between her legs. And she came for him. When he plunged into her, unsheathed for the second time, her heat and wetness nearly sent him spiraling out of control. But he grasped her hips and held on, grinding into her time and again. If this was the beginning of the rest of his life, it was starting out right.

Two hours later, sated and drowsy, he heard Hannah shifting next to him in the bed. "No really, Ben, I need to know. Are you mad?"

"What's there to be angry about?" Ben asked.

Hannah hesitated. She was in deep, and each step could be the difference between drowning and saving herself.

"You never held Logan. You didn't even look at him."

"You know how I feel about Marty, Hannah."

"Logan isn't Marty. He's a baby that can't help who he's related to."

A deep sigh escaped Ben. "And?"

"You said that you were happy that you and Samara didn't have kids."

He placed a palm on each side of Hannah's smooth face. "I *am* glad I didn't have a baby with Samara. I never took a single chance when we were together. I was never so...overcome that I wanted to." He smoothed away the wrinkles that puckered between her eyebrows. "I'm sitting next to the woman I love and she's going to have our baby."

Ben was whistling and smiling at almost every woman he saw. The obviously pregnant ones made him wonder how Hannah would look a few short months from now. The ones with babies thrust him a little further into the future. He even found himself scrutinizing the little faces in strollers—wondering how their genes would come together. Would the baby have his blue eyes? Her curly hair. His strong nose? Her husky voice. Knowing what he knew about DNA, the combinations seemed endless. It was too bad they weren't cats.

During a college biology lab, he recalled plugging in eye color, stripe patterns, and other qualities into the feline genetics program during his studies and coming up with results that closely correlated what happened in real life. But thinking about the differences between Abbe and himself, and in a generous moment, even Marty, showed him how much variation there could be. He could barely wait the seven or eight more months to meet their baby.

Although Ben wasn't one to go to the doctor often, he was grateful that Hannah's first appointment was scheduled at her six-week mark. The anticipation of knowing more was killing him. On the fourth Friday in November, they drove to Arcata to visit with an obstetrician she'd chosen.

As they neared the end of an hour-long drive, Ben asked her, "Are there no closer obstetricians?"

"Not that came recommended," Hannah responded. "There's practically a doctor on every corner in SoCal. There are billboards advertising maternity wards. I never thought about what people did in rural areas."

Ben had never thought much about it either. He was healthy. And his dad, who did need regular medical care, worked at a teaching hospital, in spitting distance of a doctor at any given moment. They drove toward the low-slung wooden medical office that didn't look much different from his, and the anxiety ratcheted up. What if Hannah had a medical emergency? Was he equipped to handle it? Where was the nearest trauma hospital, emergency room? Would she get there in time?

He was practically shaking when they were finally called into the examination room. Hannah, on the other hand, looked as cool as a cucumber. She was back in her designer sweats and low-heeled shoes. She looked like she did this every day. He didn't want his anxiety to spill over to her—but he had to wonder why she wasn't more worried.

After the nurse rolled her blood pressure machine, thermometer, and various other items out of the room on a cart, it was only a few minutes before the doctor joined them. They both shook hands with the competent looking woman in a white lab coat. She had blond hair, streaked with gray pulled back into a tight bun. Her pants were khaki, her clogs brown, and her hands unadorned. She looked sensible and no nonsense. Ben relaxed a bit.

"Dr. Clementine Lacey," she said, flipping through the chart. Did he do that? Why couldn't doctors talk to people? Why were they always riffling through something or scribbling on some piece of paper or another? "Our tests indicate that you're pregnant. Based upon what you wrote down here, you're about six weeks along. Is that right?"

Hannah nodded.

"Was this baby planned?"

Hannah reddened a little, but answered in a straightforward manner. "It was a bit of a surprise."

"That's fine," the doctor said, making a note. She asked a few more questions, all of which Hannah answered. Ben stood there feeling nervous and useless. "The nurse is going to come back and prep you. I'm going to do a pelvic exam and an ultrasound, and then we'll be all done for today."

The nurse reappeared and helped Hannah cup her heels into the hard plastic stirrups. He took the nurse's suggestion and sat near the head of the exam table. He held Hannah's hand tight as she reclined on the cold vinyl.

When the doctor returned, she washed, gloved, and lubricated her hand. Not able to help himself, Ben let loose on the questions about where she went to school, what hospitals she was affiliated with and where in the heck Hannah was supposed to have the baby? There were no hospitals in Shelter Cove.

"Dr. Cooper," she started, not once taking her eyes away from her tasks. "Women have been having babies forever. None of the three hospitals up here is more than an hour away. Your due date is in July—in the summer. So when Hannah goes into labor, you put her in the car and drive to the hospital. That's it."

With calm assurance, she answered every one of his concerns. Having a baby was normal and everything would be fine. Dr. Lacey started the ultrasound, and Ben peered at the tiny blurry picture. Then he noticed the tiniest flicker in the middle of the image.

"That's the heartbeat, isn't it?" he asked in awe.

"It is," Dr. Lacey said then frowned.

Ben's own heartbeat accelerated with the downturned corners of the doctor's mouth. "What's wrong?"

Dr. Lacey's frown neutralized, and she backed away from her close scrutiny of the monitor. She stood, grabbed paper towels from the dispenser, and wiped Hannah's belly. Officiously, she snapped off her gloves. "Nothing, that I can see," she said. "It was probably a trick of the light, but for a moment there, I thought I saw twins. Neither of you have twins in your background though, right?"

Hannah and Ben, gazes locked, both shook their heads.

"That's what I thought. Ignore my old eyes. It's that with so many women on fertility drugs these days, I feel like every other patient who comes in here is pregnant with multiples. In nature, you know without Clomid, and FSH, and IVF, twins are rare—probably about one percent of pregnancies. So the odds weigh heavily against it."

Ben's gaze broke from Hannah's and his breathing and heart rate came back to normal. He was almost resolved that this would be a normal pregnancy, they'd have one healthy baby, and all would be fine.

13

Twins.

Hannah tried to clear the image from her head. She'd left the doctor's office with Ben, and they'd shared a good laugh on the way home. Once Hannah was alone, she wasn't laughing. She hadn't been honest with Ben. Lies were piling up like dead flies on a windowsill. She hadn't been honest with Dr. Lacey either. When she'd answered the questions about the pregnancy being planned, no one had blinked with her negative answer on the question of fertility drugs.

Why would they? It made no logical sense to question her. But of course, she'd been taking Clomid over the summer, right up until she'd left Michael the first time. Dr. Stern had given her all the warnings about Clomid—one of which was the risk of multiple birth. She and Michael had talked about the possibility and the analog of a selective reduction if too many fetuses were detected. Hannah had tossed away the side effects pamphlet like a used tissue. She didn't expect them to have any impact on her.

Rather than wringing her hands, Hannah looked around for something to do. She usually spent Saturdays with Ben, but he was working the shift he'd traded to spend a half day with her at the doctor. She'd started looking at some portraits she'd been thinking of using for her upcoming gallery show. She'd probably be very pregnant by that time, but was still very much looking forward to showing, and maybe even selling some of her work.

Her damned cell phone rang. She didn't have to look to know it was Michael. In a fit of guilt, she'd agreed to one session with a counselor. Even though she'd noted it on her calendar, she had hoped Michael would forget or cancel. But it was scheduled for an hour from now over Skype.

"Michael."

"I wanted to make sure you remembered our session this afternoon."

"I'll be there."

"You have Skype installed? Is your internet speed high enough? If you'd come home..."

She cut him off. "Michael. I agreed to this one session. I will be there as I promised. See you in an hour."

Lead weighed in her chest and belly. Michael had crushed her creative spirit in the insidious way he always had.

An hour later, the screen came alight simultaneous with the pinging that indicated there was a Skype call. When she clicked on the answer icon, Michael's face came on the screen as well as a man she'd never met before. She assumed he was the therapist Michael had chosen.

A twinge twisted Hannah's gut. She didn't know if it was the baby or guilt over Michael's appearance. He was a proud and vain man made haggard by her actions. The light brown stubble on his cheeks and chin was not that of a Don Johnson devotee. His eyes were red, and his shirt collar looked like it had been chewed by mice. It was shocking to see a man who rarely left the house without a hair out of place sitting in front of a webcam looking downright disheveled.

The therapist stood in stark contrast to Michael. Dressed so well, he looked downright dandy. The therapist's camera took a full body shot of the man sitting on a high backed leather office chair, from the bottom of his spectator wing tips to the top of his ascot.

"I'm Hannah," she said in the friendliest voice she could muster, trying figuratively, to bat away the judgment she was heaping on the two men.

"Good morning Hannah, it's nice to meet you," the dandy said. "I'm Russell Deaver." Hannah tuned out as Deaver recited all of his profession credentials. Michael never hired anyone who wasn't infinitely qualified. "It's not my preference to meet you this way, Hannah. But I understand you're not willing to come back down to Orange County right now." Deaver paused. "Hannah, can you hear me?"

"There wasn't a question."

The tall leather chair squeaked as Deaver leaned back. He put his hand to his lips as if to say, 'so that's how you're going to play it.'

"As you may know, I've been meeting in one-on-one sessions with Michael for the last four weeks. He says that you're finally willing to come to the table and talk about healing your marriage. Is that a fair statement?"

Hannah paused a long time. She looked up at the cathedral ceilings in the Coopers' house as if the right answer were going to fall from exposed beams. Guilt warred with reason. "Can I speak?"

Both men nodded. "Mr. Deaver, Michael," she started. "Our marriage cannot be saved."

Michael started to speak, but Deaver put out a hand as if to virtually restrain him. "Why would you say that? What are your reasons behind that statement?"

For the first time ever, Hannah wanted to lay it all on the table. She looked directly into her husband's bloodshot blue eyes. They were starting to crinkle at the corners. When had she missed that? He wasn't the young Wall Street wizard she'd met so many years ago. She looked more closely at the screen. There were a couple of gray hairs interwoven in the blond. Michael was going to age like Drake, going from blond to gray so gradually that no one would notice until the blond was all gone. "I think the marriage may have been a mistake."

Deaver's virtual hand moved to restrain Michael again. "Can you elaborate?"

Her gaze locked with her husband's. "Michael, I married you because you were, *are*, a dear friend. I thought all we needed to build a family was mutual respect, shared values." Her stomach twinged again when Michael winced at her use of the word 'respect.'

Deaver jumped in. "Hannah, marriages built on friendship often outlast those built on passionate love. It's one of the reasons arranged marriages can work so well. Studies show that lust and passion can die out between two and four years. After that, couples that have friendship to fall back on, make it for the long haul."

Hannah sighed, hoping the hissing of her breath wasn't too loud. She knew all this, but wanted to take a chance on the love and passion. A life with nothing more than perfunctory sex, duty, and responsibility didn't sound all that appealing.

"What parts of your marriage work?"

Michael finally spoke up. "Russell, Hannah and I have always gotten along great. We have a certain synergy. When we put our heads together, all turns out well. We got Hannah's new realty business up and running and successful almost off the bat. We got this great house at a bargain basement price. It's an absolute show place—and that's all from us working together."

"Hannah, do you agree with Michael?" Deaver asked pointedly.

"Yes, he's right. All this works. But the way Michael describes it sounds like a great business partnership, not a great marriage."

"Alright," Deaver said. "Then what doesn't work for you, Hannah?"

Hannah took another deep breath. This, this attempt at therapy, this attempt at saving what was already lost. *This* wasn't working. She wanted to spare Michael's feelings. An amicable split of their relationship, money, and assets was all she was looking for. Introspection, examination of every detail of their marriage wasn't going to go well. "Michael, I really don't want to talk about this. Can we agree to dissolve our marriage without all this? I think that would be the best thing that we could do."

"Hannah, I really think we can save this," Michael said.

They weren't listening. It was if they had an agenda which didn't take her thoughts, feelings, wants, or concerns into account. "Mr. Deaver, I'm doing this session to appease Michael, but I feel like nothing I'm saying is getting through," Hannah started. She cleared her throat and made her voice as forceful as she knew how. "So here goes: Michael, our marriage isn't working.

"I hate living in Orange County. I don't fit in there— whether it's my politics, beliefs, race, whatever. I don't want to live there—but your family and business are there. I don't love you enough to make any more of an effort at this. I can't continue with our sex life. I hated it. I felt humiliated every time we got undressed. Your disinterest in intercourse—your obsession with those airbrushed models who look nothing like me make it impossible for me to come back to that. I want passion and love and a family and I've found all that here in the North Coast.

"I'm in love with someone else."

There was silence as their collective images flickered on her laptop screen.

"Michael, were you aware that Hannah had gone outside the relationship?" Deaver asked. Michael nodded. Apparently he hadn't mentioned that little fact to the therapist. "I was unaware of this. It certainly puts a different spin on things." He directed his next question to Hannah. "Is this a serious relationship?"

"I'm pregnant," she said before she could think to hold it back. "I think I'm in it for the long haul." Michael's hand barely covered his gasp of surprise. His eyes turned glassy with unshed tears. She hated the devastation on Michael's face. This is not at all how she wanted to end things. Maybe it had been right to get the truth out there. Maybe now Michael would understand that they were over. That she and Ben had a future together where Michael and she did not.

The session ended quickly after that. She imagined that Michael was going to be spending a lot of time with Deaver hashing out her betrayal. She could only thank the legislature that there was still no fault divorce, and no court would delve into her infidelity while dividing their possessions. Because all that was left was figuring who took what stuff.

The phone rang again only minutes after she'd disconnected on Skype. It was Michael. Her hope that her words would put some distance between them was going to go unfulfilled.

"Is the baby mine?" No 'hello.'"

"How could it be, Michael?" Was he delusional? They'd been trying for years and nothing had happened. He was infertile and would have to come to accept it.

"I got a call from Dr. Stern." Michael acted like he didn't even hear her question. Maybe Deaver wasn't worth all his fancy credentials. The point of therapy was learning to listen.

"Why are you telling me this? After the session we had, I don't think there's really anymore we can or should say to each other. I don't want to hurt you any more than I already have, Michael. I want us to be happy—even if that means we're happier apart."

Michael persisted. "Stern wants me to come in for new tests. There was a mix up in the lab the day my sample went in." It was as if he didn't hear a word she had said in the last five minutes or fifty. What difference could his fertility make now? She heard the rustle of paper in the background. Without any prompting from her, Michael started reading. "We regret to inform you that your test performed on September 18th may have been compromised by our outside laboratory. Pacific Center for Reproductive Health recommends that you come in for a new semen analysis. In order to assure the results you received were correct, we ask that you make an appointment for complementary testing with our new lab. The new results will be made available as soon as is practical."

If Hannah hadn't already been sitting, she would have fallen to the floor. Her knees turned to water. Suddenly, her back couldn't hold up her head, much less her five foot ten body.

"Are you going in?" she asked hesitantly. Hannah didn't want to ask too many questions of Michael. He probably needed to do this for himself. Male infertility was emasculating. She was one hundred percent sure that the results would be the same. They'd tried for years and nothing had happened. She looked down at her thickening waist. She was healthy, and obviously fertile.

"Of course. If there was a mistake and I'm able to..." Michael left the rest unsaid. Hannah carefully placed the phone down on a table, disconnecting the call. If he were able to have a child, she could come back and they could.... They could do what? She was already pregnant. The baby couldn't be his anyway. His penis had barely made contact with any part of her body that could result in a baby. In the week she'd been home, none of the encounters they'd had had been consummated. Hannah's hand slipped from the phone she was going to use to dial Dr. Stern herself.

There had been that third time that she'd banished from her mind. That middle of the night, early morning encounter when Michael had taken her from behind—when she'd been half asleep. He was always horny if he woke in the wee morning hours. She always slept facing the edge of the bed, and he facing her. If she wasn't wearing sweats or underwear, he could often arouse her. After their years together, he knew how to make her wet even if he didn't always try. That last morning, his fingers had worked magic on her flesh, and he'd taken what he wanted. Her body had betrayed her, and she hadn't put up a protest. It was done in a few minutes. Sleep had crowded out guilt.

Hannah flicked and scrolled through her phone like a woman possessed. The call confirmed what she didn't want to believe. There really had been a mix up. It was possible that Michael was fertile after all.

Ben emerged from the BART station at the corner of Market and Kearny Streets. It had been a long time since he'd been to San Francisco. The streets were still jammed with rush hour road construction, too many cars, and a million tour buses.

New York was supposed to be the biggest tourist destination in the country, but it had always felt like San Francisco should hold that title. Crossing Geary Street and heading toward Union Square, he counted no less than four tour buses in lime green, turquoise, red, and orange. Double-deckers full to bursting with visitors and their cameras though the weather was downright blustery. The lineup to get on arriving buses was even longer. Zipping his own jacket against the damp chill, he walked the short blocks toward Union Square and the jewelry store, its' two story shop window decorated with its' signature turquoise boxes and white satin bows.

Pausing outside the heavy double doors, Ben took a deep breath. He was doing the right thing. He was doing the right thing. He'd vowed never to come back to this place. The last time he'd been here, those many years ago, he'd been with Samara. She'd refused to get a ring anywhere else. And she'd refused to let him shop alone. They'd sat in a small private room looking at settings and stones for damn near three hours—until his ex had been satisfied. That one visit had set him back a pretty penny. Clearing the memory from his head, he had to remember Hannah was different. It was all different this time even though he was in the same place. But he wasn't a jewelry expert, and he couldn't think of another place to go.

At least this would be the last time he had to come here. Resigned, he pulled one of the heavy pewter colored doors open and allowed the vacuum of warm air to suck him in. The store was preternaturally quiet. There must be some noise-canceling device that muted all sounds inside the rarified walls. He hadn't walked two feet before a soft-spoken woman appeared at his side.

"I'm Elsa," she said in an unspecific foreign accent, holding out her hand in greeting. "How can I help you?"

Elsa was a small woman, with graying hair that looked as if it had once been jet black, scraped back into a bun. Her gray cashmere wrap sweater was accentuated with a silver brooch. Her other jewelry was very simple. The only incongruity was the coiled elastic bracelet and key dangling around her wrist. Everything was locked up in a place like this. He looked down at his own fraying jeans and worn boots and felt underdressed. Working with animals was hell on a wardrobe.

Time to get this over with. He wished Hannah could be here with him. But then there would be no surprise. "I'm looking for an engagement ring," he said matter-of-factly.

She led him to a quiet corner, and two maroon upholstered chairs. "When are you going to pop the question?"

"Wednesday or Thursday." He'd made up his mind on his way to San Francisco.

"A holiday proposal with family and friends?" Elsa said smiling indulgently.

He nodded. Ben wanted Hannah to know that he was no coward. Trusting was hard for him, but when he invited someone into his inner circle, he was committed. He was ready to take the next step if she was, and Ben wanted the world to know it too. They'd spend the weekend in Davis for his parents' regular holiday shindig and he'd do it there. Maybe they could be married by Christmas. He didn't want any child of his coming into the world with parents who weren't one hundred percent committed to each other. He felt a sureness, a rightness this time that he hadn't felt before. Ben chalked it up to age. Deep down in his bones he knew that this was the right time with the right person.

"Yes, but I don't live close by, so I can't wait for a custom ring. I'd like to know what you have available right now."

Elsa, probably sensing a guaranteed sale, asked a few questions and retrieved a few rings from a velvet tray behind lock and key.

Despite all the bling, he thought a simple ring would suit Hannah best. After looking through the four or five standard ring settings, he picked something Elsa described as an open curve diamond band, with a one and a half carat square cut solitaire. He held the small ring in the palm of his large hand. It looked and felt right. He was as sure of the ring as he was of his decision.

Ben paid for the ring, glad that it didn't cost as much as his car, and got the fancy wrapping. Pocketing the blue and white box in his large jacket, he left the store with a spring in his step. The damp fog had burned off, revealing warming rays of sunlight. His mood matched the weather. Looking at his watch, he hadn't realized he'd been shopping for so long. Maybe it was set up like a casino on purpose so people didn't know how much they were spending.

If he walked briskly, Ben would make it to Dottie's at Market and Sixth in time for his lunch appointment with some old friends. He felt a sudden pang. Ben missed more aspects of his old life than he had realized. When he'd cut Samara out of his life, he'd left it all behind, Marin, San Francisco, and many of the friends he'd made over the years. A lot of his college friends, and even some people he'd met later had stayed in the Bay Area, but he'd dropped out of his social life there. Two hundred and fifty miles made friendships impossible, and he'd wanted it that way in the beginning. Until Cody had brought Hannah into his life, he hadn't realized that he might not be destined for a life on Walden Pond.

With a new lease on life, he took a seat at one of the small wooden tables in Dottie's Diner. Ben marveled at how many people they could crowd into a small space. The restaurants in Shelter Cove had nothing but space. The neighboring diners were never close enough to touch.

Thinking about his clothes for the second time today, he felt like Davy Crockett. All he was missing was the beaver hat. Maybe it was time to fill up some space in that closet. He quickly dismissed his thoughts. Hannah liked him fine the way he was. And he liked the new, less self-conscious him as well. Thank goodness, it wasn't too long before Colette and Hugh came in, the self-reflection was killing his buzz.

"Ben," they both said at the same time. He couldn't believe how glad he was to see them. The strong hugs he gave them were genuine. Colette and Hugh were 'partners.' They'd been together since college, had a house, and kid and all that, but refused to marry until their gay friends could as well in every state.

"It's great to see you guys," Ben said, his heart feeling suddenly expansive. Maybe he'd been too far away and alone for too long. His heart beat like the Grinch's on Christmas day.

"We thought you'd fallen into a hole down there."

"Long hibernation."

"You were cryptic on the phone. What brings you out of your cave?" Colette asked.

Ben pulled the small box from his pocket and set it on the table. Colette gasped.

"Ben Cooper, are you getting married?" Hugh asked.

"Aren't you the dark horse?" Colette said. "Who is she? Do we know her? How did you meet anyone down there? From your e-mail it seemed like a lot of coyotes, bears, and the regular dogs and cats, with a few horses thrown in."

Ben gave them an overview of his and Hannah's meeting.

"I never thought you'd do this again," Colette said. Never one to mince words, she continued. "She's engaged too, you know. It was kind of sudden."

His curiosity got the best of him. "To the same guy?"

Colette's leg jerked under the table. Ben was sure Hugh had nudged it with his own. Colette looked down, her face contrite.

"I shouldn't have said anything. Let's hear more about Hannah."

"Guys," Ben said. "I'm a big boy. I know my wife cheated on me. It's why I left. I'm not keeping a torch alive for her. Tell me how she's doing."

"She dumped the guy she left you for when she met Tim. He's a Silicon Valley entrepreneur. His company made those little video cameras that were so popular a couple of years ago. He sold to some huge corporation."

"So she landed her billionaire," Ben said, sounding more bitter than he meant to. He pocketed Hannah's ring when the food came to the table. Colette had a lentil burger. Ben looked down at his plate and saw a lot more micro greens than had a right to exist. Maybe he didn't miss the Bay Area quite so much.

"I think it was only half a billion," Colette said, after thoughtfully chewing her so-called burger. "We got an invite to their wedding coming up in January. I think they're going to tie the knot at a vineyard in the South of France."

"You're going?" It wasn't that he was looking for loyalty. They were all adults. Colette and Hugh could have other friends. Even if their friends included his cheating ex. After all, he was hundreds of miles away and never saw them.

She shrugged. "It's the South of France," she enunciated each word. Colette and Hugh fed the homeless and rescued dogs. He couldn't see them sipping champagne in France. "They've chartered a jet for the guests." A jet. A goddamned jet. Ben shook his head in disbelief. How could he have thought he and Samara could ever have been compatible? A small town vet could never compete with dot com half-billionaire.

Hugh pushed the condiments toward Colette. "So tell us about Hannah."

And he did. Every sentence that left his mouth erased the sting of Samara's betrayal. He wasn't jealous so much as regretful. Ben wished he could have met and married Hannah years ago, never tasting the bitterness of deception.

"So, I guess it's worked out for both of you," Hugh said. "You and Samara have met the right people. We couldn't be happier for both of you."

Ben relaxed his face. He couldn't begrudge Colette and Hugh this trip. Hell, if he wasn't divorced from Samara, he'd probably want to go too. He hadn't been to Europe in years.

Hannah couldn't stop moving. She alternatively fiddled with her earrings, her headband, her remaining rings, her phone. Ben must have noticed because he turned to her with a question in his eyes.

She stilled under his gaze. "Have you spoken to your parents since we left that morning after Logan's party?"

"It'll be fine," Ben said blithely.

"You didn't answer the question."

"I've smoothed things out with Mom and Dad. We've agreed to disagree right now. It'll be the family for Thanksgiving." His emphasis on the word, 'family' did not go unnoticed.

"Did Marty usually come?"

"No. Marty has never been a part of our family celebrations. Marty goes wherever Marty goes. Abbe said he's spending Thanksgiving with Hallie's family down in Riverside County," Ben said with some finality.

Well, that was at least one less confrontation she'd have to face. They pulled up to the Coopers' house. It was the first time she'd seen the all white, two-story, gabled-roof affair in daylight. Imposing was the word for the New England style house that outshone the millions of post World War II tract homes she'd seen during the endless Realtor caravans she'd attended.

Elaine's greeting seemed a little standoffish when she pulled open the door. She embraced Hannah in an awkward hug. Hugging little old ladies was probably the only time

Hannah hated being tall. She felt like a giantess who could pick up Ben's mom with one arm.

"What year is this house?"

Elaine stepped back from the hug. "It was built in 1887—one of the oldest in the city. There's quite the history behind it. I can show you some stuff we collected in the study—later. Why don't you come in and sit down? You must be tired."

"We've been sitting for hours. Can I take a look around outside?" There must have been an acre of land around the house. That was huge in California real estate. Most of the buyers she'd sold to considered a five thousand square foot lot generous.

"Not at all," Elaine said. "Why don't I join you?" Ben's mom got a jacket from a peg by the front door and slipped into rugged looking loafers. Ben smiled, and took their bags inside.

They walked for a while, Elaine pointing out little historical facts about the property and Davis. But something about the interaction felt stilted.

"Have I offended you?" Hannah asked. She'd turned over a new leaf and wanted everything to be out in the open going forward. Never again did she want to face the awkwardness she'd had with the Keeslings.

"Oh, dear no. I'm sorry." Elaine turned to Hannah and grabbed her hands, her genuine warmth coming through with her touch. The hug this time was real. "Ben spilled the beans. Congratulations! We're so happy. It'll be lovely to welcome another grandchild into this family."

Hannah didn't know what to say. She and Ben hadn't agreed to silence. Of course, she'd shared it with her mother because that's what women did. But they hadn't talked about the three-month rule that so many of her friends abided.

"Thank you, I guess. We didn't..." It was awkward being thirty-seven and having to explain an unplanned pregnancy. It was like there was a neon sign on her head: *we didn't use a condom.*

"Oh, honey. I've been around a Manhattan block a time or two. I know that you and Ben weren't planning this. But you're both mature adults and happy about it. Am I right?"

Hannah nodded.

"Then we're happy for you. You know, Walter and I have learned a lot in the last forty years or so." Elaine paused for so long, Hannah started to consider Elaine's age and senility. Then she spoke, her voice full of quiet regret. "Marty was an unwanted baby." At Hannah's expression, Elaine softened. "I'm sure his mom loved him. But when she got pregnant, there was a lot of stress. Walter didn't want that child to be born either. It very much upset his carefully ordered world. And as you can imagine, I was quite resentful for years. But I sorely regret how we all handled it.

"Marty was blameless. If Minnie was determined to have him, we should have all done what we could to make him feel welcome from the beginning. Children are not responsible for the circumstances of their birth. But the adults around him or her are very much responsible for how they treat that child."

Hannah tried to swallow past the lump in her throat. Elaine was so right. She'd been a surprise to her parents, and while she knew they loved her, Hannah had often felt like she had put their lives on hold, held back their respective careers, and ended their marriage. If her mom could have continued to tour with her dad... Even if she'd had a baby with Michael, she may have somehow projected that on her child—her sacrificing the city for Orange County, giving up her artistic career, choosing a safe marriage. Hannah vowed right then to make sure the baby she was carrying always felt wanted and loved, no matter what.

"You've been quiet," Elaine said as they passed a wooded section of the property and what looked like a dilapidated paddock gate. Through some young trees, Hannah saw an old barn.

"Did you ever keep horses here?"

"No, never. The previous owners were descendants of the original builder. He was some kind of horse nut. There were a lot of horse properties back then, before it all got developed and subdivided. Walter and I always talked about turning that barn into something; a playhouse for the kids, a library for him. We never got to it.

"If it were up to Walter, he'd tear it down. But I so love the history of it. You know what it's like coming here from New York. We grew up in an area steeped in history with the old carriage houses in Manhattan, brownstones in Brooklyn. California developers would plow everything down if given half a chance. I like to think of it as my stand against the constant Western spirit of 'new, new, new.'"

They walked and talked for a half hour more. Hannah's stomach growled, giving her hunger away. She didn't want to end her bonding time with Elaine. It looked like her child was going to be blessed with wonderful grandparents.

"Sorry," she said, putting a hand over her stomach.

"Nothing to be sorry about. I was always starving when I was pregnant. Let's get you a snack. Dinner won't be ready for a couple of hours yet."

Hannah genuinely liked Ben's parents. It had been awkward at first, with them showing up at the house on Sea Court. But she was glad they were going to be her baby's grandparents. After all the years of awkward in-law dinners and worry about the future, she finally felt content. As soon as Michael consented to the divorce, all would be okay.

Abbe and her family arrived as dusk was falling, and the Coopers prepared to celebrate the first night of Hanukkah. She was glad they came early. Despite the snack Elaine had made for her, she was starving. The family gathered in the large dining room, and Hannah, not wanting to intrude, stayed back from the festivities. Abbe's six-year-old son got the lit Shamash candle from Walter, and lit the one candle on the right of the menorah. He was very proud of himself for having done such a 'big boy' task. After the prayers were said, they sang a few songs, then Elaine and Abbe went to the kitchen to get dinner.

"You okay?" Ben asked. He sat next to her at the ornately carved dining room table.

"I'm fine," Hannah said, smiling. "A little hungry."

"Then you're in the right place. Mom doesn't cook that often anymore, but she still goes all out for the holidays. It's got to be hard on her this year with the first night of Hanukkah back to back with Thanksgiving. But she wouldn't hear of skipping either. Thinks it's important for the kids to have traditions."

Elaine didn't disappoint. She brought out platters filled with latkes, brisket, and kasha varnishkes. It reminded her so much of New York. She'd grown up having these dishes at her friends' houses, but it had been a long time. Hannah wasn't shy about eating and helped herself to a satisfying helping of each dish, topping her latkes with both sour cream and applesauce.

After dinner, she watched Abbe, Ben and the kids start the dreidel game.

"Hannah, you can't sit there. You have to join us!" Abbe beckoned her over.

She pulled her tired body from the hard little couch in the family room and got down on the floor with the kids. It had been years since Hannah had done this, so Abbe's husband, Isaiah explained the rules and they were off. Abbe crowed when she won the gelt, and Hannah had to laugh despite her heavy heart, thoughts of extracting herself from Michael weighing her down. Abbe was like Ben in so many ways, but different, more outgoing, louder, bawdier, but genuinely nice. The Coopers were a family she could grow to love.

When Isaiah ushered the kids off for a potty break, Abbe held nothing back.

"I guess there's not much to do up in Shelter Cove," she said.

"Abbe—" Ben's voice held a warning.

"What? She's pregnant. It's not like it's a secret that you've been doing the deed up there."

"It's a lovely town," Hannah put in diplomatically. "The beaches are scenic, and Cody has enjoyed the trails through the redwoods."

Abbe leaned against Ben. For a moment, Hannah imagined them as children sharing this same closeness. "I can't imagine you being a father, Benji. I remember when you couldn't even put your shoes on the right foot. And remember that girl you went to prom with in high school? You were so nervous about your first time. Didn't I end up buying condoms for you?"

Ben colored. It was the first time she'd seen him blush. Walter hid a smile. "Abbe, that's enough. I hear your children clomping down the hall now," Ben's father said. With the children settled on the floor, Walter said, "Now let's get this game going. I'm going to beat the pants off the two of you. I have years of experience at spinning."

She didn't win a thing, but it was the most fun she'd had in a long time.

Hannah was coming out of the powder room, when Ben pushed her cardigan into her hands. "What?"

"Come with me," he said, urging her out the back door.

"What about your parents? Should we tell them…"

"They'll figure it out. C'mon."

Silently, she followed him across the lawn, past the paddock and toward the old barn. "What's in there?" she asked, shrinking back, imagining all sorts of creepy crawlies.

"You'll see."

Ben pushed open the door, she stepped in hesitantly, entering another world. Fairy lights twinkled, illuminating a small loft area in the barn.

"Can I go up?"

"Of course."

Carefully, she climbed the narrow wooden ladder and hoisted herself up to the loft. There was nothing more than a futon mattress covered by a soft wool blanket, and the lights. So simple. So perfect. Ben came up right behind her and settled himself next to her on the cushion.

"When did you do all this?" she asked, gesturing to the lights.

Ben laughed. "I didn't. Abbe set this up years ago for smoke outs. When you and Mom were walking, I wondered if it was all still here. I brought out the sheets and blankets from the linen cabinet, plugged in the lights, and the heater. It was a miracle they both worked."

Hannah leaned back against the rough wood wall, her feet and legs toasty from the blast of heat from the small metal box. Ben disappeared for a minute and moved stuff around in a far corner of the loft. He brought back two pillows, from the old couch she'd seen downstairs.

"Thanks."

"Things will probably be crazy this weekend and I wanted to spend some time alone with you."

If her heart could melt, it would be a puddle on the floor. She grabbed his hand in hers and leaned over to kiss him.

"I didn't come here to seduce you," he said, putting a hand in the middle her chest. She raised her eyebrows. "Okay, not quite yet. I...After Samara, I didn't think I'd ever trust anyone again, let alone trust myself. I don't know what your divorce was like, but mine was shit. Samara wanted to spend hours divvying up the stuff, and I wanted out."

"Your lawyer must have loved that."

Ben grimaced. "Probably cost me more, but I let him handle all the pots and pans." His look sobered. "After today, I don't want to talk about it ever again, but I need to get this out.

"It was hell being cheated on. It was a blow in so many ways. To find out someone you trusted, up and had sex with someone else—then lied about it." He shook his head, his eyes closing at bad memories. "It's taken me some time to trust my judgment." He reached and fingered the hair that had fallen in her face, pushing it back. "I know we haven't known each other forever, and this little one," he placed a hand on her abdomen, "has made things a little more urgent. But I want you to know that I love you, and him or her." He paused again. For a moment, Hannah thought he was going to propose. Instead he said something so Californian, she had to laugh. "I think it's going to be a great ride."

Great ride was not "let's get married." Hannah didn't know if she was relieved or not that there was no ring forthcoming. A thought slammed into her head like a sudden migraine. She should tell him about Michael. It was now or never. If he found out, she didn't know what would happen. But he couldn't find out. She'd fly down, make Michael see sense, and get back to Ben. Not every secret in a relationship was meant to be shared.

"You're quiet. Sometimes you seem so far away," he said, his large hand wiggling her leg.

"I'm here. Thinking about what you said."

Then he kissed her. All talk, all worry, everything but Ben vanished. Where she expected fierce passion, she got gentle lovemaking. His kisses were soft, his touch delicate.

"Ben, I might be pregnant. But I'm not going to break. I promise."

She was pretty sure he'd heard her, but his approach didn't change. He smoothed her hair back and kissed her forehead, her ears. She shivered when his tongue traced the whorls of her ear, and licked at the pearl studs she wore. She slipped her hands under his sweater and tried to pull him closer, urge him to take her quick and hard. But he wouldn't budge. Pleasure warred with guilt. He was going too slow. She was thinking too much.

The more she pulled at him, the slower he went. Caressing her stomach with feather light touches. Rubbing his thumb over her bra, glancing off the nipples that grew hard at his touch. He eased her clothes off slowly. His hands seemed to touch every one of the fine hairs on her arms and legs. Her skin pebbled in the warm air. One more of his feather light touches and she thought her skin was going to catch on fire.

Hannah couldn't remember if Michael had ever touched her this reverently.

Damn him. *Damn* him. Damn *him*. She refocused on Ben, touching and kissing the most desirable man she'd ever known. She *had* to push Michael out of her head. He was intruding on the most perfect moments of her life.

When Ben finally entered her, sensation blotted out the world. She could only hear and feel the man moving over her. By instinct, she wrapped her legs around his waist and pulled him deep. With his exhalation of breath, she knew he'd finally lost control. She nearly died at the sound of his control slipping away. This, this is what she needed.

"Oh, God, Hannah, I don't know if I'll ever get enough of you."

She would never, ever get enough of Ben Cooper.

Thanksgiving morning, a few of Walter and Elaine's friends trickled in. Abbe's kids had stayed overnight—giving the parents a much needed break—but they were back by noon to help with the kids and the meal. Everything would have been perfect if it weren't for the phone that persistently vibrated in her back pocket. Slipping away to the back paddock, she finally took Michael's call.

"Happy Turkey Day." Her tone was less chipper than the words belied.

"Why are you ignoring me?" he complained.

"Michael, it's Thanksgiving. Last night was the first night of Hanukkah. When exactly was I supposed to take your call?"

"And now you're Jewish? Did you find that part of yourself, too?"

"Michael," she said, injecting a note of warning in her voice. Hannah never tolerated disparaging anyone. She'd had too much of that in her life.

"I'm sorry, but we were always together during the holidays." Something in his tone made her shiver.

"Michael, your family is only forty-five minutes away. Are your brother Kendall and his partner down for the day?"

"You're my family," Michael said, ignoring her. One- way conversations were becoming the norm.

"Michael, I know this is hard. I can fly down next week and we can talk about this in person."

"I plan to see you before that, Hannah. I don't want to spend the holiday alone."

"Michael," she said firmly. She'd been far too solicitous. "We're not together anymore. Nothing is going to change that. I'm very sorry that it's hard for you. But we both need to move on with our lives. Why don't we agree to meet on Tuesday?"

"Did you tell him the baby may not be his?"

Another shiver coursed through her. Alarm bells started to sound in her head. This was going to be anything but convivial. She should have listened to her mother. She should have told Ben about Michael. She should never have told Michael about Ben. Hannah had to head this off before the Michael disaster spilled over into her life with Ben.

"I'll call you in a few hours. I'll give you my flight times and you can meet me at the airport. Deal?"

But he'd already hung up.

Hannah called Southwest and made flight reservations from Sacramento to John Wayne Airport. It would be the best ninety-nine dollars she ever spent if she could get Michael out of her life once and for all. She made her way back to the house.

Ben cornered her in the dining room. He looped his arms around her neck and pulled her in for a kiss.

"Where'd you go?" he whispered into her ear. She shivered, with need instead of fear this time. It was going to be a long few hours before they could be alone together.

"A few crazy calls. I'm going to fly down to Orange County on Tuesday to tie up some loose ends."

He came back down for a more serious kiss this time. She felt like a high school student, kissing against a locker. Hannah was both aroused and cognizant of the inappropriateness of the setting.

"Come with me," Ben said, dragging her to the family room. "I think you're going to want to stick around for this."

She took the glass Ben proffered. "Sparkling cider," he said in answer to her querying gaze. The cool liquid felt like heaven in her parched mouth. Ben stepped away and got his own glass. Such a festive family to drink sparkling wine and cider on Thanksgiving. He opened a drawer in his parent's secretary and retrieved something.

Above the din of a dozen people talking, drinking, and laughing, Hannah heard the doorbell ring. Someone let the guest in, and Hannah didn't think anything more of it. Probably another friend of the Cooper family. Good thing Elaine had enough food for a crowd.

Ben clinked a heavy gold letter opener on his glass, and the crowd quieted. As if on cue, those who had been in the kitchen with Elaine or in the library with Walter drifted toward the family room.

"I have something to say," Ben said. The crowd grew quieter in anticipation.

"As most of you know, my life has had a lot of ups and downs over the past few years. Mostly down. Things started looking up when I met Hannah Keesling. Cody may have been the best thing that ever happened to me." The crowd laughed. "I'm sorry, Hannah," he said looking anything but sorry. "But I can't keep something this big a secret. Hannah's pregnant!" Noises of surprise came from those who didn't know. "I couldn't be happier."

"Oh, really! Who's the father?" Everyone but Hannah laughed at Abbe's joke.

Hannah looked away from Ben when she heard heavy shoes on the wood floor.

Michael.

Ben, oblivious to the new guest, knelt in front of her in a timeless gesture. A turquoise box appeared as if out of nowhere. She knew what was coming, but couldn't stop it. Hannah couldn't stop this any more than she could stop a speeding freight train. Even though she knew it would end in a crash.

"Hannah, I knew the day you walked into my clinic, that you were going to change my life. I didn't know how much. You saved me from myself." Out of the corner of her eye, she could see Elaine nodding. "I want to have you, have this baby with me for the rest of my life. Hannah Keesling, will you marry me?"

As everyone realized what was happening, the crowd went silent. Now that the time had come for her to give her answer, Hannah didn't know what to do. She yearned to say yes. She wanted to shout her acceptance, and was on the verge of doing that when Michael cleared his throat noisily. She broke eye contact with Ben, looked up, meeting Michael's blue eyes— the coldest she'd ever seen them.

She shook her head. He couldn't do this here. He couldn't do this to her. They were over, done with. All that needed to happen was for them to sign some papers. But Michael didn't look done. The train was about to crash. Hannah closed her eyes and waited for the bang, the inevitable twisting of metal, the screams from passengers. Instead, she heard Michael's voice.

"She can't marry you, Ben Cooper," he said. Hannah's heart tripped. It went from hundreds of beats per minute to utter stillness. Without blood pounding in her ears, she could hear muted gasps from the crowd. "Hannah is already married—to me."

14

A trickle of laughter escaped Ben before the sound lodged in his throat. "Abbe?" he croaked as if she'd made a joke. Abbe shook her head very, very slowly. He turned back to Hannah. She could hear the clomp, clomp of Michael's shoes on the one hundred and fifty-year-old wood planks as he advanced on them.

She looked down at the man she loved as his face changed from happiness, to puzzlement, to anguish. "Hannah?" Ben stood. The velvet box thudded to the floor, forgotten. Michael's hand, possessive on her arm, prevented her from rescuing the ring.

Rounding on Michael, she pointed a finger at his chest. "How did you..."

"Find my iPhone."

Jerking her arm from his grasp, she looked at Ben, but couldn't force a word past her lips.

"Is he your...husband?" he said, his voice going hoarse with betrayal.

She caught his hand. There was a glimmer of hope in Ben's eyes—like this was some cruel prank. But it was not an episode of *Candid Camera*, or *Punk'd*. There was no comic relief around the corner. "Yes, but..." As she had from Michael, Ben pulled his hand from hers like it was on fire. The explanation died on her lips.

"But here's the kicker, Ben Cooper," Michael continued. "The baby could be mine."

Hannah got no chance to explain. Ben was out the door. Squealing tires raced from the curb, the sound reverberating through the thinly insulated house. She turned to Michael.

"Hannah, I love..." Though she'd never been a violent person, she slapped Michael as hard as she could and ran to Ben's room. She slammed the door and clung to the mussed bedcovers before the few happy memories they'd shared in this room began to fade.

Love someone, get lied to, be betrayed—rinse and repeat. What had he done in a past life to have this happen to him three different times? He lifted his head from his hands, glancing around the darkened interior of Hannah's car. All he could think about was driving to some big box mega mart, and buying and putting some kind of very large firearm to his head.

At that moment, he was supremely thankful for the Brady bill. In seven days, maybe he'd want to harm himself a little less.

Fuck it. He wasn't going to be a naïve little wuss like the last time. He jerked open the glove box and pulled out the registration and insurance. "Hannah and/or Michael Keesling," both documents read. There was an address in Newport Beach. He rifled through the remaining papers, as if he needed more proof.

Something metallic clinked to the carpeted floor mat. He punched the overhead light on and felt below the passenger seat. When he sat up, an engagement ring, much larger than the one he'd bought, rested in the palm of his hand. He fisted the ring and banged it against the driver's window. Instead of the satisfying crack of glass, he pulled back a sore right hand. The howl he released would have scared the neighbors if the car's soundproofing hadn't kept it contained.

The downstairs rooms were in near darkness. Ben didn't know how long he'd been gone, but everyone had left. He started the slow climb up the long staircase. He didn't want to come back here, see Hannah, suffer the pity of his family, but he didn't have anywhere else to go. He didn't even have a damned car. He was an ass for letting Hannah convince him to drive her fancy, schmancy car with all its bells and whistles. And that damned ring—he'd done it again. Lost himself—changed his whole life around for some cheating woman. Maybe *he* should be the singer. He was warring between blues and a country music guy done wrong, when he opened the door to his childhood bedroom.

Hannah was sagged into Ben's bed, her eyes puffy and nonseeing. His tiny mom sat next to her, her thin arms wrapped around Hannah's back. His father was there too, sitting in the wingback chair looking thoughtful.

His sister emerged from the bathroom, damp washcloth in hand. She was the first to notice his intrusion on their little tableau. "Ben! Where have you been? We were worried about you. The way you peeled out of here..."

"Oh, Benji," his mom said. Her voice was the one woman pity party he'd wanted to avoid. "Abbe, Walter, let's go," his mom said, standing up. "I think Hannah and Ben need to talk."

Abbe handed Hannah the washcloth and all three members of his little nuclear family left him alone with her. It took all the will in the world for him to keep still, leaning against the wall by the door. He crossed his arms for good measure. Damn it, she was even beautiful all red-faced and puffy-eyed. He wanted nothing more than to open his arms, take her in his, and tell her that everything was going to be okay. But everything was *not* going to be okay. Hours ago, he'd pledged to spend his life with her, but she'd already made that pledge with someone else. It was time for her to go home and fulfill her own vows to someone who was not him.

"Where's Michael?" It wasn't what he'd meant to lead with. But he'd kill that bastard if he was anywhere within a ten mile radius of his family. Justified anger was obviously making the guy unstable.

She looked up at him, tears still leaking from her reddened eyes. Silence stretched for a long time.

"I don't care," she answered, her own voice hoarse. She looked away as fresh tears sprung from her eyes.

"Are you married to him, Hannah?"

More silence. Then a small nod.

"Did you file for dissolution?"

Head shake.

"Are you at least separated?"

"I told Michael it was over."

"When?"

Hannah's glistening eyes shifted away. She dabbed at her face with the washcloth Abbe had given her.

"Look at me!" He tried to keep a cool head, but he could hear his own voice rising. "When did you tell Michael it was over?"

Those brown eyes he'd thought so trustworthy met his. "After I met you—"

Lies, lies, lies. Ben turned away. He opened the door and strode into the hallway. He'd take the real guest room. He needed the oblivion of sleep. Tomorrow, he'd figure it out. Tomorrow.

Her voice reached out to him in the hall. "Ben, wait." She ran out to stop him. Hannah pulled at his shoulder to turn him toward her. He turned, but shrugged her hand away. "I was planning to leave him anyway..."

"You take the car back to Shelter Cove. I'll find another way home," he said.

"No, you take the car. I need to go back to Newport."

"You're going back to him?" He hated the desperate note in his voice. Of course she was going back. Michael was her husband. Not him. Never him.

"No, I'm going to file for divorce."

"What about Cody?"

"Can you take care of the dog? I'll be back for him."

Details settled, he turned away again.

"Ben…"

He'd forgotten something. Ben reached into his pocket and pulled out Hannah's real engagement ring and wedding band.

"I think you shouldn't keep something so expensive in the glove compartment," he said, pulling her free hand toward him and folding the glittering jewelry inside.

He didn't turn around again. If he saw her one more time, he'd throw all good sense to the wind, pull her to him, pardon all her sins. But he wasn't God. Her sins were too big for a mere mortal like himself to forgive.

"Goodbye, Hannah."

He didn't even ask about the baby. It couldn't be Michael's. They'd only had the one encounter. What happened with Michael could barely be called intercourse. Hannah looked down at her hands, bare of rings. She was dogless, manless, and likely homeless. Her phone weighed in her pocket like rocks. No reason to turn it off now, the jig was up. Michael knew exactly where she was.

The thought that the baby inside her could belong to Michael was eating her up. Knowing full well the clinic was closed up tight for Thanksgiving, she dialed the number anyway. Hannah listened to the message wishing her a happy and fruitful holiday season. The Pacific Center for Reproductive Health wouldn't be open until Monday. Goddamn, Monday. The wait to find out the results of Michael's test was a prison sentence.

The yawning hunger turning her stomach inside out propelled Hannah from the isolation of Ben's room. She'd tried to ignore it, but she finally had to give in, when her head started to float away from her body. If it were only her, she would have holed up in the room and expired from hunger. But she wanted the baby inside of her, and it would need energy. She pushed open the swinging kitchen door only to find Walter sitting alone at the small breakfast table having a lonely turkey dinner. Michael had ruined Thanksgiving for this wonderful family.

"I'm sorry..."

"There's nothing to be sorry for. Come, sit. I'll get you a little something."

Walter was surprisingly spry and adept without his wife around. In no time, he had a plate full to heaping with turkey and all the fixings.

"Thank you," Hannah said. Walter sat across from her and continued working away at his meal. "I don't know what to say..."

"Do you love him? Ben, that is?"

Hannah didn't hesitate. "Of course. He's the best thing that ever happened in my life."

Her stomach growled again, and she picked up her fork. They ate in silence for a while.

"I went for it, you know," Walter said.

"Went for what?" Hannah said, putting down her cutlery. The sound of heavy silver hitting china reverberated off the walls of the stark white kitchen.

"The one great love."

Hannah leaned back in her chair, sensing a story was coming. "I'm sure you think I'm a shit. I cheated on my wife with my secretary, had a child I lied about. Now I'm *that* old guy, one foot in the grave, trying to make amends."

What was she going to say? She hadn't walked in his shoes. But she did think he was kind of a shit.

"I love Elaine. I want you to know that. I love Abbe and Benji with all my heart. All three of them are the best things that ever happened to me. But when I was about your age, I got the itch. They called it a mid-life crisis back then. I didn't get a cherry car or a lot of gold jewelry. But I had some of the feelings that you probably had. I wondered if I'd done the right thing. You've met Elaine. She's a whirlwind. She almost single-handedly raised the kids, researched and edited my work, volunteered for the temple. That woman kept my life together, but she wasn't the sizzle.

"Then I met Minnie. She was the sizzle in the steak. That woman got me. She was a terrible secretary. Couldn't alphabetize her way out of a paper sack. But she got *me*. Instead of organizing my shirts, my kids, my papers—she asked me about who I wanted to be."

"But why did you marry Elaine, then? Why didn't you wait?"

"Who waited in those days? She got pregnant. Marriage is what was expected. People weren't holding out until their thirties or forties waiting for their one true love. It wasn't the idealistic fifties, but the realistic seventies."

"Is that fair to Elaine?"

"Probably not. Look, I'm going to level with you. I married her because she would make a good wife. Did make a great wife. Does make a great wife. Minnie, though, was the love of my life. When you pass seventy, you get a lot of perspective. If I had to do it all over again. I'd have held out for the love of my life."

Hannah was taken aback. She didn't know why she hadn't seen that coming a mile away.

"I understand why you did what you did. Not saying it was the right way to go about things. But I *get* it. I honestly don't know if Benjamin will ever forgive you. He's always been hard on people who don't live up to his high moral standards. But don't give up on him. I think he's your Minnie."

Walter didn't have to tell her that the conversation they had could never leave that room. But knowing this about Ben's father, made her love Ben a little more. When Abbe came bustling into the room looking for a late night snack, asking what they had been discussing, another lie rolled off her tongue. Hannah vowed to make it her last.

"We were talking about what a great cook your mom is. Would you like some pie?"

After getting out of the compact rental car, Hannah found herself standing in front of her own house late Monday morning. She rang the doorbell. The chimes' eight notes echoed off the walls. She waited a minute and rang the bell again. Relief flooded through her. Michael wasn't home. She slid her key into the door and entered. The plan was to get the rest of her stuff, move it to storage, and move on with her life. Whether Ben ever took her back or not, Michael had to be out of her life. The stunt he'd pulled in Davis was needlessly cruel. She would never forgive him.

Before Hannah entered the bedroom to get the rest of her clothes, she made a beeline for her office. Her MacBook was in Shelter Cove, but Michael's work laptop was in the top desk drawer. If he hadn't taken it to work, she wondered where he was today. No matter. She opened the lid, and typed LOVEHANNAH into the small square box. Gratified that the password was still the same, she opened his browser. Hannah scrolled through his bookmarks until she found what she needed.

She picked up the landline on the desk and dialed. After the receptionist's long and perfunctory greeting, she got down to business.

"Hi, this is Hannah Keesling. I'm calling about the retesting results for my husband, Michael. He was part of the lab mix-up."

"Oh, hi, Hannah. Lilly here. We're so very sorry about that. Let me put you on hold for a bit. I'll get the nurse to get your file and she'll pick up the extension. Thanks."

Tuning out the softly voiced ads for surgical and non-surgical conception methods, she looked around the room. Despite the years and moves with Michael, there wasn't much she wanted to keep. A few framed photographs, maybe. Some knickknacks that her mother had sent from Copenhagen joined the mental list.

The familiar voice of the nurse they'd met several times came on the line. "Hannah?"

She snapped to attention. "Yes. Thanks. I was calling about Michael's results."

Static filled the line as the nurse hesitated. "Due to doctor-patient confidentiality and HIPAA laws, I can't discuss Michael's medical file with you."

"What are you talking about?" Hannah asked. "We've both called and gotten results in the past. I'm sure that Michael was the one that called about the uterine fluoroscope..." she fumbled at the unfamiliar words "...thing." Unseen by the nurse, she waved her hands emphatically.

"I'm sorry." The nurse's voice got faint as if she were moving the receiver from her ear to the cradle on her desk.

"Wait! Didn't we sign some kind of form that allowed you to share medical information?"

The voice came back to the line, strong again. "Michael revoked his waiver. Again, I'm sorry." The nurse disconnected the call. Michael had revoked his waiver? How in the hell was she going to find out if he was really infertile? Shit, fuck, damn. Hannah cursed, calling herself all kinds of a fool. She slammed down her receiver when the insistent bleat of the broken dial tone pierced her haze of anguish.

Okay, that was a problem for another day. Setting aside paternity, she could still get her stuff. Michael hadn't yet revoked her right to be in their house. Hannah advanced on the bedroom like a woman hell bent on an important mission. Why was it so dark in here? Flicking on the light switch, and moving to draw open the heavy curtains, she was shocked to find a hand on her wrist. Shock gave way to fear. Hannah screamed.

"Michael! What the hell? You didn't answer the doorbell. I thought you weren't home."

Pulling her hand away, she pulled open the curtains and lifted the blinds behind them. Harsh southern California sun flooded the room. Michael folded his lanky body on the severely mussed bed. He must have been in there all along. Looking at him more closely, she noticed that he was fully dressed. Though his clothes looked like they'd done ten rounds in a boxing ring.

"You came back," Michael said, hunching over. He eased off his shoes and dropped the heavy leather onto the thickly carpeted floor. They barely made a sound.

"I'm here to get my stuff. That's all, Michael. I'm not staying. I won't be back again."

"I love you. Hannah. I'm sorry about Thursday, that was...that was kind of crazy. Deaver warned me against it, but I couldn't...can't let you go."

"What happened at Dr. Stern's office? The semen analysis?"

"The baby could be mine, Hannah."

The deep thudding in her chest slowed. "Are you saying the first result was a mistake?"

"Why do you love him more than you love me?"

"Michael, I can't. No, I won't answer that question." She sat on the bed, grabbing his upper arms in earnest. "Are you fertile? Tell me. I need to know." When he didn't answer right away, she shook him a little.

He eased her hands from his arms, and laid back down, turning his back on her. If he wasn't going to answer her most pressing question, Michael was a waste of her time. Hannah got the giant suitcases down from the top shelf in the walk in closet and started putting her remaining clothes in. She moved the luggage to the foyer, and grabbed the very few things that were important to her, half-finished songs and camera lenses. When her broker's van pulled up to the driveway, it was probably the only time she was grateful that she'd been a real estate agent. Her broker staged houses, and always had ready transportation and storage. They loaded the van, she locked the front door, and left her life with Michael behind once and for all.

Hannah thanked her lucky stars that Grady Martinez could see her that day. While she waited in the subtly decorated reception area, she filled out the intake form.

Grady stood when she entered, embracing her and bussing her on the cheek. "Hannah, I haven't seen you in a while. Not since that mess with the Hendersons, I think. I was so glad you got them to agree on a price for that house. What brings you here?" he asked, sitting and leaning back in his high backed leather chair. "Don't tell me you need a divorce," he joked.

"Actually, Grady, that's exactly why I'm here," she said, sitting down in one of the two wooden seats when he forgot his manners.

The easy smile fell from the attorney's face. Instantly sober, he said, "I, uh, didn't expect that. I assumed you were here about a client. Okay." He stood again to close his office door. "Is that my form in your hand?"

Hannah nodded, and proffered the clipboard. He separated paper from wood, and left the single page form on his desk, unread. He then gave her the spiel about confidentiality. She'd already had a big dose of confidentiality that day. She didn't know if she could take any more secrets.

"So what's the story?" he asked expansively.

"Michael and I..." she started. That wasn't true. No more lies. "I want to end my marriage to Michael."

"Why?"

"I thought 'why' didn't matter in divorce anymore."

"You're right," he acknowledged with a slight nod of his head. "I like to get all the facts on the table."

"It was a mistake to get married in the first place." The truth, laid out like a corpse on a metal gurney.

Grady looked unsatisfied with that explanation. "Is there someone else? For you, for him."

"I met someone, yes. But I was going to leave regardless."

"How does Michael feel about this? Does he want a dissolution?"

"No. Does that matter? I assumed..."

"You assumed right. One person can dissolve a marriage. Even if the other party objects, the court will end it. I like to know what we're up against. When a spouse isn't ready to end it, they can make a lot of trouble."

He picked up the form. They ran through the litany of questions about the where and when of the marriage, the property they owned together. "You didn't check any boxes. But I know you don't have any kids, unless you've gone all Angelina Jolie on me. And you're not pregnant right?" he asked, getting his pen ready to tick the little box that had caused her so much consternation in the waiting room.

She started to speak. He paused, his pen hovering over the small square on the bottom of the form.

"Are you pregnant?" he asked, disbelief in his voice.

"Yes."

"Is Michael the father?"

"No." Even she could hear that her voice lacked conviction.

"Are you sure?" She could hear the phone ringing in the reception area, cars starting and stopping outside, the heat turning on, then off. "Hannah?"

"I'm sure the baby isn't Michael's." Then the whole tale spilled out, about them trying to get pregnant for years, about the confirmation of Michael's infertility, about Ben, about the possible lab mix up.

Grady listened, rapt. "Um, okay. I can file the papers and start the proceedings, but you won't be divorced until the baby is born."

"Why?"

"Courts like clean breaks, and children are messy," he said. Then he shook his head as if clearing away the cobwebs. "Let me explain it this way. The court is going to start with the presumption that the baby is Michael's."

"What?" Hannah was sure her outrage could be heard in every office in the suite.

"I'm not saying we can't rebut that presumption. And in many, many cases, the husbands don't want the responsibility of a child who is not theirs, but I don't think you have that here. So...unless Michael is willing to disclaim paternity, or unless there's conclusive testing and the court determines that the baby isn't his—you're in this until—when is your due date?"

"July fourth of next year."

"Well, perhaps July fourth will be your independence day."

Ben ignored the knocking on the door. His parents broke one of their lifelong rules and came in anyway. He was sitting in the same wingback chair his father had occupied on Thursday night.

"What's this, an intervention?"

"Kind of, Benji," his mother said. She straightened the bedcovers, and threw open his windows letting in the winter chill. "You haven't left this room in days."

"I'll be out of your hair tomorrow morning."

"What about Hannah?"

"What about her?"

There was silence among the three of them for a long time. Then his mom spoke.

"I'm really sorry, Benji. I thought it would be different this time. She was from New York. She seemed like such a nice girl."

"Why would it be different?" He pointed to his dad accusingly. "I'm probably hard wired for this sort of thing. It's like a fucking family curse."

Abbe came into the room. "Ben, this is not Dad's fault."

"Why do you always take up for him? He cheated on Mom. He betrayed us. He wants to share his legacy with some bastard child."

"Hannah's child may be your bastard child very soon, Ben," his father said quietly. "People in glass houses," Walter stopped, shrugged, and left the Chaucerian reference incomplete.

"That's not fair. None of this." He jabbed a finger first at his father, then Abbe. "None of this is my fault."

"Oh, woe is you," Abbe said, her voice full of exasperation. "The common denominator in all this is you. Excluding Dad, this is as much your fault as it is Hannah's."

"It's my fault that Hannah is as much of a lying witch as Samara was?"

"Obviously you're attracted to duplicitous women. Everyone and their brother knew Samara was cheating on you. How in the hell you didn't notice is beyond me. And what did you really know about Hannah before you got her pregnant? Did you ask about her marriage? Did you even look her up on the 'net?"

"So now I'm an idiot if I don't investigate the women I love. I'm a fool for trusting them?"

"If the shoe fits."

"You're blaming the victim? For a supposed feminist, that's rich."

"Thank goodness I'm not a fragile fucking flower," Abbe said, taking the insult in stride. "All I'm saying, Ben, is that you're blaming Dad or Marty or Samara or Hannah. Except for Marty, I'm not saying that you were in the wrong. All I'm saying is that if you keep winding up in the same situation— you must be doing something. The definition of insanity is— "

"Doing the same thing over and over and expecting a different result," he finished. Maybe he was plain crazy, *loco*,

fou. What was the word for crazy in Danish? He was probably
that too.

15

Brooklyn. The never changing smell of piss, shit, vomit, and body odor greeted Hannah at the airport. New York City. At its core, it never changed. Despite the smell, Hannah took a deep breath while wheeling her carry-on luggage through the boarding ramp. For the first time in months Hannah's heart and mind were quiet. Dorothy was right. There is no place like home.

On the long cab ride down Atlantic Avenue from Jamaica to her father's house in Brooklyn Heights, she recounted the neighborhoods she'd spent much of her childhood in, East New York, Williamsburg, Bedford-Stuyvesant, Cobble Hill. So much had changed since Brooklyn's much maligned reputation though the 1980s. Gone were the crack houses and vacant lots. Infill housing and lots of yuppies had changed the community.

Sometimes she missed the edginess of the gang and drug infested years. 'Giuliani Time' had changed the city forever. Nowadays, it was too many sushi bars, coffee shops and hipsters in fedoras for her taste.

As good as his word, her dad was waiting on the stoop when her cab pulled up. He'd been gone a lot of her childhood. But he'd more than made up for it in the last few years. He was there whenever she needed him.

"Daddy!" she cried. It was her first word when she was an infant. She hugged Shay, enveloped in the all-too-familiar smell of cologne and cigars. Tears leaked from her eyes. "You've got to stop smoking," she admonished.

"Hannah, banana. I'm too old to stop. I've all but given up scotch and fast women. Let me have this one thing."

She pulled back, wiped her eyes, and looked at her dad. When had he turned into an old man? She'd been taller than him since she was sixteen, but he looked even shorter than the 5'6" he'd always been. She suspected he was nearly bald under the beaten leather driver's cap he wore tilted at a jaunty angle. His neatly trimmed moustache and beard had turned gray years ago. But underneath the jowls, gray hair and hat, his coffee brown face creased with a smile letting her know she was wanted unconditionally, and loved. She pulled him in for another tight hug. His hands smoothed her hair and patted her back, giving her much needed comfort without judgment.

"Have you really given up booze and women?" Hannah asked doubtfully. She pulled away and they carried her bags into the house.

Shay shook his head. "Maybe I haven't given up everything. But I am slowing down a little."

Hannah didn't care if he smoked, drank and played the field. She only wanted her dad to live a long and healthy life. As he led the way into her childhood home, she pushed past her father and ran into the main rooms on the first floor, sighing in satisfaction. Everything was the same. The butter yellow walls of the living and dining rooms may have been refreshed with new coats of paint, but in every respect that mattered, everything was as she remembered it. Her father's mahogany grand piano stood prominently by the tall front windows. His turntable stood to one side of the black marble fireplace. Incongruously, an iPod dock stood quietly next to it.

"Daddy, I thought you said you'd never listen to electronic music," Hannah said in surprise.

"Ah, shit. I had to change with the times. Can you believe that releasing an album on vinyl is now considered an 'artistic' choice? I had to get this to hear the new stuff coming out these days. Some of it's even good."

The kitchen was a surprise. The old red enamel rotisserie oven she'd grown up with was still there, but a new stainless steel refrigerator and dishwasher were fitted into the freshly painted cupboards.

Her dad followed her in, his leather slippers scuffing along the floor. She looked at him questioningly. This was a man allergic to change.

"What? I listened to what you said about keeping it fresh, saving on the electric and water bills with more efficient appliances."

"Oh Dad, that was my now retired Realtor talking."

"Well, I have been thinking of selling."

Hannah's heart, which had been calm for the first time in weeks, sped up again. Tears pricked at the back of her eyes. Though she hadn't been here in years, this was the place she always thought of as home. She tried for a light tone. "What? Seriously? Dad, why would you sell? This is a great place."

"It's a big house. I don't have a wife or child living here anymore. I'm paying to heat a lot of big rooms. They're doing some new co-ops in Williamsburg that I've been keeping an eye on."

"Williamsburg? I rode by on the way in. It looks better than I remember. But in my mind, it's still a lot of burned out buildings and muggers. Cupcakes and coffee shops couldn't have changed it all that much."

"It's not like here, but it's certainly not the boonies. I played a couple of gigs there this year."

"Oh, God. Was it all twenty year olds in flannel and facial hair?"

Her father had to laugh. He nodded. "Maybe."

Hannah went back to the living room and plopped down on one of the green tufted couches in the room. Williamsburg and Times Square may have changed, but at least the furniture here hadn't.

Her father put Jackie McLean on the turntable, and sat across from her on a twin of the couch she was sitting on.

"Where's Michael?"

"I left him." She hadn't given her father any reason for coming to New York, except she wanted to see him during the holidays.

"Mmmm," her father replied. He got a cigar from the box, but seeing her frown, resisted lighting it. Instead, he nestled it in the pocket of his button down shirt.

"Have you seen Jackie lately?" she asked.

"He died seven years ago, honey. A lot of the old cats are gone. Hard living and longevity don't mix."

"I've been singing."

"I'd heard."

"ASCAP?"

He laughed, a genuine belly laugh. "Those payments take a year and a day. Nope, an ear to the ground is all. Joe Sheppard and I used to jam back in the day. Funk Fiesta has done some arrangements of my stuff. My daughter performing was a big deal. Even if it was out in the sticks. And I had to hear it from somebody else."

"I'm not as good as you—or Mom even." Suddenly shy, Hannah got up and retrieved her music folder from her bag. She thrust her two songs at him like a child showing homework for inspection.

Sheet music in hand, Shay moved to the Bechstein and started plinking out her tunes. He nodded. "Sing these for me."

With him accompanying, she stood stiffly next to the piano like she'd done as a teenager, and sang the two songs she'd performed with Funk Fiesta in Eureka. First, the song about a troubled woman, then the song she wrote for Ben. Professing her love was as embarrassing the second time around as it had been the first.

"This song wasn't for Michael."

"I'm pregnant," Hannah announced without ceremony. She leaned against the piano for support.

Her father shot forward, his elbow striking a discordant note against the ivory keys. "And you left Michael?" His voice was filled with confusion. "Should I congratulate you?"

"Michael's not the father," she said.

Her father's face was inscrutable. The Wall Street wizard and Brooklyn musician had never seen eye to eye.

"Who is the father?"

"Ben Cooper."

"This is the first I'm hearing of this." The gossip from Eureka had been limited to music. "Is he worthy of you?"

"Daddy!" He'd never thought anyone she'd dated had been good enough for her.

"Seriously."

"I think he's the one."

"Which one?"

Was he being deliberately obtuse? "The man I'm meant to be with."

"I thought your mother was the one, and she's in Copen-hagen. If he's not here with you now, something's wrong. Wouldn't you say?"

Hannah started crying again, this time from sadness and despair. She blubbered out the whole story while her father nodded, pulled the cigar from his pocket and lit up. She confessed. He filled the room with thick smoke.

"I'd never thought Michael would have put up a fight. Gotta give him props." Shay shook his head ruefully. "Bigger balls than I'd have expected on a white man."

"It's not funny, Dad. He completely ruined things with Ben."

"Look, I was never a fan of Michael. You know that. But he's always loved you. He married you. He's never betrayed you. Why should he step aside?"

"It wasn't a real marriage."

Shay jabbed a thumb toward the open window. "I was there at your wedding right around the corner. Seemed real to me."

"You know that's not what I mean." Hannah had barely admitted the truth to herself. It was a struggle to tell the truth to anyone else, much less her father. She'd always wanted him to think the best of her. "I settled."

Her father put out his cigar, and rose to lift the sash on one of the huge front windows. She watched the smoke curl and seep around the old wood, thick with decades of paint. Shay leaned against the windowsill.

"So Michael Keesling wasn't 'the one?'"

Hannah shook her head slowly.

"Why did you do it, baby? Your life was okay here. Maybe you weren't meeting the right guys, but you were taking pictures and singing. You seemed happy."

"I didn't want to be forty and single, and childless. I was afraid of ending up alone. Like aunties Carol, or Mary, or Joyce." She'd grown up with these women, friends of her parents. They were strong, single women living in New York. They never seemed lonely, but they were certainly alone. "I wish I'd met Ben first."

"I'm alone. It's not so bad."

"But you had Mommy and me first."

"That's true, I guess. Your mother never wanted to be alone."

"Axel is nice enough, but she loved you best."

"And I still love her, dearly, Hannah. I treated her badly and I lost her. I hope you weren't following my example."

"It wasn't like that," she said, ducking her head. They had never had a straight on conversation about his road trips or his infidelity. From the arguments and insinuation, she put together that he was easily swayed by backup singers and groupies while on the road. "I was planning on leaving Michael anyway." When her father's eyebrows rose, she continued, "No, really. We're not compatible in any way that counts."

"You didn't know this before you stood before God and country at First Unitarian?"

She nodded. She did know it. "I thought it would be, he would be—good enough."

"A lot of people do it that way. Your mother Freja's doing that now. But you were never that girl, Hannah. You always lived life to the fullest. How long did you think you'd be able to live in the little box that a day job and kids put you in?"

"It was really, really stupid. And I think I hurt Michael really, really bad. And I hurt Ben worse, and the whole thing is a fucking mess." The tears came in earnest again.

Her father got up and came back with a glass of seltzer. "Can't have anything stronger these days, I guess."

She drank thirstily, then burped loudly. It broke the tension and they both laughed a long time. They ordered in Chinese from her favorite restaurant and talked about other things. When she was bustling around the small galley kitchen, throwing away boxes and tucking the leftovers in the fridge, she heard Shay's voice from the dining room.

"You know you're welcome to stay as long as you like."

She came into the room, wiping her hands on a kitchen towel. "Thanks. I hope it's okay if I stay through Christmas. After that, I want to go to Copenhagen. Mor," she self corrected, "Mommy said I could stay with her and have the baby there."

He nodded, suddenly looking a little sad. "I guess girls need their mothers at times like this."

Hannah wearily climbed the creaky wooden steps to the top floor of the four-story building. Her dad had never changed her childhood bedroom except to remove the posters, pictures, and stuffed animals. She'd moved up to the attic space in her teens, happy to spread out away from the scrutiny of her parents.

All her books were still there and her plastic cube of a Mac from high school had stayed in its prominent position on her desk.

She looked at the bedside clock. It was only nine-thirty in California. She lifted the receiver of the novelty phone she'd thought was so cool twenty years ago, watching the neon glow. It still had a dial tone. She wondered if her dad had kept her separate number her parents had gotten out of desperation. No matter, she dialed the number she'd memorized the first time she'd called it.

Ben answered on the second ring. She could hear Cody whining in the background. Ben had probably figured out that she spoiled the dog with nightly treats. A painful squeeze gripped her chest. She missed the man and the dog desperately.

"It's me."

There was a long pause on the line. "I can't do this, Hannah."

Do what. Talk to her? Love her? Forgive her? "Please don't hang up," she said. He hung up. There was nothing but a dial tone. The sound that had been so welcome moments before, mocked her now. A digitized voice advised her to make a call or put down the phone. She placed it back in the cradle.

Despite her best efforts, she was going to end up alone.

Hannah woke to the sound of her cell phone buzzing near her ear.

Michael.

She made up her mind right then. If he wasn't going to behave rationally, then he was going to get the same response Ben had given her.

"Hello Michael." His voice cut in and out. She made her way downstairs to the little deck her parents had built years ago. Hannah shivered on the warped planks, wishing she'd thought to wear a sweater. The signal was good out here. She looked up at the sunlight as it filtered through the maples bare of their summer leaves. "I'm in Brooklyn at my dad's house. But I'm sure you already know that."

"I won't ever do that again."

"Do what, Michael? Stalk me? Humiliate me?"

"What in the hell was I supposed to do, Hannah? Stand there while you ride off into the sunset with your vet in shining armor?" He paused, recalibrated. His voice was much calmer when he spoke again. "I got the papers from Grady. I guess you're serious."

Hannah brushed dead leaves from the old wood chaise and sat down.

"Dead serious, Michael."

"Do you want to marry that other guy?"

This had to be the most awkward conversation she'd ever had. Life hadn't prepared her to discuss marriage prospects with the person she was already married to. "I think I do, Michael. But after Thanksgiving, I'll be happy if he ever speaks to me again."

"I talked to my parents. It was long overdue. They've been real asses sometimes, but I've got them straightened out. I talked to my brother, Matthew and he's willing to help in any way that he can."

"What are you saying?"

"I'm saying that you can come back."

"I was unfaithful."

"I love you, Hannah. I always have. I know why you married me." Hannah's heart beat a little faster. Every woman had secrets she kept from everyone, even her best friend. How could he know the one thing she'd never told anyone? "How long are you in New York?"

The change of subject threw her. She answered without thinking. "I'm leaving for Copenhagen on the eighteenth."

"Staying with your mom."

"She's one person that'll take me in no matter what."

"I didn't throw you out. You chose to leave. You can always come back."

"Are you going to look at the papers?"

"I will. I promise."

One long, cold week later, Hannah was debating whether she was big enough for warm maternity clothes when her father's doorbell rang.

"Can you answer that?" Shay yelled. He was in the kitchen, cleaning up after breakfast. Her father was a great cook, but he rarely took the time. It was a pleasure waking up every morning to some variation of grits, eggs, and toast smothered in gravy. Getting up from the table, she realized her pants were tight and too thin for this weather. She'd never survive New York, much less Copenhagen unless she got something a little warmer. But getting maternity clothes seemed like it would be going overboard. She wasn't even showing yet.

Without pulling aside the lace curtain and looking through the large glass panel, she pulled open the door. California had softened her. Too late, she realized she should have checked to see who it was. Hannah shouldn't have been surprised.

"Michael."

A Lincoln Town car idled, double-parked at the curb. Of course Michael would hire a car service. At Michael's cue, the driver opened the trunk and took out Michael's Tumi weekender. "Can I?"

"You can come in out of the cold." She gestured to the bag the taxi driver had in hand. "I can't stop you from staying in New York, but you can't stay here."

The driver brought the bag up the stairs. Tipping the driver, Michael entered her father's house.

"Who was it, honey? I'm not expecting anyone." Throwing a dishtowel over his shoulder, her father came into the living room where Michael stood awkwardly with his bag. "Michael Keesling. I have to say you're the last man I expected to see." He looked at his daughter. "Hannah?"

"It's okay, Dad. I was going out anyway. Would you like to come?" She directed her question at Michael.

"Sure."

"Daddy, I'm going shopping. I'll be back in a couple of hours."

Shay looked dubious. "If you're sure."

"It's fine, Dad."

Hannah pulled her old down jacket from the hall closet, and stepped outside. Michael followed her dutifully. She walked toward the Court Street subway station. "I guess I wasn't too hard to find this time."

"Who moves in New York?"

They both said, "New York inertia," at the same time and laughed. For the first time in weeks, there was no tension between them. Michael was for a moment, back to being the close friend she'd had for years.

They rode the N up to Herald Square. For the first time in her life, all the holiday decorations and elaborate window displays didn't make a dent in her surly mood. As a kid, she'd loved pressing her nose to the glass at Macy's, Bamberger's, and A&S, peering at the wonderlands the designers created. Despite the holiday crowd, Michael didn't complain once as Hannah went through a few floors of Macy's and a few other stores, getting a mix of maternity clothes, and some things in bigger sizes. The outsized stomach pouches made her laugh too much to seriously consider purchasing them. Michael was funny, charming, and helpful. It was like being reunited with her old friend—not the sullen, narcissistic asshole she was divorcing.

"Let's check the bags," Michael said, gesturing to an escalator moving down. They left all her shopping bags at the counter in return for a solitary claim ticket. "So which Szech-uan place do you want to hit?"

Hot, spicy food had always been one of Hannah's favorites. It wasn't nearly as popular on the west coast where other re-gions dominated Chinese food and culture.

After wandering through mid-town, they finally settled on a place on West 39ᵗʰ Street. Michael took the initiative and ordered all her favorites.

"About Ben," Michael said.

His name alone caused her stomach to bottom out. Hannah cut him off with a frown and a swift movement of her hand. "The only way this is going to work is if we don't talk about Ben. Okay?"

Michael nodded.

Hannah put down her chopsticks. "Are you going to tell me?"

"What?"

"The results of the retesting?"

Michael turned his face toward the large plate glass win-dow. He watched the comings and goings of the eclectic New Yorkers getting their spicy fix. "I know why you married me." That again. "I've been puzzling it out. We used to get along great. We hung out, saw movies, ate out, and walked this city dozens of times over. Remember that time we decided to bike across the Brooklyn Bridge?"

She did remember. They'd gotten bikes from the shed be-hind her dad's house. It had been a last minute impulse to try out the new so-called bike-friendly Manhattan. They were going to cross the bridge, then take the much-touted Greenway bike trail along the Hudson River side of the island. Neither one of them had thought to check the weather, and they were drenched in a late summer thunderstorm, halfway across the Brooklyn Bridge. Soaked, they'd biked back across the bridge and holed up in her apartment under the Manhattan Bridge overpass waiting out the downpour. Of course, they'd gotten undressed and in the steamy apartment, while they were waiting for Michael's clothes to dry, Hannah had let her guard down. That was the day their relationship had changed from friends to lovers.

"I remember," Hannah said softly.

"I fell in love with you that day." Shit. Was this going to be true confessions? She couldn't take any more crushing guilt. She started to speak. "No, let me finish. I've always liked you, from the day I first met you. I'd been angling for a way to meet you for months. We had a lot of the same friends, but every time I saw you at a party or something, there was always some guy keeping you all to himself." Hannah had to acknowledge there had been a lot of assholes in those days. One after another. They had dominated her life, and not one of them liked to share. Although that hadn't stopped them from sharing the love with women everywhere. "Then you were alone at that gallery opening for that guy with the horrible pictures."

"Oh, God. The one with nothing but pierced women's body parts."

"I think you'd broken up with someone. Anyway, it was the first time I'd ever seen you by yourself."

"Was that the first time we talked? Really?" She had to admit the memory was vague. She'd been coming off a bad breakup with another unsuitable guy she thought she could tame. She was searching her memory, had this one been a drinker, unfaithful or both?

Michael grimaced. "You were a little tipsy. We sat in that Greek diner while you poured your heart out. I got you home in a cab. Then you started dating another guy, and I didn't see you for a while."

Ah, the singer. Hannah remembered that one. He'd been on the road most of their relationship. "In between guys, you called. We'd hang out, then you'd disappear again."

"Did you think I was using you?"

"It's okay. I wanted to be used. Slow and steady wins the race. Isn't that the lesson of the Tortoise and the Hare?"

Hannah shrugged. She leaned against the booth, sated. She declined the To Go box the waiter offered, and was glad when the table was cleared. She requested more fortune cookies and more hot, black tea.

"After your thirty-fifth birthday, you changed. You finally started looking at me as a man, not a buddy. You were flailing and I was there to catch you."

"The wedding," Hannah said, caught up in the long-dormant memories he was rousing. She'd taken him as her friend/date to yet another Connecticut wedding. It was trite, but she started to feel like she was going to be a bridesmaid forever. It was about the same time that her 'auntie' Joyce had been diagnosed with ovarian cancer. Hannah had done what she could to support Joyce. But at the end of the day, Joyce was alone. She didn't want to be Joyce in twenty-five years.

"I courted you in my own inept way. You married me because you thought it was time. You married me because you wanted to settle down. You married me because you wanted children and a father for them."

Hannah couldn't look at Michael. He'd known all along. She hadn't fooled him one bit. "Why did you do it then?" she asked, her voice rough with self-reproach. Her secret was out. Her secret had never been a secret. He'd known the worst, and married her anyway.

"Because I loved you. Because I thought you'd fall in love with me eventually. It works in arranged marriages. Most of the time, the couple ends up loving each other. The divorce rates for those marriages are lower than those in so-called love matches. Because I thought I loved you enough to make it work."

"Why are you telling me this now?" Hannah asked, her voice hoarse.

"Because I waited before. I can wait again," he stated plainly.

"Did you think our marriage worked?"

Michael nodded. "For me it did."

She'd been avoiding this conversation for years. No, avoiding wasn't the right word. She'd never planned to have this conversation. "It didn't work for me, Michael." Hannah wanted to cry for not being able to will her heart to do what it should, what would be right, what would smooth everything over like the wallpaper she'd glued over horsehair plaster walls when she was a teenager.

She looked at the man across from her. Objectively, he was good-looking. Everyone always told her he was handsome. He was generous, and could be nice. He was a banker, for Christ sake. For every ninety-nine percenter out there who hated bankers, there were three Seven Sisters alumnae, Junior League volunteering, Lilly Pulitzer wearing women who loved bankers. There were a thousand women in this borough alone who'd crawl on top of her not-quite-dead body to get to him. Why couldn't she want him like that? Was there something wrong with her?

"Why?"

"I don't think you want to hear this."

"I'm a big boy, Hannah," Michael said, pulling himself up to his full height against the red vinyl booth.

Hannah took a deep breath. She was about to set the Brooklyn, Manhattan, and Williamsburg bridges on fire. "You didn't support me."

"What? I paid the bills. I told you that you could do whatever you want. How have I not supported you?"

"Since we left New York, you've never been to one of my shows. Not when I was singing. Not even the gallery show of celebrity portraits."

"I was busy making a living for us, Hannah. *You know*, I think you're very talented. How is *that* not enough?"

She shook her head. "I don't want to argue with you. I'm only answering your question."

"You don't look like you're done. What else?"

The waiter absentmindedly refilled their glasses. She was so glad she wasn't in L.A. A west coast restaurant host would have tried to turn over the table ten times by now. "You treated me like your maid, Michael."

"I told you that you could hire whomever you wanted to do whatever you needed. I've never asked you to cook or clean or do my laundry."

"That's true. But you expected me to arrange it all. Who's the gardener? The housekeeper?" He shook his head. "I had to interview everyone, hire everyone, supervise everyone. That took time away from what I wanted to do. I wanted a marriage that was a partnership. I didn't want to be your property manager."

Michael sat back, crossing his arms in front of his chest, a sure sign he didn't like what he was hearing.

"What else, Hannah?"

She dropped her voice, although no one was listening. "Our sex life is awful."

"I don't think so. Maybe not often enough," he tried out his 'poor me' smile.

"Michael, you spend more time looking at porn than looking at me."

"You said you didn't mind me looking at porn."

"Michael. I'm not twenty. I know that men like to look at other women. I never worried about you being unfaithful. What I don't appreciate is you looking at other women when we're together."

"But I love you Hannah, not them."

"It doesn't feel that way."

"The irony of this isn't lost on you."

"Michael—" her tone warned him that he was treading on dangerous ground.

"Can't you believe me on this? *I* don't want anyone but you."

"It doesn't pass the Dr. Phil test. He'd skewer you in a heartbeat."

"Is it really the porn?"

"I don't give a shit about the porn, for the most part, Michael. I feel like you don't really want to be with me. Maybe you like the idea of me. Maybe I'm still exotic to you. I don't know. But you never really want to kiss me. There's no foreplay. You kiss me once, rub me 'down there,' then want a blow job. You never want plain vanilla intercourse."

Michael looked away. Hannah excused herself. The bottomless water glass had filled her bladder. She did not want to ride the train back home with her legs crossed. Michael's head was bowed when she returned. With effort, she scooted her newly expanded figure back to her spot on the bench.

"I'm sorry. I thought you wanted to hear the truth."

Michael looked up, laying his hands on the table in supplication. "Here's the truth, Hannah. I can't control myself when

I'm with you. You turn me on so much that I come as soon as I'm inside you. If I kiss you or touch you, it goes even faster. It really isn't you. It's me."

"Really?"

Michael colored—something he rarely did.

"Why didn't you tell me this before?"

Michael leaned back against the booth, his eyes focusing past her. "Hi, I feel like a jackrabbit when fucking my wife. Oh, and I can't get her pregnant, either. No, not emasculated much."

The lull between lunch and dinner was over. The restaurant was filling up again. Waiting customers were milling about in front, rubbing their hands together and stamping their feet for warmth.

Hannah had been so wrapped up in their memories and feelings, that she noticed for the first time Michael was missing an appendage.

"Where's your Blackberry?"

"In my suitcase."

"What if—"

"What if, what? The market crashes. Our companies spiral around the drain. The holiday shopping season collapses?"

She nodded. "All that. You're never without e-mail." He'd reminded her of the Ari character on Entourage. That phone was always in his hand.

"I did all that to support you, us. If there's no us, none of that really matters, does it?"

"Let's go," she said. They backtracked to Macy's for her bags. Michael popped into Duane Reade for a second, claiming forgotten toiletries. After that, the train ride back to Brooklyn was mercifully short. The silence stretched between them.

Hannah couldn't figure out if knowing any of this before would have made a difference. Would she have driven north? Would she have given it another chance? Should she now? Why was this so damn complicated? She loved Ben. She thought she was carrying his baby. No, she knew she was carrying his baby. The train ground to a halt at Court Street. They both rose and she waited a beat for Michael to take the bulk of the bags. He didn't. Maybe the atmosphere of the restaurant was getting to her. Nothing had changed. She moved quickly to get out before the doors closed. MTA subway conductors weren't known for their patience.

She trudged along and stopped at the stairs to get a good grip on the bags before she began her ascent. Finally, Michael took the bags without a word. She looked up and saw a few stars winking faintly through the bare branches of the Brooklyn maples.

Art Pepper was on the turntable and cigar smoke filled the living room when she and Michael entered.

"Didn't know if you guys wanted dinner."

Hannah looked at her phone. "I'm going to turn in. I know it's only past five in California, but I'm tired."

Her father cocked his head and looked at her sideways for a long moment. "Your mom was really tired during the beginning of her pregnancy. I swear she slept about fifteen hours a day. Freja beat the cat, hands down, for most sleep a mammal could get."

She leaned down to kiss her father's perennially rough cheek. Even with the gray stubble, it was so much softer than it had been when she was a child. "Good night, Daddy." She'd leave Michael to him.

Hannah took the bags and carried them all to her top floor room. Her father still used the bigger third floor bedroom as a studio. Michael could either get a hotel room or maybe her dad would let him sleep in the maid's room. Either way, it wasn't her concern anymore.

Her phone rang. The 530 area code was unfamiliar.

"Hello?" Hannah said uncertainly.

"Abbe Santos." Ben's sister. Hannah's hesitation came through on a gasp. "I'm not mad at you or anything," Abbe said. There was one person in California still speaking to her. "I hear you're in New York."

"Ben mentioned it?" She felt like a giddy thirteen-year-old crushing on a guy. Too bad her biggest worry wasn't whether he'd go to the dance with her.

"He asked me where the 718 area code was."

"Do you think—?"

"Will he come around? Hannah, I don't have a fucking clue. He's currently doing the Ted Kaczynski disappearing act again. It took him two years to emerge the last time. I don't think he has the luxury of time now. But I'm not in control."

"Is he okay?"

"Other than fucking devastated, hollowed out and raw, he seems fine."

"What should I do?"

"I don't freakin' know. I was hoping you'd have some ideas. I think he really loves you. That's why he took this so hard."

"Didn't he love his ex, Samara?"

"Not like you. I think that was more about his ego being bruised. She's off to marry some billionaire—no, for real—a genuine Silicon Valley rich guy. That would stick it to any guy worth less than, say, a billion. You're a whole different matter. He proposed to you in front of the whole family. He was really excited about the baby and you guys' future. The whole fucking thing. Sort of like the silver lining on a really bad rain cloud."

"I filed for divorce."

"You should have done that about six months ago."

"Abbe. I've done all the groveling I'm going to do. He hangs up on me. I'm in New York until the eighteenth. After that I'm going to stay with my mother."

"Where's that?"

"Copenhagen."

"As in Denmark. Clogs, and tulips and shit."

"Clogs, yes. Tulips, no. I think you're thinking of Holland. But yes, that Denmark. My mother moved back after she divorced my dad."

"Why did she leave your dad?"

"Infidelity, probably."

"Karma, man."

"If you talk to Ben, tell him I love him. I'll try to call him from there. You never did say why you called."

"I don't know. I drove up there to see him in person—to make sure he wasn't going to slit his wrists. I didn't want your dog going all Alive on him. I called to tell you he's messed up. To find out if you're coming to get him. To tell you the dog seems okay. Cody's kind of nice, actually. I don't know. I thought maybe I'd figure out a fix. But I guess it is what it is. Don't give up on Benji, though. Oh, and have a safe trip."

After cutting the tags, repacking her clothes, and taking a shower, Hannah thought she heard a knock at her door. She got up to pull it open, "Daddy–"

It wasn't her father. It was her husband. She stood, barefoot on cold wood.

"Michael–" She pushed the door toward him.

"Give me one last night." He pushed back.

Hannah pulled open the door and moved her body away from the opening. Michael's thin cotton jersey pajamas would be no match for the cold December night.

He rubbed his hands together after she'd closed the door. "It's a lot warmer up here."

"It's the attic. Always a great place to be in the winter."

Michael walked along the walls, most lined with books on shelves, on the radiator cover, along the back of the bed.

"I forgot that you used to read a lot." Hannah went back to rearranging her clothes. He sat on a chair and thumbed through her collection of coffee table books featuring photographers important on the New York scene. "What changed?"

Hannah put her clothes down and leaned back on the double bed. "A lot changed. Getting married and moving to California was like growing up. Talk about putting away childish things. So, some of this had to go. I had to change. Despite how it may sound, I don't blame you for everything. I made some bad choices. I didn't stand up for myself. We obviously didn't communicate," she said, alluding to their lunch conversation.

Michael put down her books, and came to lie on the bed beside her. The large room suddenly seemed smaller and darker. During the day it was lit with skylights—but those same openings seemed to suck the light out of the room now.

He grabbed and held her hand, and they were silent a long time. She had tried so hard to make everything perfect. After she'd married him, she'd stopped being single, stopped feeling desperate. Michael was supposed to be her ticket to a life different from her parents. She'd messed everything up, and nothing could ever be the same with Michael or Ben ever again.

"I really am tired."

He reached over and snapped off the light. "Can we talk like we used to? We used to stay up all night—talking. Do you remember that?"

She did remember, of course. They'd been friends first. But it all seemed like a lifetime ago. They talked when she lived in Brooklyn. They'd talk at his little Manhattan apartment. They talked and laughed in that Silver Lake house that she'd loved. They never talked in Orange County.

"What is it like being pregnant?"

"It's not much different from not being pregnant. I'm a little tired, and my clothes don't fit." She patted her expanding waistline. "I imagine that part will only get worse. The tiredness should go away soon."

"You're still beautiful."

"Michael, you don't have to say that."

"I never thought you were exotic. I don't know why you said that, today. That hurt."

"I know that." She did. Michael was not racist. "Maybe it's because of how your parents act."

"They're another generation, Hannah. I'm sorry that they behave shitty at times, but they do mean well. I don't think they harbor any ill will toward you. They grew up with people who only looked like them. The only black, Latino or Asian people they see are on TV or at the grocery store or whatever. I think they're uncomfortable around you. They don't know what to say or how to act."

"I'm a human being."

"I'm sorry."

"You never stuck up for me."

"I feel like I've messed this up three ways to Sunday."

They were quiet for a long time. She went to the bathroom and brushed her teeth, and dressed in a sleep shirt. She got under the covers. Michael was already under the covers, in nothing more than his boxers.

She turned, ready to sleep. Michael had other ideas. He started stroking her hair and her arm, bare from the biceps down. It raised goose bumps on her arm. She turned to face him, arms outstretched in protest.

"Michael—"

He silenced her with the press of his lips to hers. That was all the answer that she was going to get. Hannah wanted to push him away, tell him it was all wrong, but guilt kept her hands pinned to her sides. Hannah tried not to focus on that kiss. She'd never liked the way he'd kissed her, as if it were something to get over with before getting to the good stuff. Michael threaded his hands into her hair. He placed his lips everywhere, her eyelids, nose, cheeks, chin. He licked the shell of her ear, sucking her lobe into his mouth and biting it, gently. When he pulled the duvet down, she shivered at the night air. Michael mistook that for a reaction to what he was doing.

His hand was under her shirt, rubbing her back. The hand moved, sliding between her underwear elastic, and cupped her butt in his hand. He stopped kissing her.

"I miss this, Hannah. I miss you. We can do this, us, again. I don't care if the baby isn't mine. I'd raise it like my own."

"Michael—"

"We could come back to New York."

"Please—"

He pulled her shirt over her head, and her panties off. She could tell Michael was trying to hold himself back. He took one nipple, then the other in his mouth. Betrayal was her middle name. She tried to hold back, but it felt good what Michael was doing. A moan escaped.

"Oh, God, you turn me on so much," he said through clenched teeth.

Michael did something he never did. He kept his underwear on. He rolled her onto her belly, and gently massaged her shoulders, her arms, her back. The tension of living so many months with indecision eased. "Turn over." She did. He sat astride her, his knees on either side of her hips. She closed her eyes so as not to witness her duplicity. He massaged her neck, her breasts, touching everywhere except her most sensitive center. Involuntarily, her back arched, and Michael finally touched her there.

She made no move to touch Michael's erection pressing against her insistently. Michael did something he never did. He parted her legs and kissed her softly, lovingly. She held her breath, curled her toes, tried to hold off the ripples of pleasure radiating out. When Michael squeezed one nipple, then the other, she couldn't hold back any longer. She bit her lip to keep in her cries, but she could feel the pulse of her orgasm nonetheless. She knew Michael could feel it too. He didn't say a word as he shucked his own clothes. He reached back in his pocket for something. Hanna heard the distinctive rip of a condom wrapper. God, was this her life? Her husband didn't want to have sex with someone who could be carrying some kind of disease. "Michael, if you need that. Maybe..."

"Shh. It's not what you think." Then he entered her. Hannah steeled herself for the usual two or three strokes before he grunted his satisfaction. She tried not to let the pleasure build for a second time because it would never be fulfilled.

"Michael?" she said breathlessly, questioningly. The coil was turning, tighter, tighter. It wasn't long before the dam broke, and she came a second time. Michael finally came with his own hoarse shout of satisfaction.

"Shit. I hope Shay didn't hear. I don't want to have to explain this over breakfast."

Michael silently padded to the bathroom without a word. He came back and handed her the shirt she'd discarded earlier. He put on his own pajamas and laid down next to her, pulling up the duvet.

"What? Why?"

"The condom is called 'delayed pleasure' or something stupid like that."

"What does it do?"

"I think you saw what it does."

"Oh."

"Hannah, I'm not a complete moron. I hear you. I get it. This started out all wrong, but I think we can make it work. I think we proved it could work between us in bed. If we can fix this, we can fix the rest."

"But what about the baby, Michael? Could it be yours?"

He let out a long, defeated breath. "No, there's only the most minute possibility that the baby is mine."

"So our—no, your—test wasn't one of the botched ones?"

"No. What I told you in September still stands. I'm infertile."

"Why couldn't you tell me that earlier?"

"I wanted the baby to be mine, Hannah. It's what we wanted. It's what we were trying for. If you'd gotten pregnant six months earlier, you would have never gone north. You'd have never met *him*. You'd have loved *me*, stayed with *me*."

It was true. Maybe her dissatisfaction wouldn't have shown up. Maybe it would, but in a year, or five years. With a toddler or grade-schooler in the mix, it would have been long past the point of no return.

Hannah swore softly to herself. She hadn't thought about Ben in hours. She'd had sex with her husband and she felt as guilty as sin.

16

Hannah popped one of the K-Cups into her father's coffee maker. Four minutes later, she was working on her caffeine high. She could give up alcohol for nine months, but she didn't know about coffee.

Layered in flannel, her father made his own coffee and joined her at the dining room table.

"I hope you know what you're doing."

The sandstone and brick house had been built in the mid nineteenth century. Surely he couldn't have heard anything. Hannah couldn't remember the last time she blushed. Heat and mortification spread up her arms, and down her face and neck like bad hives. She did not want to talk about sex with her dad. She hadn't wanted to do it at fifteen and she certainly didn't want to do it now.

Play it cool, Hannah. "I'm still going to Copenhagen," she said neutrally.

"How does Michael feel about that?" She shrugged. "How does that Ben guy feel about it?" Her left shoulder lifted and fell.

"What are you doing, Hannah? I love you, honey. Don't get me wrong. But you're pregnant. You have no house, no job, and no plans. I know you're not sixteen, but it still smells like a disaster waiting to happen."

She wasn't going to cry. She wasn't. Why did her dad have do this? She'd been reduced from thirty-seven to seventeen in less than ten seconds. "Look, you know I'll help you out. You can stay here, or at Water Street." He'd bought an apartment for her in her twenties. It was leased to tenants now. The stairs creaked. Michael was coming down. "I want you to seriously consider this. It's not just you anymore."

Hannah tried not to pull back when Michael leaned in to kiss her full on the lips. "Good morning. That coffee looks good."

Her father pointed to the kitchen. "It's in there."

Michael disappeared into the galley kitchen and was back ten seconds later. "Where's the pot?"

"It's a K cup," her dad said. Michael looked perplexed. "Hannah, can you?" Michael asked. He always asked. She'd always complied.

Her father tried to hide the look of disgust on his face. "I'll do it."

Like a good host, Shay came back with coffee, milk, and sugar on a small tray. Without her mother, he'd become quite domesticated. He didn't sit down again. Instead he belted his robe, gathered his cup, and said, "I've got a rehearsal today." He looked directly at Hannah. "You need to think about what I said. Especially if I have to serve notice." The stairs creaked again, this time as her father shuffled up.

"Serve notice on who?"

"The Water Street apartment."

"Your dad still owns that? I thought he was planning to sell when we moved to California."

"He didn't. Got a firm to manage it. He offered it back to me this morning."

"Did you tell him we're thinking of getting back together?" Michael leaned in to kiss her. She turned her head this time.

"I never said–"

"Were you throwing me a bone last night?"

She could not get this right to save her life. Someone was always angry at her. "I'm human, Michael, if you press my buttons, you're going to get a response."

"Were you turned on at all last night?"

Hannah had never been a diplomat. She didn't work at the United Nations for a reason. A lack of tact was her distinct weakness. She dodged. She feinted. She'd already declared herself before God, their families and all their friends. Why wasn't that enough?

"What do you want me to say?"

"What do I want? I want you to say, Michael you're a god." He quirked his mouth in an odd half-smile. "You could try: I love you. Let's have the family that we've always planned."

"And when the child comes out with curly dark hair, or blue gray eyes, what then?"

"Then we love him or her like a child should be loved." He paused for a long moment, looking at her critically. "I looked in the mirror this morning. I'm not exactly the hunchback of Notre Dame. Are you even attracted to me? Have you ever been?"

She had promised Ben, she'd never lie to him. Maybe she should extend that to everyone. Maybe it would be her new year's resolution. January was too long to wait. She'd start now.

"You're a wonderful guy, Michael." For someone else.

He sat back, crossing his arms across his chest, face as closed off as his posture. "Stop spinning me, Hannah. Can you answer this one question?"

"Any woman would be happy to—"

"But not you, right?" He jabbed an angry finger in her direction. "What about you, Hannah? I'm not asking you about all the women in California or even the available women in the tri-state area. Bottom line it for me. The woman I love, the woman I'm married to doesn't want me."

She ducked her head. If she said that one little three letter word: yes, all could be okay again. They could fly off into the sunset in New York or California. He could be a dad to their one child. She could pursue music and photography. But what would happen when the baby grew up and moved out? Would she be back in the same place, only in her mid-fifties? She did not want to live without exploring the possibility of happiness. She looked into his blue, blue eyes, decision made.

"No."

"No what, Hannah?"

"Please don't make me say this, Michael," she whispered. She could feel the trickle of tears running down her cheeks. His eyes watered in response to hers. He shook his head, imploring her. "Say it, Hannah."

"I think I want a divorce."

"Think?"

She took a deep breath. "I want a divorce, Michael Keesling." Her voice didn't quaver. "I don't want to be married to you anymore."

"Now I feel like shit." He turned away, hiding the hurt she knew would be in his eyes. "Are you sure? This is the last time I'm going to ask. If I walk out this door today, I'm not coming back."

In one month, two men had turned their back on her. Hannah's stomach clenched. She was giving up something that had been good enough for years, for the unknown. Ben may never take her back. She may raise her baby alone, and die alone like one of her spinster 'aunties.' Resolving not to regret what she said, she spoke. "I'm sure, Michael. I want love, not obligation, not possession. You have never been able to give that to me. Last night didn't change that."

Michael's blue eyes grew as cold as the winter sky outside. Where there'd been warmth, there was now distance. He stood and walked upstairs. Maybe five, maybe fifty minutes later, he came back down dressed, overnight bag in hand.

He placed his cool lips against her cheek. The kiss felt like a slap.

"Where will you go? Do you have a flight booked? You can stay here instead of JFK or something. I'm sure it would be okay with Shay," Hannah said, trying to fix the one problem she could.

Michael was silent. He shook his head. "This is goodbye, Hannah."

He showed himself out the front door. It slammed, the heavy wood crashing against the brass. In one fell swoop, she'd lost her husband and everything that she'd worked toward over the last years, forever.

17

"You didn't have to make the trek," Hannah said to her dad.

"It's only Newark. I've got some music," Shay said, gesturing to the iPod in his pocket and oversized noise-canceling headphones hanging around his neck. "It'll be fine."

Hannah tried not to cry. She was not the crying type, but her emotions were on overload. Gesturing to her bags, she said, "Well, the days of seeing me to the gate are over, so we should say goodbye now. That security line looks seriously long."

"Hannah Banana," her dad said, enfolding her in his arms. With those two little words, the tears came in earnest. He hadn't used that term of endearment in years. Twice in the same week was her undoing.

"I'm sorry to cry on your coat," Hannah said, pulling back. The salt tinged tears left tiny dark brown spots on her father's leather jacket.

"Stop apologizing, honey. Call me when you get there. Tell your mother I said hello."

"Okay, Daddy."

The seven-hour flight was uneventful. Unable to take the sleeping pills Hannah favored for transatlantic travel, she dozed fitfully. Her heart twisted with guilt whenever she thought of those last moments with Michael at her dad's dining room table. Whatever his flaws, he was a fundamentally good man. And she'd been careless with his affections. Utterly careless.

Hannah realized she'd probably used the fact that he loved her to get what she thought she wanted. And when she didn't want him anymore, she'd casted him aside. She shifted in the uncomfortably hard airline seat. It wasn't that she hadn't loved Michael. It was that going from friends to lovers had been the biggest mistake of her life. She'd lost her friend years ago. That hurt more than losing her marriage.

Every single person spoke to her in English, and she replied to every single person in Danish. It was always this way. Even with the immigration of non Scandinavians to Denmark, people never assumed she could be Danish. There were so many people who looked like her mom, and spoke the first language she remembered hearing, that she felt like she was coming home. But her skin color and curly hair always caused people to treat her like an 'other.' Hannah couldn't remember how many conversations she had with waiters, or shop owners explaining her origins after she spoke to them in their shared native tongue.

After she cleared customs, Mor and Axel were waiting for her. Freja was still intimidatingly tall, blond-haired, blue-eyed and slender. Her shape was the mirror image of Hannah's. It was like looking in the mirror at a paler, blonder, older version of herself. Up close, Hannah could see gray hairs mixing in with the blond. There weren't many people at the airport that early in the morning, and most of the kiosks and shops were closed. The wood floors and baffled ceilings muted whatever noise remained from the tired travelers. Mercifully, the train ride to her mother's flat was short.

Orange. Sometimes it felt like everything in Copenhagen was orange. The walls of her mother's living room, the slim Scandinavian chairs, the colors in the framed prints on the walls. The apartment was small by American standards, but her mother and Axel had made it cozy after almost a decade.

Axel put her bags in the small second bedroom, which was mercifully not orange, although the candy floss pink wasn't much better. Her mom pulled out her trusty kettle to make them tea.

Although Hannah's mother spoke to her in Danish, upon Axel's entrance in the kitchen, she reverted to English. Like most Danes, he was fairly fluent, but she hoped the nuance went over his head. He was okay. He loved her mother, but they'd never gotten close in the last ten years. As selfish as it seemed at thirty-seven, she wanted her mom all to herself. She was relieved when he announced that he was going to work.

"So you've closed the door on Michael," her mom said after Hannah told her about her time in New York.

"It was the right thing to do. He may be upset now, but hopefully he can find the right woman for him."

Her mother's disdain for the decision was written all over her face. "This was a big mistake you will regret, Hannah."

"I think I'll regret not trying to work things out with Ben more."

"And what do you know about Ben? You knew him for hat, a month or two. And you're giving up all the years you knew Michael. He loved you, married you, and even said he'd stay with you if the baby wasn't his. Where is Ben? Shut away somewhere in the wilderness of California? You're here, pregnant and alone, and he has not been man enough, loved you enough to be with you?"

She felt like a whiny teenager, but said it anyway. "But I love him, Mor."

Her mother shrugged derisively. "I loved your father. All that love and passion and good sex is not enough." Hannah shook her head, and drank more tea. She did not want to think of her mother and father having sex. "Oh Hannah, grow up. You are old enough to deal with this."

Hannah was getting angry. "Neither you or Daddy were ever fans of Michael. I never saw two more morose people than the two of you at my wedding. But now you're both acting like I killed a puppy in cold blood now that I've left him."

"Your dad and I probably weren't fair. We're both artists and it seemed odd for you to be marrying this banker, with all his designer clothes, and little luxuries. He seemed so vain, and to always be distracted by work. It was rude, I thought, for him to be tapping away on that phone every time the three or four of us had a meal. But from what you've said over the years, my position softened. Maybe your father has as well. No matter how flaky or flighty you've been about your careers, he's always supported you. You've always had a nice place to live, a nice car. And now I know he was willing to take you back after you cheated on him and got pregnant with someone else's baby."

"If you want frankness, then I'll give you frankness. Michael was terrible in bed. And I'm tired of shitty sex. It's only ever been good with two people—"

"Lucas and Ben," her mother finished.

"How did you—"

"I have known you your whole life, Hannah. So the sex was good with them? Yes?"

Even with her mother in the room, Hannah felt a shiver from her belly to her sex.

"Yes, very good."

"I am saying. It's not all there is. The sex was very good, passionate, with your father. But he was never around." Hannah resisted the temptation to put her index fingers in her ears and sing 'la, la, la.' She loved her mom and dad equally and didn't want to have to think of them struggling through the same things she did. And even though she knew the facts of life, she never wanted to think of them having sex. "He also had passionate sex with every backup singer in the world. Maybe the sex with Axel is not as passionate, but he's caring, giving..." Freja had been puttering around the kitchen, but stopped in her tracks to jab her finger pointedly on the butcher block table top, "...and most of all he is here, every day and every night. I do not have to wonder."

Hannah lost her breath first. Then her nose started tickling. Tears were around the corner. She tried to keep them in, but she couldn't catch her breath, keep her shoulders from shaking.

"Oh, honey. I'm so sorry. I didn't mean to come down on you." Hannah's soft cries turned into big, noisy, messy, sobs. Freja put down the dishrag, ran to her daughter and knelt by the kitchen chair. She drew Hannah into her arms as she cried. Freja shook her shoulders gently. "What could be so bad?"

"It's not as simple as you make it out to be, Mor. He makes me feel so bad about myself."

"Did he hurt you, honey? Tell me."

Hannah took the deepest breath she could and coughed. "He needs other women to have sex with me." The look of shock on her mother's face was enough to start the tears leaking again.

"What are you saying?"

Despite the mortification washing over her in wave after cresting wave, she told her mother about her husband's need to look at other women while she pleasured him. The way he treated her like an object to be possessed, not a woman to be loved. Freja's swift intake of breath was full of condemnation.

"I never knew. I thought we shared everything."

"I didn't want you to hate him any more than you already did. I'd chosen him. I had to live with it."

"You didn't have to live with it. You never did. Daddy and I have always been here. Why did you stay so long? How could you have thought of having a baby if things were like this?"

"Where would I go?"

"But you're a smart, talented, and beautiful woman."

"You're biased."

"Honey, there are plenty of men who will love you the way you are."

Hannah threw up her hands in surrender. "Who? Where are they? They all leave me, Mom. Lucas left. Ben left. Every single one in between walked out on me. Michael may have had his flaws. But I knew he would never leave me."

Her mother held her hand for a long time, finally squeezing it and standing up. She picked up the dishrag, wrung it out, and laid it over the chipped porcelain sink.

"So tell me why is Ben so wonderful? Why are you willing to give up everything for a chance with him?"

"He's ethical. He loves his family. He loves animals."

"What do you mean by ethical?"

"He has a strict moral code that he lives by."

"Such as?"

"He doesn't believe in casual sex. Despite the societal pressure to date as many women as a guy can, he doesn't do it."

"Go on."

"He doesn't tell lies. He has always been truthful, in his feelings about his ex-wife, in his feelings about his father's infidelity, in his feelings about me."

Hannah felt the prick of tears in the corners of her eyes, again. It had to be the hormones. She hadn't cried as much in her life as she had in the last three months. "When he found out I was pregnant, he didn't waver, didn't hesitate. He asked me to marry him in front of all his family and friends. Once he does something, he throws his full heart into it."

"That seems the opposite of you, right now."

That hurt. She wasn't this dishonest, deceitful person. She had handled the whole breakup with Michael badly. It would probably always be her greatest regret. "But he makes me want to be better. Being with him made me want to commit to my art once and for all. I wanted to commit to him. I don't ever see myself wanting to leave him."

"If you knew all this about him, why could you not wait? You should have put Michael behind you and then pursued a relationship with him. He might have respected you for that honesty."

"I know it was impulsive. But he was what I needed."

Her mother was silent for a long time, seeming to consider all that Hannah had said. "Maybe you have that something extra that Shay and I didn't have. Maybe I am wrong and it is something worth saving. But it seems that you have really botched it up. How are you going to fix it?"

The tears leaked from her tired eyes and ran down her cheeks again. She was so tired, from jet lag, from early pregnancy, from going through the emotional wringer.

"I don't know, Mor. But I'm going to try."

18

Ben Cooper was no neophyte. But once he'd ditched his cell phone, everyone had treated him like he was in the dark ages. The clinic was nearly empty save for Ben, a few pets in surgical recovery, and the overnight technician. He turned to the computer, hating himself for what he was about to do. But it was time to delve into the University of Google. Shaking the mouse to awaken the computer, Ben opened the browser and started to type in the omnibox.

Samara Gold, who'd dumped his last name like a sack of garbage, was first. She really was marrying a half-billionaire. From her Facebook updates—he couldn't believe people made their lives public—he saw her engagement photos. He couldn't quite work out what had happened to the guy she'd left him for, but figured he'd been cast aside when a richer model came along. Ben looked down at his hands. They were still. All the anger and hostility were gone. Finally. He didn't know when they'd left, but he didn't feel any of the bitterness that had been eating at him for the last two years.

He scrolled down the page for a little while. There was Samara's life for all to see. Clicking the back button a few times, Ben got out before he went any further down that rabbit hole. Didn't people value their privacy? Relationships were in the past because that's where they belonged. He couldn't imagine connecting with old high school friends on Facebook. He didn't know how Abbe did it. The last thing he wanted were inquiries about his look-alike half-brother, the bastard child of his father. His shame had bounds, and he liked to keep it under wraps.

He started typing again...Hannah. He had to stop because his hands did start shaking this time. He banged his fist on the computer keyboard in frustration. Why her? He should have followed his instincts and skipped dinner that first night. She wouldn't have starved to death.

Ben leaned back in his office chair and closed his eyes. He still wanted her. How fucking stupid was he? He still wanted her. But she'd lied to him, big time. All those years he'd looked at his mother and considered her weak and stupid. And he was no different. Was the baby even his? If they got back together, and that was a big IF, would he be willing to raise someone else's kid? Did he want to see Michael weekend after weekend for the next eighteen years?

He finished typing her name in the box, and clicked search. A few real estate listings popped up. But there was nothing older. It was as if she'd appeared on the web a few years ago. Then he remembered, her *other* name. He typed Hannah Morrison in this time. Bingo. She had a website. Two websites. He had no idea. He clicked on the first. It was a virtual photo gallery. Ben clicked through some of the photos. There were actors and people he guessed were celebrities. On a personal snapshot page there were even pictures of the Lost Coast and Cody. He looked down at the dog snoozing at his feet. Even the dog was online.

He went back to the search results. She had a Wikipedia entry. Did everyone? Geez. His heart started when he saw the picture of her on the right side of the page. It was grainy, and out of focus, but it was Hannah. She was singing in some nightclub, from what he could tell. She was the daughter of famous musician/songwriter/band leader Shay Morrison and singer/songwriter Freja Lauritsen.

He knew that, or most of it, at least. It said she'd been a regular in various cafes in Los Angeles, and that she was an active songwriter. He looked down at her discography, surprised that she'd co-written a very popular song with her father. A pop song he'd heard on the radio a million times. He'd proposed marriage to someone he knew nothing about.

This Hannah online seemed so distant from the Hannah he'd known here. He clicked on a link to another 'official' site. There she was, a more professional portrait this time. Her beauty hit him like a punch in the gut. There was a link to music, and he hit the play button. Nothing. He looked around his desk and turned on the speakers he never used. Her husky voice hit him full on. She was singing a bluesy song about being done wrong by a guy.

He closed the website with a swift click on the 'x.'

Marty Wexler was next. It looked like he'd been the one to follow most closely in their father's footsteps. He was an associate professor of engineering at Sacramento State. He clicked on the link next to Marty's name and was rewarded with a picture of a man who looked a lot like him. Damn his father for messing up the family dynamic. Why could no one keep it in his pants?

He clicked in the search box again, and jabbed in his request. Of course, the *New York Times* would have a long article on rates of infidelity in the U.S. It was the first result. All the studies referenced confirmed his continued naïveté. Everybody was cheating. Men, women, young, old, with children, and without. Of course, there were no studies on whether cheaters continued to cheat. He'd never asked his mom if his dad had cheated again. He couldn't imagine she'd put up with it a second time.

Ben nudged Cody. It was time to go home. Nothing was to be gained from this. Nothing. Before he shut off the computer, he e-mailed the woman who filled in for him. If he timed it right, he could go home, pack, and be in Davis in the morning.

It was nine o'clock at night in California. Hannah's hand trembled on the phone. She had to press the long string of numbers three times before she got it right.

He answered, the deep voice she loved sounding bone weary. "Hello."

"Ben, it's Hannah. Please don't hang up." When the connection held, she continued, "I'm so sorry. That's all I wanted to say. I'm sorry, and I love you." Those were the only words she got to say before he hung up the phone. A lump the size of Texas formed in her throat at the sound of the line going dead.

"I thought you'd be down here sooner or later," Elaine said. She sat a mug of coffee and a dried pear and cardamom scone before him on the kitchen table. He stared down at a burn mark he'd made about thirty years ago when he'd dropped a lit match on the table. His mother had ended his firebug tendencies that day.

"I wanted to see how you're doing. And I thought I'd check up on Dad when I knew he wouldn't be home. You haven't said much about his heart since those couple of days you spent at my house."

"Your dad's fine. You know that." She sipped at her own coffee, looking out the window. "You want to know why I stayed with him." He was glad she'd taken the lead. After his and Abbe's discovery, he had never talked to his mother about this, ever. It was the elephant who'd stomped around and moved into his parents' living room. It was true that elephants lived long lives with excellent memories. She looked past him through the window again. "It's complicated."

Of course it was complicated. He'd discovered that for himself. The rational, thinking, well-educated part of him couldn't even fathom taking Hannah back. His heart and lizard brain wanted her near him, no matter the emotional cost. His mom abruptly stood up, sloshing his coffee. "Come here," she said. He hadn't touched his scone yet.

She led him to the dining room and motioned for him to sit. From the bottom of the china cabinet, she pulled out one thick photo album.

He stopped her. "Ma, I've seen the photo albums before."

She shushed him, pulled up one of creaky wood chairs right next to his, and started flipping the pages. For about fifteen minutes, his mom turned the yellowed plastic leaves, and he looked at pictures of himself and Abbe—with new bicycles, with missing front teeth, in tacky party hats. Sometimes his father was there with a book in hand, often working at his desk with one or the other of them playing on the floor. His mother was hardly in any of the pictures.

"Where are you?"

"I was taking the pictures, Benji." Ben suddenly flashed forward. One day his mother would be dead and there would be few pictures of her. He'd been so angry with her on and off for years, but she'd always been there.

"What is it you want me to see, Ma?" he asked, resigned to the lesson she was drawing out.

"The two of you look happy. Your world was ordered and stable. I never wanted to take that away from you." She took an envelope from the back of the book—the kind that contained negatives. Instead of old color reverse film, she pulled out a single photo. He knew who it was the instant he looked at the eyes. Marty. "What do you *see*?"

"That's Marty, right?" The boy looked to be about eight years old in the picture.

"Yes, that's him. But what do you see?"

Ben studied the picture. It was Marty, with a seventies bowl haircut, wearing too-short cut-offs, and a short sleeved plaid shirt.

"He doesn't look like they had much money."

"That's true. Look again."

Ben picked the small square picture up in his large hand. Under all that hair, Marty wasn't smiling. A new train and some other shiny toy was next to him, but he still looked sad. "Oh," he nodded in understanding.

"He was the saddest little boy. Not all the time, I think. But he didn't look happy. I never wanted to see a face like his on you or your sister. That's why I stayed."

"But how could you trust Dad after what he did? Did you ever worry that he was going to leave you for..." He couldn't say the name in front of his mother. "...her?"

"He promised. And I believed him. I think he realized he'd made a big mistake. I don't think he ever did it again." She paused a long time. "It wasn't like it is now. I didn't grow up in a time where people divorced at the drop of a hat. Your dad made a mistake—a very big one—but I loved him, and I loved you, and I was willing to work to make it better."

"Was it better?"

"You're not really asking about me. You're asking about Hannah," she said matter-of-factly.

He put the picture back in the envelope, closed the album, and leaned back. "I still love her."

"Of course you do. Betrayal doesn't erase the love."

"She has a husband."

"She won't have him for very much longer, I expect."

"I'm not sure I'm the father of her baby."

His mom sighed. "Look, Ben, if you take her back—you're going to have to take the whole package. That child she's carrying did not ask to be born. And he or she certainly didn't ask to be born in these particular circumstances. Who would? But the child is innocent. That's what I've been trying to get you to understand about Marty. I want you to get something I didn't understand until it was too late. The reason you and your sister don't know Marty is because I shut him out of our lives. I didn't want someone else's baby interfering with what we had here. I didn't want a reminder that your father might have loved someone else. But that wasn't fair. You and Abbe wouldn't have been any less loved if he'd been in our lives. And now, your dad and I are scrambling to make up for lost time. But it'll never be the same for me, or you, or Marty. I wouldn't ever want that baby of Hannah's to think it was somehow second class."

"You'd accept it even if it were her husband's?"

"Not it. He or she. There's a little person coming into this world." She smoothed back his unruly hair like she'd done so many times when he was a child. "To answer your questions, Ben: unequivocally, yes. If that's what you decide. That child would be my grandbaby like Abbe's kids." She stood and tucked the album away. "I think you need to talk to your father."

Ben's jaw clenched. "About what?"

"About this. You need to forgive him. I think it would go a long way to helping you work out what you're going to do about that woman you love."

He tried not to grind his teeth. "I've got to go, Ma."

"Go where? Aren't you staying here overnight? You're not going to make that long drive back without even eating something."

Ben cast away the years of etiquette his mom had drilled in his head and walked out the door. He needed to leave before his head exploded.

"Making the rounds?" Abbe said when he showed up unannounced several hours later.

"Turns out that you can't really stop by people's houses with such short notice at my age. Too many small kids in the schedule."

"And I'm the exception?"

"Abbe," he pushed his way past his sister, dropped his coat on a chair, and made himself comfortable in her small living room. Ben pointed to the cold hearth. "Do you ever light this?"

His sister ignored him. "She's in Copenhagen."

"Denmark?"

"Yup."

"How in the hell do you know that?"

"I called her."

"You have her number?"

"Why are you really here?"

Ben rubbed his face, his tired eyes, his roughened jaw. When had he last shaved? "How did you forgive him?"

"Isaiah!" Abbe yelled. Ben heard a faint response from the back of the house where it sounded like her husband was bathing the kids. "I'm going to get drunk tonight. So you're in charge." Her husband shouted his acquiescence without so much as a protest. But then, who would buck Abbe? Suddenly he felt very sorry for Isaiah.

"What's your poison?" When Ben started to speak, she put a hand on his arm. "Don't say wine. That shit will take forever. I mean real liquor."

Ben didn't drink spirits for a reason. He needed to keep his head clear, in case of emergency. He'd also suffered through one hangover too many after his divorce. Hangovers at sixteen were an inconvenience. Hangovers at forty were deadly. "Bourbon, neat." To hell with it. He'd be Abbe's problem tomorrow.

Abbe and Isaiah had a little room between their kitchen and living room that held all the junk that belonged nowhere.

An abandoned foosball table stood collecting dust in one corner. Ben brushed a stack of bills aside and sat in an old office chair. Abbe camped out on a beanbag. Where in the hell had she gotten that?

"You need to forgive him."

Ben shook his head and took a big sip of his drink. "Why is everyone saying that? You all sound like experts in pop psychology. I expected more from a real psychologist. What's with all this forgiveness?"

"Oh, fuck. I *am* going to sound like an episode of Dr. Phil. Look, forgiving him will make you feel better. You should forgive Samara too."

"Maybe I should forgive Osama Bin Laden too, right?"

"Ben. What I mean, I think, is that you have to make peace with what our dad did. It was purely *his* fault, not Marty's, not ours. For the other things, I think you need to forgive yourself."

"Forgive myself? I've never ever done anything wrong."

"Well, Mr. Holier Than Thou, you've been beating yourself up for Samara for years. I know you wonder why you weren't enough for her. You got the big house, the big practice, all of that overpriced shit and she left you anyway. I know you're really beating yourself up about Hannah, too. If you'll excuse my butting in, I don't think it's the same mistake."

Ben finished the first bourbon, and helped himself to another. He added an ice cube this second time around. "Tell me what's wrong with me."

"I'm not sure why you married Samara. But you picked a trophy wife. You're a great guy, but I think you've always felt inadequate. Maybe because of what Daddy did." Abbe shrugged. "I think she filled the gaps you thought you had. She wanted more. She always needed more attention, more money or more stuff to fill whatever her hole is."

"I think she's got it now."

"Daddy's the hard one, you know."

"Mom said she regrets not having Marty in our lives."

"It's probably mean to say this, but that's her shit. I'm fine not having grown up with Marty." He let her kissing up to their dad slide for the moment.

"Mom showed me some pictures this morning. The kid looked really sad."

"Then maybe his parents should have thought of that before they got into bed together."

"You don't sound like you've forgiven dad."

"I have, Ben." Abbe closed her eyes. "Do you remember me going into therapy when I was in school?" He did. She'd said at the time it was a requirement before she could get her Ph.D. in clinical psychology. "I hashed all of this out then. I couldn't let the rest of my life be defined by choices I had no part of. He did a shitty thing. A really shitty thing, to Mom, to Minnie, to Marty, and to us, too. But I love our father. And I have forgiven him. That doesn't mean he wasn't a big ol' asshat for twenty years. Not to sound like Oprah and Dr. Phil all rolled up into one, but I've put aside the resentment. It's done. There's no going back. My childhood was fine. My life is fine. And I'm really grateful to them for that. I've watched the news. All this could be a whole lot worse. I have a messy house, crazy kids, and not enough sleep, but these are first world problems. They paid for my education. I'm not scratching out a living from the dirt. I think you need to get over yourself and choose to be happy." Abbe grimaced at the trite saying. "Sorry."

Ben finished his second bourbon. "I'm canceling your satellite TV and magazine subscriptions."

"Damn, I sound all full of pop culture aphorisms, don't I?" Ben nodded. "It's going to be a bitch going back to work. The clients aren't going to take me seriously."

When he was safely back in his hideaway, his home, the phone rang once. He snatched it up without thinking.

"Ben, it's Hannah. Please don't hang up. It's Christmas today. I'm in Copenhagen with my mom. I promise I'll never lie to you again." He hung up. She didn't even know that he'd never celebrated Christmas.

"Jesus, Dad, what are you doing here?" Ben shouldn't have been surprised when his dad pulled up to his garage the Saturday after Christmas. His mother and sister had probably harassed and harangued Walter into making the long drive.

"That's a fine welcome," his dad said grumpily, snapping off the radio and stepping out onto the gravel.

"Where's Mom? Did you drive up here all by yourself?"

"I'm not planning on dying anytime soon, Ben."

Ben gestured vaguely. "I'm taking care of your house. You could have called if you needed to check up on it."

"That's not why I'm here. I drove all this way because you've avoided talking to me."

"What do you mean? I'm talking to you right now."

"You never once asked me for advice about Hannah."

Ben could feel his jaw working. Tension shot straight from his shoulders up the back of his skull. He could tell he was going to have one hell of a headache in a few hours. He needed to head that off. Without a word to his father, he dropped the garden tools on the floor of the garage. Toeing off his boots, he struggling with the sticky door, upping his frustration. He shoved it open with his flat hand, ignoring the sound of splintering wood. Finally in the house, he went straight for the kitchen sink. One glass of water and two ibuprofen later, he glanced back. Walter had followed him, closing both the garage door and kitchen door with more gentleness than Ben had been able to muster.

He needed to sit down. He picked the couch. Wrong move. The memory of Hannah, wrapped only in a throw, smacked him in the gut. She was the only woman who'd ever been in this house. The only woman he'd ever made love to here. Ben got up and stalked outside to the deck. There was sureness, a consistency out here. The ocean was always moving. The waves always came in and rushed back out. High tide and low were as predictable as the phases of the moon.

His dad walked out, leaning over the deck railing.

"You've got a great view here. This one eighty deck is something else."

"You have the same view."

"Not quite." Walter turned his back against the railing and stared directly at Ben—blue gray eyes meeting blue gray. "I was really surprised when you moved out here."

"You guys did."

"We were looking for somewhere to retire. And after six months out here, your mom and I realized, it was too slow. I'm so glad I listened to her about keeping the house in Davis. But you, Ben. You stayed. I would think it would be hard being a single man living out here like this."

Ben grunted noncommittally.

"I liked Hannah. She has a lot of spunk. Knows how to go after what she wants."

Ben ground his teeth. Two ibuprofen had not been a serious enough prophylactic. "I don't want to talk about Hannah. And I don't want to talk about Hannah with you." He had never discussed women or relationships with his father. He did not want to start now.

"Do you plan to hate me forever?"

Ben was startled by the hurt and resignation in his father's question. "I don't hate you."

Walter pulled up a chair on the opposite side of the table from Ben. He opened his hands in supplication. "Hate may be too strong a word. But we've been no more than ships passing in the night for the last twenty five years. You've been angry with me for so long, it's something I live with."

"I think I have a right—"

"You *had* the right to be angry. I messed up. You win, okay. In the big cosmic game of life, you win. But we need to get past this. *You* need to get past this."

"Why does everyone—"

Walter slammed the side of one hand against the palm of the other. "Because you're not being fair to yourself."

Ben's throat constricted. He hated himself for still feeling this way. "Why did you do it?"

Walter was silent so long, Ben didn't think he was going to answer. "Because I loved her."

"Did you want to leave Mom and marry her?"

"Yes." His father's honesty all these years later, startled him. It hurt that his father had loved someone who was not his mother.

"Why didn't you?" Maybe if he'd left, it wouldn't have been like rubbing salt in an open wound, year after year.

"Because I loved you and Abbe more than I loved Minnie."

"But you loved Minnie more than Mom? If it weren't for us, you would have left Mom."

"It's not that simple—"

"You drove all the way here. If you didn't want to answer this question, you should have stayed home."

"In a different world, I would probably have divorced Elaine and married Minnie."

"Why don't you do it now? Do you still love her?"

"I owe it to your mom to honor our marriage vows."

Damn, his mom was the consolation prize. "Are you joking?"

"No, Benjamin Aaron Cooper. No, I'm not joking. What kind of man would I be to hold on to your mother during her best years? When she was nurturing my children and helping my career, only to abandon her when it's all done. Where would she be then? I don't think in good conscience I could leave an older woman all on her own."

"Do you talk to Minnie?"

"Sometimes."

Jesus. He hadn't expected that. "You don't still... You haven't..."

"She lives in Nashville."

"There are Jews in Tennessee?"

"I have never cheated on your mother again. I made a promise to her. A renewing of vows, I guess, and I've kept to it."

Ben knew the rest wasn't his business. But curiosity ate at him. It was a craving that would finally be satisfied. "How did Mom find out about Minnie and Marty?"

"Before your mom worked—got a job outside the house—I should say, she volunteered a lot. At the temple, at your preschool, with the less fortunate, whatever. Minnie babysat for you guys on occasion. Abbe was only a toddler, and I thought she was oblivious, but I think she might have said to Elaine that she'd seen us kissing. Little children can be unflinchingly honest. Your mom questioned me, and I lied. I didn't know what to say. Here was a woman who'd had my two babies, and there I was fooling around with someone else who made my heart go boom. Then Minnie got pregnant. I think Elaine suspected, but she never asked."

"When did you tell her?"

"After Marty was born, Minnie struggled. Her parents were far away, and I didn't want her to leave and take my son. I had to support her, or she would have gone back to Tennessee. So I told your mother and begged her forgiveness. She relented on the money. At least she was generous in that way. But she refused to have him in our home. She refused to have the two of you meet him. I should have pushed on that. But I was grateful that she was staying with me. It was still the 1970s. She could have divorced me, taken you to New York, and I'd probably have never seen you again."

Ben went into the house and brought back coffee for himself and his dad. He didn't think he'd been unfair to his dad, Walter *had* put their family in jeopardy for selfish reasons, after all. But it was the first time he really saw his dad as another guy with human failings. By now, Ben knew that parents eventually fell off their pedestals for every child. Instead of a gentle descent, his father was knocked off. He hadn't stopped loving him. He'd stopped believing that his father was omnipotent.

"Do you want to talk about Hannah?"

Pain radiated from his shoulders to the back of his skull as his body tensed. His teeth and jaw weren't going to survive this year, much less this lifetime. He shrugged, trying to look

casual. Trying not to look like he'd been hollowed out. "Do
you still love her?"

"God, yes," slipped out of its own volition.

"Do you love her enough to get past the beginnings of your
relationship?"

"So what am I going to tell our child?"

"You'd tell him or her that you saved Hannah's dog. That
is how you met."

"But what if they—?"

"It would be a long time before any child of yours asked
those kinds of questions. A very long time."

"But we found out."

"Don't compare my situation to yours. It's not the same.
Hannah doesn't have any other kids. She has a husband, soon
to be ex, I assume. Maybe one day your kids will know that
Mommy was married before. Nothing more ever needs to be
said."

"But *I'll* know."

"And that's a decision you'll have to make. Whether *you*
can live with that knowledge."

His dad stayed for a couple of days. It was nice. It was as
if all the anger had gone. For the first time in years, he was
able to talk to his dad without a pain pill or a drink. They
took the dog to the beach, on easy hikes his dad could manage.
Three days later, his dad pulled the Camry out of Ben's garage, and pointed it in the direction he needed to go.

"Are you going to be okay on the drive?"

"I'm fine, Benjamin. I'll call as soon as I get home."

He patted his old man on the shoulder, still a little shy with affection. He'd gotten out of the habit of hugs and kisses with his father when he was sixteen. "I'll see you guys, soon, I hope."

"I hope one day you'll come around about Marty."

Ben tensed. It hurt, hearing that name. Not as much as before, but it still hurt. "One thing at a time, Dad. One thing at a time."

19

"Ben, it's Hannah. Please don't hang up."

"How far along are you?"

Hannah's lids dropped briefly, her breath hissing out slowly. Maybe he still cared. "It's week twelve. The baby is supposed to get fingernails, toenails, and vocal chords this week."

"Why are you calling me?"

"It's New Year's Day. I wanted to say Happy New Year and I love you."

He hung up.

"Ben, it's Hannah. Please don't hang up."

"How many men have you slept with?"

"I don't think this is a good idea..." The silence stretched. She pulled the phone away from her ear. The phone light was still lit. The connection held. "Why do you want to know?"

"Answer me, Hannah."

This was math that no woman wanted to do. She quickly counted on her fingers. At least she didn't need to extend the counting to her toes. "Ten."

"Fuck," Ben said on a swift intake of breath.

Hannah laced her voice with all the sarcasm she could muster at six in the morning. "I guess that would be the operative word."

"Did you love any of them?"

"I love you, Ben."

"But who were the others?"

She sighed, but reluctantly began her recitation. "My first was my high school boyfriend. I was fifteen, I think. My college boyfriend Lucas and I were together for three years. You know about Michael. The rest were different guys in the music scene. Or who I met taking pictures. You meet a lot of people in New York."

"You didn't answer my question."

"It's been ten total, including you." Hannah tried, and probably failed, to keep the exasperation out of her voice.

"Not that one. The other. Did you love them?"

Little white lies, and tact, and dishonesty were nice to hide behind. She'd erected a wall of half-truths she'd hid behind for the last five years. All this bald truth was killing her. Who could love her after knowing everything? "No, two. Lucas and you. It was a long road to get from there to here."

"Where is here, Hannah?"

She was tired. The rested feeling she'd had after a good night's sleep was evaporating. "I don't know, Ben. I'm hoping for the best, but planning for the worst."

"What's the worst?"

"That you never forgive me, and I have to raise my baby alone."

"Where would you go?"

"Here where my mom is or New York where my dad is. Either place. It looks like I'm going to need all the help I can get."

Anger flared in her gut at the thought of being alone. She lashed out the only way she knew how. "Have you loved every woman you had sex with?"

"Yes." She should have expected that answer, but it was still a punch in the gut.

Most people weren't one hundred percent honest in their everyday lives, much less their romantic relationships, Hannah thought as she answered every single question Ben slung at her, this one being no easier than the last.

"Have you ever cheated on anyone else?" he asked during one of their brief phone calls.

"Never, Ben."

"Of those nine other relationships—make that eight—you've never cheated before."

"This is why I didn't want to give you a number. It's not at all cheap or sordid. I was monogamous with everyone I was ever with. Except, well you know."

"Have you slept with anyone since you slept with me?"

"Michael, obviously."

"When is the last time you slept with your husband?"

She closed her eyes. She could tell this one little lie. He would never know. She could deny, deny, deny. But if it hadn't worked for a consummate liar like Pinocchio, the truth would probably come out. "Ben, please don't do this."

"Don't do what? Answer me."

"When I was in New York."

"What?" His outrage covered the distance between them faster than the speed of sound. "You couldn't help yourself?"

"Before I came to my mom's house, I was with my dad in New York." Ben was silent, but he hadn't hung up. "Michael showed up on my dad's doorstep."

"He does a lot of that."

"And we went shopping, had dinner, and we talked. He wanted to get back together."

"There's a shocker."

"Sarcasm doesn't suit you. You're not that kind of guy."

"Then you what—fell into his bed?" he asked, ignoring her.

"You did this once. You of all people should know that ending a marriage is complicated."

"I never slept with Samara after I found out she cheated. Never wanted to." That settled it. He was a saint. She was a sinner.

"I don't know what to say that's going to make this okay. It happened." She had no intention of sharing Michael's inadequacies—or his attempts to overcome them. She'd hurt, betrayed, and emasculated that man enough for one lifetime. "We both knew it was the last time."

"Are you sure—this time?"

"I'm sure, Ben. Very sure."

"Good night, Hannah." He hung up.

"Why did you marry Michael?"

"Because I didn't want to die alone."

"Did you..." Ben paused for a long moment. "Do you love him?"

"I love Michael, but I'm not in love with Michael. I never was. It was something we talked about in New York. I met Michael years ago. He was one of a group of friends. After I broke up with somebody, he started pursuing me. All of my friends were married. One of my mom's friends got sick and she said the greatest regret in her life was not having picked one not-so-perfect man to spend her life with. I thought she was right. There are so many women in New York with so many rules, that some perfectly okay guys slip from their grasp. They wake up forty, alone, and regretful. I thought marriage would eliminate all of that seeking, all of that doubt. I made a choice. It took one major life decision out of my hands."

"That seems very calculated."

"It was a calculated effort to make my life what I wanted it to be. Marrying Michael was a safe choice."

"What was so safe about marriage? It's a jump into the abyss."

The truth. The truth. The mantra played in her head. "God, only my mom knows this," Hannah said, lowering her voice, mortification seeping through her veins. "I had my heart broken once." She paused. Her throat closed up. She pulled the phone away from her ear and shook her head angrily. All these years later, it still hurt to think about this, talk about this.

"And?"

"His name was Lucas." The shaking breath she took was long and deep. "Lucas Campbell. He was the first person I ever fell in love with. He...we were together in college. His family didn't really approve of me. He dumped me. Took me two full years to emerge from that hellhole. I never wanted to go back there again."

"But you got married, what, more than ten years later. It doesn't follow that this guy had much of an impact. It was your first heartbreak. We've all had that. We all get over it."

"It's not like it sounds. A few years ago, I got very emotional. I've always made bad decisions with my heart. Instead, I decided to make a very rational decision with my head. I wanted to control my life. If I married Michael, I knew I couldn't be hurt like that again."

"Do you regret it?"

"No," she said, clearing her throat. "Because I learned a very important lesson."

"Which is?"

"I discovered that friendship isn't love. A relationship and a marriage needs romance and passion. Fraternal love isn't enough." He didn't ask the next question. Hannah answered it for him anyway. "Ben, I love you in the second way. The moment I met you, I knew my life was about to change. You aroused that long forgotten passion in me. I want you in my life. I want you in my bed. I want you to be the father of my children. I can't imagine loving anyone else now that I've loved you."

"Good night, Hannah."

She'd put it all on the table. The ball was in his court, now.

Hannah heard the rumblings of her mom and Axel starting their morning routine. With only one bathroom, it would be a while before she got a turn. She pulled her laptop from her bag, a plug converter, and booted up. Switching to English, she typed Lucas Campbell into the search engine. As she scrolled through the results, she realized she hadn't done this in a few years. When Lucas drifted away from their college friends, she used to look him up every six months or so, tracking his movements across the northeast. It had probably been five years since she'd done this, but the internet had evolved too. It only took about five minutes before a picture popped up from a popular professional social networking site. She sat back in the hard plastic chair and looked out at the slate roof of the building next door. She clicked on the picture, and it expanded before her eyes. There he was, Lucas Campbell in all his middle-aged glory. Hannah held a hand to her heart, felt it beating a normal rhythm. Devastation didn't rip through her gut. Only mild curiosity replaced the usual free-fall.

She read his bio, from the bottom up. He'd graduated from Vassar, gone to graduate school at NYU, and worked at a series of jobs in publishing. According to his company's web-site, he was an associate editor at John Wiley, acquiring and editing non-fiction book titles. One of his authors was a Nobel Laureate. That was it. He was another Joe like everyone else. A few more clicks and she found he was still married to Anne Campbell, a woman she knew he'd met in graduate school.

Three more clicks and she found his address, a two bed-room condo in Williamsburg. She clicked back to the begin-ning and looked at the picture again. He was older, heavier, with close-cropped hair and reading glasses. She could see some of the guy she once knew and loved, but this was just another man, another New Yorker she'd once known. How had she let her relationship with this one person control so much of her life? She closed the lid on the laptop. It was a love lost so long ago. She stood and stretched, realizing she needed to relieve the insistent pressure in her bladder. She didn't want to lose the man she loved now. Devastation would tear her inside out this time.

"Ben, please don't—" Some time during the last few weeks, he'd stopped hanging up on her. He was finally listening to her, but he was asking questions as well. Hard questions.

"Why did you leave Michael?" Because Michael didn't love her, he loved the idea of her. Because she was tired of being a trophy. Tired of caring for a man who did not care for her. Because she wanted more. Craved more. Craved Ben.

"Because I felt stifled," she said. "I'd changed everything in my life and I wasn't happy." It was all she felt comfortable saying. He had a way of making what had seemed rational and well thought-out appear foolish in the light of today. But she'd made a mistake, realized it, and tried to fix it. Shouldn't she get extra credit for that?

"You were running away from your own decisions."

"I made a bad decision. I needed time to decide whether to stay or go."

"If you'd gotten pregnant with him, would you have stayed?"

Hannah patted her rapidly swelling body. What woman wouldn't do anything to protect her child? "Probably," left her lips on a weary sigh. How could she prove her loyalty to this man? She would never hurt him again.

"If you hadn't met me, would you have stayed?"

But she hadn't stayed. On her way to Oregon, she'd already made the decision. "No."

"Do you always run away when things aren't going your way?"

"I don't run away."

"You were running away when you met me. You're in Co-penhagen now. Five thousand four hundred miles feels like running away to me." He'd counted the miles.

"Where else would I be?" Her brain flicked through images like a slide projector—through Los Angeles, Newport Beach, New York, Copenhagen.

"Here." Hope bubbled up through her chest. "Good night, Hannah."

"You wrote 'Melancholy Moon?'"

The mention of the song startled her. "You Googled me."

"About time. Don't you think?"

She wanted to share all of her life with him, and owed him an explanation for this glaring omission. "My dad and I co-wrote it when I was a sophomore in high school."

"Hannah, that was the most popular song of 1993. I danced to that ballad at my senior prom. This must have been huge in your life."

But she had spent years downplaying her art. Out of habit, she said, "It only made it to fourteen on the Billboard chart." Of course it had been huge. It had been her third trip to the Grammy awards. The first time she'd been invited in her own right, not as her father's 'date.'

"Who sang it? I would have remembered seeing you."

"Mariah Carey recorded it."

"How in the hell do you sell a song to Mariah Carey?"

"We don't sell songs. The singer performs them."

"How do you get paid?"

"Are you sure you want to hear this? The whole thing is kind of boring."

"I'm listening, Hannah." He *was* listening. He was *listening.*

She didn't want him to hang up. They were building a connection slowly, step by step. She was sure of it. "The record company pays nine cents for every copy of the song sold on an album or CD, or whatever. Then, a producer or promoter pays when the song is performed. Now there's money for downloading on iTunes and other sites, but none of that existed when we were teenagers."

"So if you sell a million albums..."

"Then you get about ninety thousand dollars."

"Jesus. How many sold?"

"I think about ten million copies."

Ben did a quick calculation in his head. "That's almost a million dollars."

"Thereabouts."

"Did your dad give you the money?"

"As a teenager? You've got to be kidding me. I got nothing. It was one thing he and Mor could agree upon. He bought an apartment that we co-own. We also share the royalty payments."

"Mor?" he asked.

"My mom. It's the Danish word for mother."

"Have you sold any other songs?" He was curious, interested. Like in the beginning.

"A few, though nothing as popular as that."

"Like what? Have I heard them?"

Hannah named one or two others he might have heard of.

"Jesus." His voice held incredulity. "Why did you stop writing? You seem to have a knack for it."

"Michael didn't think the music business was compatible with a family."

He hated hearing that name. It twisted his gut almost as much as Marty did. But Hannah's past would never go away. It would always be right there staring him in the face.

"I have to go now, Hannah." He placed the phone back in the cradle.

"When will your divorce from Michael be final?"

"After the baby is born." Ben's sigh carried over North America, the Atlantic, Northern Europe, but she felt almost like his breath was there on her cheek, whooshing past her ear. "You of all people know there's a six month waiting period in California. And my lawyer tells me that no court will grant a divorce to a pregnant woman."

"Is the baby mine?"

"Yes, Ben."

"Has your husband agreed to relinquish parental rights?"

"I haven't talked to Michael since New York."

The hope burgeoning in Hannah's heart bubbled over. "Does that mean you'll take me back? That we can all be one family?"

"I'm not there, Hannah. But you're probably having my baby, and that's not a lifelong commitment I'm willing to share."

"I'll talk to him."

"Goodbye, Hannah."

It was three long days before Michael answered any of her calls.

"What do you want? I thought we'd agreed to talk through lawyers. Are you stalking *me* now?"

"We don't need to spend seven hundred dollars to have this conversation. What I have to ask you is personal."

"Go on."

Her heart sped up, and a sick feeling started low in her belly. She used her spare hand to rub at the sweat on her upper lip. "Will you give up paternal rights?" In the silence, she could hear faint noise in the background. Michael sounded like he was on the patio in their, no his, backyard. "Michael?"

"So this is it, then? Five years, and poof, it's over."

"It's been over for a long time, Michael."

"A couple of months isn't a long time, Hannah."

"I left in September."

"But you didn't tell me you were *leaving*, remember? Excuse me for needing a moment to catch up."

Hannah took a deep breath. This was quickly going to devolve into another argument if she didn't nip it, now. "Are you willing to give up your parental rights before the baby is born? Grady says it'll get us divorced after the six month mark, rather than waiting until July."

"And you can't wait to get me out of your life, can you Hannah?"

"I need to be divorced from you, Michael. We need to stop hurting each other. There's no other way."

"Is he going to step up to the plate? Be a father to your kid, no matter what?"

"I think so."

Hannah Keesling's name and a nine-four-nine number lit up on the little green screen. Cursing himself, Ben picked up before the second ring could finish.

"You're back in California?" he said in lieu of greeting.

"This is Michael Keesling, Hannah's husband." Ben's hand balled up involuntarily, while a similar ball of anger settled into his gut. He looked at his hand and relaxed it. What was he angry about? Michael had probably been as much of a victim as he'd been. Could he blame the guy for going a little nuts when his wife waltzed off? "Are you there?"

He unclenched his jaw to answer. "Yes, I'm here."

"Hannah called me." Ben was silent again. Once Michael realized there wasn't going to be much back and forth, he continued. "She wants me to relinquish any parental rights I may have to her unborn child."

Michael had said her, and not our. "Is the baby yours?"

Long pause. "No. There's really no chance of that. I'm sure Hannah's told you all about that."

A tiny prick of joy burst through Ben. He chastised himself silently for the uncharitable delight he'd briefly taken in another man's tragedy.

"She didn't give me any details."

Michael laughed ruefully. "She's like the blood-brain bar-rier, little passes through. I've loved Hannah a long time, longer than you've known her." His sigh was long and exas-perated. "Despite all that, she chose you. I'm not going to let her child be raised without a father, no matter what happens. So I'll give up my right to custody to this baby, but only if you're going to step up to the plate." An ultimatum, from her husband. This had to beat all. "You're very silent, Ben Cooper. Are you going to man up, or what?"

"I..." he faltered.

"If you don't love her enough, say it. She's an easy woman to love, but a hard woman to live with. I know. She has a lot of flaws. She's judgmental, and obviously unfaithful. I'm will-ing to forgive all of that. I'm going to be a father to her child. And I'll fight like hell to stay her husband if you can't do this. I have Hannah, and all the time in the world. So you let me know what you decide."

Michael hung up before Ben could answer. Not that he did answer, or would answer, or knew what to say. But he did know one thing. Michael was an asshole. How could he say those things about Hannah? She had a lot of flaws? She was hard to live with? Other than her being unfaithful, which wasn't so much of a flaw, but a blunder, she was damn near perfect, or damn near perfect for him. She was warm, and funny, and beautiful, and as easy as hell to have in his house and his bed. "Fuck." Cody's head rose. Had he said any of that aloud?

The phone rang in his hand. He placed it down, staring at it while he shook his head from side to side. Ben didn't need a repeat performance with stalker Michael. He looked up when Hannah's voice poured through the machine in the next room.

"Hi, Ben, it's Hannah. I guess you're out now. I called Michael. Okay, I'll try again later."

Ben strode into the only cell phone store in Garberville, as soon as it opened the next morning. He picked up the first phone he saw on the display pedestal, plunked down his credit card, and signed away two years of his life. He didn't want to miss another call from Hannah. If she had an emergency or needed to share something about her pregnancy, now she could reach him anytime. The whole trip from his office and back only put his patient schedule behind fifteen minutes.

He poked his head into the lobby of the vet clinic to see how long the line was. Grateful that it was empty, he dialed the string of numbers Hannah had given him in December. Her "hello" was tentative. She sounded like she was in a restaurant. He looked at his watch. It was nine o'clock there, so it was probably a safe guess. He remembered that Europeans tended to eat dinner late.

"It's Ben," he said. "I wanted to give you my new number."

"New?"

"Are you at a restaurant?"

"Hold on," Hannah said. "I'm out with some of my cousins. I've been here two hours and will probably be here two hours more. You have a cell phone?"

"In case you have an emergency."

"I'm in Denmark."

"Call me if anything happens with you or the baby."

"Oh, okay. I have to go back."

"Goodbye, Hannah."

"Do you want me to stay for her visit?"

"No, Mor, you have work to do. I can do it on my own." This was something Hannah felt she should do without her mother.

An hour later, the buzzer sounded and Hannah let up a gray-haired woman. The midwife carried a large tote, which she laid in the foyer.

"Would you like coffee or tea?" she asked the woman in Danish, after introducing herself.

"Tea. Thank you. And I'm Adalena Erichsen."

While they waited for the kettle, Hannah and Adalena sat at the kitchen table, exchanging pleasantries.

"How are you feeling? You seem big for twelve weeks."

"I'm very tired. Mor says it will get better in a few weeks. But it's all I can do to get up, bathe, and eat before I want to lie down again."

Adalena nodded as if she'd heard it all before.

"Where is the father? You are American? Is he there or here in Denmark?"

"He's in America...in California," Hannah clarified, anchoring Ben in a country over two hundred times bigger than Denmark.

"It's warmer there this time of year," Adalena said, making small talk. Hannah made tea while the midwife took her medical history, ticking boxes on a paper file. "Were you on any medication during the last year?"

"My doctor prescribed Ambien. I couldn't sleep." She gazed out the kitchen window above the wood stove. "I was also taking Clomid."

"You were having problems conceiving?"

"No, as it turns out. My...former husband was infertile. But in the U.S. drugs are given as a first resort."

"I'm confused. Your baby's father is not your husband."

"No." Her tone discouraged further discussion.

"Where would you like to do the examination?" Even on this cloudy day light poured through the large windows. "This is a very bright flat, we could do it anywhere you feel comfortable."

Hannah escorted the midwife to the large bedroom she'd been using. The midwife took a small plastic machine from her bag—the parts attached by what looked like an old-fashioned telephone cord.

"I'm going to do a quick pelvic exam, a breast exam, and listen to the heartbeat, okay?"

Hannah nodded and took off her sweat pants. The pelvic exam was quick and painless. "That didn't hurt at all."

"Pelvic exams should never hurt, dear. It's a matter of knowledge and patience. Lift your shirt, please."

Hannah complied, acquiescing to the palpitation. "You will have no problem nursing. Your breasts are built for suckling babies with these large nipples."

"Um, thanks." Hannah pulled down her shirt over her breasts, embarrassed at Adeline's frankness. After warming the lotion in her hands, Adalena smoothed the gel on her belly. Then she pressed what looked like a microphone to her belly and held the speaker side to her ear. Hannah heard what sounded like whale calls from a nature documentary. "Hmmm. I'm going to change the batteries." She rummaged around in her tote and exchanged one nine volt battery for another.

"What is this called?"

"It is a Doppler fetal heart monitor. I am trying to hear the heartbeat of the baby, count the beats per minute, make sure he or she is healthy. Quiet please for a moment, while I try this again." This examination took longer than the other two. After more than ten minutes of listening, applying more gel, and moving the microphone around and around, she finally looked up at Hannah.

"There are two heartbeats. You are having two babies—twins."

"Oh," Hannah said, nonplussed. "I...oh."

"It happens, you know. With the drugs, the chances are far greater. Put on your pants and we will talk in the living room." Hannah did as she was told and sat on one couch, facing the midwife on the other.

"So while I do not normally recommend more than two ultrasounds during pregnancy, I would like to have this confirmed, and to see what position the babies are in." She pulled off a slip of paper. "Call this clinic and make an appointment. Have them call me with the results." Hannah was amazed that Adalena could be so businesslike after delivering that news. Gobsmacked, she needed time to acclimate. One baby was a life changer. Two...at the same time was a sea change. She turned to the midwife, who it seemed was still speaking. "We will also need to discuss your birthing options. Have you read the pamphlets the doctor gave you?" Hannah nodded, she had. "Do you think you'd like to give birth here or in the hospital?"

What had seemed so esoteric all the time she'd chased the dream of having a child, was becoming a cold, hard reality very quickly.

"Can we do it here, even if I'm having twins?"

"Yes, of course. Should complications arise later in the pregnancy, we can reevaluate. But for now, we can assume that you'll have a normal delivery. So do you think you'd like to do it here?"

Freja's hospital experience in 1970s New York City scared the shit out of her. She knew they didn't gas women or do twilight birth anymore, but the thought of going to a hospital wasn't welcoming. "Yes, I think I would. What preparations do I need to make?"

Adalena laughed. "Nothing for now. All that will come much later after week thirty-six or so. For now, you need to make sure you are eating and sleeping well."

⊘❧

"Ben, it's Hannah."

"Cody misses you." Did he miss her too? She didn't want to ask. The answer might devastate her.

"Is he alone all day?" Maybe she did run away. A sudden wave of guilt overwhelmed her for abandoning her dog. First she'd taken Cody from the only life he'd ever known with her and Michael. Then she'd left him.

"I take him to work with me."

"What about the motion sickness?"

"He's mostly outgrown it. Probably a puppyhood thing. Stopped feeding him breakfast, and he's been fine."

"I have to tell you something."

He sighed as if she were about to drop the weight of the world on his broad shoulders.

"It's not about Michael or anything like that. It's about the baby ... no, babies. I'm having twins."

He was silent for a long time. "They don't run in my family. What about yours?" His response was as cold as the Pacific Ocean in winter. She shivered in the chill morning air. The heat would go on in a second. Axel liked a warm apartment in the morning when he got ready for work.

"I was on Clomid when I got pregnant. It stimulates..."

"I know what it does, Hannah. Because you and your husband were trying to conceive, right?"

"Yes."

He hung up.

Despite the heat and tea, her morning chill never abated. For a week, Copenhagen was cold, bitterly cold. Hannah's mom insisted the weather was no different from that in New York, but no matter what Hannah did, she couldn't get warm. The knee length down coat with its fur tipped hood didn't help. Neither did the big sheepskin-lined boot, nor the bulky gloves.

"Ben, it's Hannah. Please don't hang up."

"What time is it there?"

"Six o'clock on the morning. I'm nine hours ahead."

"So they're probably fraternal twins."

"Probably, although my midwife told me that there's no way to tell."

"Midwife? This isn't the 1800s. Aren't you seeing a doctor?"

"I'm not sick."

"But that's what pregnant women do."

"Can't dogs and cats give birth without a doctor? Don't you send them home to work it out? I haven't heard that you have a birthing section in your clinic."

"Mmmm."

"This is not the U.S. I saw a doctor and he referred me to a midwife because prenatal care, birth, and postpartum is what she does. If anything comes up, I'll go to the doctor. Otherwise, I'll assume that everything is okay."

"I'm okay with the midwife, if she's going to assist. You'll be at a hospital anyway, surrounded by doctors."

"I haven't decided."

"Haven't decided what?

"Home birth is an option. I think I want to do it here with my mom by my side."

"Hannah, twins are a high risk pregnancy. Don't you—"

"You know what, it's my decision alone, Ben." She took the phone from her ear and pressed the end button.

The next morning, as she had so many of the past mornings, she did not call him. Instead, she joined her mother for an early morning coffee in the kitchen.

"You're here early."

She grabbed her mother's hand. "I wanted to spend some time with you."

"Why aren't you talking to Ben this morning?"

"You knew I called him?"

"The flat is not that big. I peeked in a few mornings ago when I heard talking."

"To check that I was not a raving lunatic?"

"To make sure you were okay. You looked serene when you were speaking with him, so I left you alone." Freja looked at the small wall clock. "Are you going to call him before too late?"

"No, Mor, I don't think I'm going to call him. I've been pursuing him since day one. It was the wrong thing to do, you know, without breaking things off with Michael, but I don't regret it. I'm tired now. I have to figure out how I'm going to be the mother of twins. How I'm going to support the three of us. Where I'm going to live. I've been waiting for nearly twenty years for a man to come save the day. First I was waiting for Dad, then Lucas, then Michael, and now Ben. It's time I saved myself."

"I think you're making the right decision," Mor said smiling weakly. "I'm sorry that all this had to happen for you to finally focus on what is important. But I am glad that you are looking to the future, and putting yourself and your children first. It is about time."

20

Ben pulled to the side of the road. He turned and looked in the back of the truck. The dog looked fine. Then he pulled the still shiny phone from the cup holder. Nothing. No messages, no texts, no calls. He'd heard nothing from Hannah for two weeks. If something had happened to her or her babies, he would have heard, surely. His sister seemed to have Hannah's number. Quickly, he thumbed in her cell number.

"Abbe, it's Ben."

"New number?"

"I got a new cell in case Hannah needs to reach me." He heard the sound of rustling as Abbe moved the phone away from her ear. "What are you doing?"

"I'm writing this number down. So I can text it to everyone I can think of when you hang up."

Once that would have made him laugh. "Whatever."

"Geez, Ben are you okay? I was writing it down, but I was kidding about texting anyone. I know you like your privacy now that you're a freaky recluse. Every time I see you, I'm afraid you're going to have one of those lumberjack beards."

Ben rubbed his jaw covered with a week of stubble. He'd shave tomorrow. "Have you heard from Hannah?"

"Seriously?"

"Abbe, can you answer the question?" Ben said, trying to keep his voice in check. His sister was mostly funny, except when she wasn't.

"No, I haven't talked to her since she left New York. I think she texted me her number in Denmark a few weeks ago. Do you need it?" He heard the clunk of metal against wood as she pulled open various kitchen drawers. "Haven't you guys been talking?"

He could hear Abbe bustling in the kitchen and her kids arguing in the background. The sounds of normalcy made him feel a little better. It was only *his* life that had gone off the rails. "She's been calling me every night since Christmas, up until a couple of weeks ago. We're having twins."

There was a loud crash. "Holy shit, no! Congratulations, that's so cool. Are you jazzed? Or…Ben, I don't know if I should be happy and rooting for you, or setting you up with an attorney who can handle custody arrangements."

"I can't answer any of that. I thought Hannah and I were working things out, but she stopped calling."

"You're using the phone right now. Now that you've gotten that skill back, why don't you call her?"

"It doesn't work that way."

"What? Do you not have the number? What time is it there, anyway?"

"It's four in the morning," he answered without thinking. He'd added nine hours to the time so often over the last few weeks; he could do it in his sleep.

He heard his sister tell one of her kids to stop riding the broom, and the other to stop chasing the cat. Abbe got back on the line. "So, wait a few hours and call her. I'm not getting this conversation. Did I miss something?"

"She. Calls. Me," he explained.

"Oh, I get it. You're the injured party. She begs for forgiveness, and you grant absolution depending on the day of the week, the phase of the moon, or whatever criteria you have. Geez, have you converted to Catholicism? You sound like a priest. Does she have to say 'Hail Marys' too?"

"You know what Abbe, I don't need this. If you haven't heard from her, then fine. I have to get home anyway." He ended the call with an angry flick of his finger, and started the car.

He'd barely unharnessed Cody from the truck, when the phone started ringing. He raced into the house, and picked up the kitchen extension without checking the caller id.

"Hannah?"

"It's Michael."

"What do you want, Michael?"

"You haven't given me an answer. I got the papers from my lawyer. I can sign everything, including giving up parental rights to the baby, and then Hannah and I can be divorced after the waiting period. If I don't sign these documents, then Hannah and I will stay married."

Michael had said baby. He didn't even know that there were two babies who would need a father. "Sign them, Michael. I'm the babies' father." He slammed down the receiver. In the yawning silence, there was clarity. He knew what he had to do.

Hannah pushed the duvet off, not caring about the cold air, as she dived for the ringing phone on the table between her bed and the couch in the room.

Her own number stared back at her.

"Michael. You got the papers." Grady had sent over her proposed settlement, giving Michael all the personal property he wanted. Selling the house and the rest, and dividing the money some day in the future when it was all said and done. He'd also drafted documents that would absolve Michael of any responsibility for their children.

"I'm not going to sign them."

Hannah looked at the image of the windows dancing on the back of her eyelids. This nightmare was never going to end. "Why not, Michael? I thought we agreed to divide the stuff. We're not talking heirlooms. We're talking Pottery Barn."

"Not that one, Hannah. The other."

"But you're not the father, Michael. Ben is."

"I'm not going to let your child go fatherless. I'm not that guy. You know what it's like to have a dad come and go in your life. You shouldn't do that to your child.

"I love you. You're pregnant. We made plans, we have this house, your SUV. We can be that family we planned. I read something that said over ten percent of men are raising children who are not their own without even knowing it. I know it, and I'm still willing to take you back. We can do this, Hannah. Come home."

"What about Ben?"

"I called him, Hannah. I've talked to him twice. I told him I'd have no problems giving up custody if he promised me he'd man up."

He hadn't called. It had been over two weeks and Ben hadn't called. She knew she'd been doing the heavy lifting, trying to repair what they had. She knew all along it had been a long shot. She had hurt him too deeply. She was the last betrayal he was going to stomach. "Sign the papers, Michael." Hannah hung up and quietly put the phone back on the table before lying down, pulling the blanket up as high as it would reach.

Copenhagen was a lot colder than San Francisco. Ben was glad he had kept his old coat from his days in Ithaca in the far recesses of his closet. He shoved one bare hand in his pocket. He hadn't been able to find anything resembling real gloves in California. He wheeled his carry-on to the ground transportation sign, happy that the second language everywhere appeared to be English. When his turn came up in the cue, he handed the address he'd gotten from Abbe, scrawled on a prescription pad, to the taxi driver.

"*Tak*."

"I'm sorry, I don't speak Danish."

"English, then," the driver said, his own English heavily accented.

"Yes. Thank you. I'm going to that address."

The driver squinted at the paper. "Maybe twenty minutes, okay?"

"Yes." Two days standing in line in San Francisco getting an expedited passport, and nearly twenty hours on planes and in three airports, and he'd see Hannah in twenty minutes. He looked at his hands, achingly cold, but rock solid on his lap. He wasn't nervous at all.

Twenty minutes later on the dot, the driver deposited him on the corner of Peter Hvitfeldts Sraede and Krystalgade. He thrust a few thousand kroner through the window, and took the slip of paper back. He looked up at the brick and stone buildings. He walked down the street a ways, matching the numbers on the building to the paper in his hand.

He looked at the names on the buzzers. He had no idea what Hannah's mother or stepfather's last name was. Nothing stood out in the sea of foreign looking names with 'oh's slashed through, 'a's and 'e's joined together. Fortunately, the door opened, a pierced and tattooed man rushed out. He grabbed the door and walked the four flights to the right apartment number, 402. He pulled his phone from his pocket, and dialed

Hannah's phone. He could hear faint ringing from inside the flat, and muffled voices.

"Hannah, it's me, Ben. Please don't hang up."

"Ben?" Her voice questioned.

"I'm outside your front door."

He heard the patter of feet rushing to the door, and heavy locks being turned. In seconds, Hannah stood there in the doorway in scruffy jeans, a big lumpy sweater, no makeup, hair sticking up on one side. She had never looked more beautiful. He dropped his suitcase, the paper in his other hand falling to the floor unforgotten, and he gathered her in his arms, momentarily surprised at the bump of belly between them. Ben loved Hannah the way she was, and that was more than enough.

ABOUT THE AUTHOR

I write crazy, beautiful love stories because I believe storytelling is magic. I love complicated heroines with secrets, strong heroes who fall hard, and a long winding road to happily ever after. When I'm not writing, I love to travel to witness the diverse tapestry of humanity, photograph the beauty of the world, visit museums, and watch live theater. I live in West Hollywood, California ten miles from the nearest airport.

I haven't found my own happily ever after, but I'm not done trying. Join me at Fifty First Dates, the Podcast, as I try to find my Mr. Right or maybe Mr. Right Now.

#50firstdates #joliemoore #crazybeautifullove